T O N Y   G U E R I N

Tony Guerin was born in Listowel, Co. Kerry, Ireland, in 1938. He presently divides his time between living in Dublin and Ballybunnion. He has written three novels, *Tomorrow is a Lovely Day* being his first published.

His first stage play, *Cuckoo Blue*, was produced in 1998 by *Danny Hannon's Lartique Theatre Company, Listowel.* It was played to sell out audiences in *St John's Theatre, Listowel, Siamsa Tíre Theatre, Tralee* and the *Cork Opera House.* The internationally renowned film actor Patrick Bergin bought the film rights to *Cuckoo Blue*. Tony wrote the film script.

His second play *Hummin* was toured nationally in 2002 by *Waterford's Red Kettle Theatre Company.* He wrote the film script of *Hummin* in 2003.

In 2001 he wrote the play *Solo Run.* It was produced by the *Lartique Theatre Company in St. John's; Siamsa Tíre,* and the *New Theatre, Temple Bar, Dublin.*

His next play *'Laird of Doon'* was produced by *Joe Murphy's Upstage Theatre Group* in 2008 at St. John's again. *Because of cast commitments the Laird has not yet travelled.* Guerin's new one act play, *Costa from the Moon,* a two hander, is awaiting production.

ACKNOWLEDGEMENTS

I would like to take this opportunity to thank those who have supported me in many, many ways down through the years.
Tomorrow would never have seen the light of day but for the generosity and encouragement of Eamon Griffin of Intacta Print, Waterford, and the wonderful Janet Carey; they not alone stitched my raw material onto a disc but designed the cover as well. Genius! I thank Jim and Margo McGrath of the Oyster Tavern, The Spa, Tralee; Eddie Holly of Cedar Builders Dublin and Arklow; Mary Keane and all the Keane family; McMahon family; Eddie McNulty; Maurice Mulcaire; Dr. Jim and Peggy O'Carroll; Eric Browne; Bert Griffin; Mike Joe Thornton; Joe Guerin; Weeshie Fogarty; Frank Lewis; Lorcan Curtin; Kevin Quinlan; John Grubb; Jim Nolan; Ben Hennessy; Jimmy Murphy; Cyril Kelly; David Browne; and especially my friend Martin McMahon for his forensic treatment of my script.
I thank the great Danny Hannon of the Lartigue Drama Group, Listowel, who put my first play, Cuckoo Blue to flight having received it from Mike 'Batch' Nagle, Marine Hotel, Ballybunion, Solo Run soon followed produced by my great pal, Denis Mahony of the same Lartigue. In stepped Ben Hennessy of Red Kettle Theatre Group, Waterford, to produce Hummin. Red Kettle are truly the people's theatre group. Vicar Joe Murphy's Upstage Group put on Laird of Doon in St. John's, Listowel. There, Cathy Tolin and Trish McMahon ensured the Laird was kept sweet.
Two very industrious committees I must give special mention to: Spearheading Writer's Week office are Muiri Logue and Eilbish Wren, and the industrious Cara Trant, who runs the Seancaoi Centre, aided and abetted by the ever hospitable Noreen Pathwell.
I am deeply indebted to Prof. Brendan Kennelly for his foreword, and Christine Dwyer-Hickey, Danny Hannon and Noreen O'Connell for their contributions. And I thank Billy Keane for launching my book and Deirdre Walshe and Owen McMahon for doing the readings. There are those who say Danny Hannon has a lot to answer for.

Tomorrow is a lovely day

by Tony Guerin

Published in 2009

ISBN 978-0-9562548-0-1

No part of this publication may be copied, reproduced, broadcast or transmitted in any form or by means, electronic, mechanical, photocopying, recording or otherwise without prior permission from the author.

Printed by: Intacta Print Ltd. South Parade, Waterford. 051-871777
Cover Design/Layout: Janet Carey 051-871777
www.intactadesignstudios.com   www.intactaprint.ie

Brendan Kennelly
PROFESSOR OF MODERN LITERATURE, TRINITY COLLEGE.

This is a most unusual book. I think this is because Tony Guerin, a writer of unique individuality, writes a novel which at times feels like a play, such is the fluency of the dialogue in 'Tomorrow is a Lovely Day'. In fact it is not surprising that Guerin turns dialogue into a narrative which carries the reader along with ease and conviction. I believe that 'Tomorrow is a Lovely Day' is a unique work of art and will attract readers who appreciate a writer turning the ordinary into the extraordinary with fascinating skill and style.

for Eileen

CHAPTER 1

He didn't have the courage to go ahead with it, he concluded, having visited several sites that afternoon and justified his rejection of each for one reason more trivial than the other.

He had been to this part of the city earlier and now returned when the world of commerce had closed its doors. Industry and chatter of stall women had gone. Traders who transported their households onto streets and, where needs be, had muffled offspring in prams among trays, baskets, and boxes, all laden with rich colourful harvest of garden and orchard. On this hard November day nothing remained of the Camden Street nomads but piles of rubbish awaiting the dump truck.

David O'Leary's dark eyes stared at their absence. His mind did not pursue beyond the lone thought 'they are gone' and then the peep into his mind of those sidewalk merchants ended.

His twenty seven year-old, six foot, twelve stone frame, dressed immaculately from handmade shoes to bespoke pin striped suit stood sideways to the road and shop fronts. The gabardine's turned up collar protected him from the harsh north westerlies. Earlier that day he had asked the woman the Religious Goods' Shop in Cathedral Street for a rosary beads, and when she handed the beads across the glass display cabinet he made no move to take it but asked, "Could I have one that is blessed, please? Also, a little picture of the Sacred Heart and the Virgin Mary?"

Religion had not been practiced in David O'Leary's home in Dublin. His mother, Emma, a Dublin woman, was indifferent and his father, Tim Pat, a West Cork man, saw priests as the embodiment of religion and to whom he referred as a 'greedy self indulgent shower of hoors'. No son of Tim Pats was going to suffer the mental castration it had taken him years to purge himself of. It would never be a total purging – it sometimes got at him: more sediment of hell than heaven remained. Tim Pat was satisfied with the end product of the non-denominational education he had decided on for his son David, but for one reservation, he reckoned David lacked street cuteness. Country youth had it inherently while their city counterparts, especially the middle class bracket, lacked that elixir, this, Tim Pat firmly believed.

Memories of his holidays in West Cork came flooding back to David as he stood looking in the window of the Religious Goods Shop before entering. As clear as if it had been yesterday, he recalled his grandmother in her soft lyrical accent reciting the rosary as she sat in her great big armchair with the beads and special prayer book that contained as many mortuary cards and holy pictures as pages. Each of those pictures had an allotted time to be held in her hands along with the ever present beads while prayers were in progress. All knelt except Gran, who said she had been granted special permission by the Pope to sit because of her arthritis. David had told everyone in his class of g ran's arthritis and the special permission from Rome. In the parlour of his grandparents' farmhouse - not at home - he had learned the Hail Mary, Our Father and The Apostles' Creed.

David never ventured on his own into the parlour where the rosary was said – the parlour was spooky; all those pictures of solemn bearded men, Our Lord with a dagger through his heart, Our Lady with the Baby Jesus on her lap whom he knew would be nailed to a cross. Each gnarled varnished frame held an eerie silence and timelessness. Those pictures watched his every move from the minute he stepped into the room; even when he wasn't looking, they were watching him. He knew this; he could feel their eyes on him. He was afraid of that room where God and his angels hung on the papered walls.

David confided his fears in his father Tim Pat who told him, 'They did me too, son, as well your aunts and uncles. They hung in the kitchen, we hated them there. One weekend when your grandfather and grandmother were away in Dublin we shifted them into the parlour.

There was ructions in the house for weeks, but they never shifted them back. Superstition, you know, superstition!"

It had been David's first time hearing the word 'superstition'; and pronouncing it as best he could, repeated it in that high pitched fashion that was the signal for Tim Pat to explain the meaning of a word.

Tim Pat diligently answered all queries from David, mindful of his own parents', negligence or inability, or then again it could have been the sheer volume of questions from such a large family that caused them to hush questions sideways.

"Your grandparents' thinking went round in circles until they believed that God made us move the pictures. Their mistaken reverence caused unreasoned fear: superstition".

Nothing was as obvious as the enlightenment on David's face, a rich reward for his father who encouraged inquisitiveness. "Oh, I see, Daddy, you put them in the parlour because you were afraid of them like me".

"Correct, son, and your grandparents were afraid of something else!"

All the memories of West Cork came flooding back, his crouching marsupial fashion beneath his kneeling father as gran's cascading holy water splashed without warning in all directions during the rosary. Gran, his father, the parlour, and the word 'superstition' were with David as he stood waiting to be served in that religious shop in Cathedral Street.

The late-fifties woman inside the counter searched his face. She did not know what she was looking for; it was the way he had spoken, the way he cowered, tried to hide inside the gabardine that caused her to worry. Why, she worried, was this customer making an apparent clandestine operation out of so simple a purchase?

The hesitation and the scrutiny was not lost on David, but, motionless he stood looking directly down avoiding the woman's eyes. She was unable to leave the young man's presence without something further being said to trigger her into serving.

She found working in the religious shop heavy going. She had always worked in the grocery trade and enjoyed it but since commencing work in this shop two years previously her friendly cheerful disposition had left her. She could not get accustomed to the odd-balls; the shop was a magnet for them. What could be the matter with this young man? She worried as she fidgeted with the small crucifix that hung round her neck on a slim gold chain. She felt a clamminess all over and heard herself say, "a blessed beads, I see, a blessed beads." She withdrew her hand indicating the proffered beads were not blessed. Nothing in the shop was blessed; if he wanted them blessed he would have to take them to a priest in the Pro-Cathedral across the road. Looking at him, she was certain he would not do this. The purchase of the beads was very important to him. She would lie rather than see him walk out without them. Pondering a moment, she remembered her husband's beads in the pocket of her coat in the rest room.

'Certainly, Sir.'

Going to the rear of the shop, she returned and placed her husband's beads along with the two holy pictures into his palms. The reverence with which he received the items left her feeling like she had delivered the Blessed Sacrament. She watched as he precisely placed them in the pocket of his gabardine. Not looking up, he took a wallet from the inside pocket of his coat. His long white fingers awaited the demand for the requisite cash.

"Four pounds, please, sir. Those beads are specially blessed, and tomorrow is a lovely day!"

She said the words wanting to put bounce into them. Her voice was false. She did not know why she said the latter part of her statement, or the way she said it, but believed it to be important. Their eyes met momentarily as he handed her a five pound note. Turning on his heel, he was gone out the door not waiting for his change.

She rung the four pounds on the cash register and placed the one pound change in a charity box. With unsteady hands she lit a cigarette and welcomed the deep drag of nicotine into her lungs. She visited herself with inadequacy; she believed she should have done more; what more she was not sure of. She made everyone welcome to the shop but especially those troubled. She hoped they found succour in their purchases. The ones that impacted on her most she said a fervent prayer that God might help them. She had to say it to salve her conscience. It never totally relieved her as she mulled over these people when she returned home to her husband after work.

Her husband had encouraged her to take a job in a grocery shop when their family was reared. The confidence she had gained and the extra few pounds brought a freshness to their lives. She switched to 'The Religious Goods Shop' because it paid better. It was affecting her; she was given to brooding, became moody, had become too reliant on God, needed to go to church each night to talk to him. Her husband had cautioned she would break her health if she continued to work in that shop. He advised there were people who could handle that situation without any problem but not her; she should return to the grocery trade.

No matter the inconvenience, her husband insisted on going along with her to the church, and because of this she kept his beads at all times in her coat pocket. The beads poorly parried distraction as her husband's mind wandered everywhere but to God. At best, they kept him from picking his nails while his eyes swivelled curiously in all directions. On leaving the Church the beads were returned to the custody of her coat pocket.

As the weeks went by and the effect on his wife became more apparent his advice was firming into the form of an order.

After the encounter with the young man in the shop that day she went directly home. She announced she was going to Church before dinner. Her husband, who had an Irish stew ready for serving, took a longing look at the simmering pot and then looked at his bothered wife. Without uttering the shouting protest of his hungry belly they left the house together.

When they knelt in the church she did not hand him his rosary beads. He nudged and requested, 'Beads'. Instinctively she put her hand to her pocket; remembering, she placed her face in her hands and burst into tears. Gently, he took her by the arm and they left the Church. Steering her to the side where darkness hid them he enveloped her in his arms. She continued sobbing; he contemplated life without her; he shuddered. Gently drawing away from his wife, he said, "You are cold, can't afford to have our bread-winner laid up, but we are not leaving until you tell me what in the name of God happened to you today?"

She related the story of her day, before finishing, added: " I'm handing in my notice tomorrow and going back to the grocery. It's as simple as that. God has given me directions".

As they walked out the gates of the Church he commented: "Fair play to God he took his time with his directions. Seeing as God is in such a generous mood you might ask him to push the stew to one side otherwise the arse will be burned out of the saucepan by the time we get home".

Together they laughed as only happiness laughs.

CHAPTER 2

Having left the shop, David went left onto O'Connell Street. Unmindful of the traffic he stepped onto the roadway. With head down and hands sunk deep into his pockets he went diagonally across heading for the GPO.

No thanks to his observance of the Safe Cross Code, David now stood in a queue in the GPO being urged forward by a woman gripping a squealing child, until it was his turn to be served. Having bought one letter-card he strayed to the octagonal writing desk. Unable to fix on a formula of words, he decided to address the letter first. He had difficulty beginning the message; would he say "Dear Whore", or just "Whore". He decided on the latter. If he changed his mind he could add in the "Dear".

A pipe smoking dapper elderly man watching David's hesitancy remarked in a strong Dublin accent, "I can empathise with you, friend; always had difficulty organising priorities when faced with a letter-card. Letter cards are all about priorities, that's what the gaffer used say, priorities!"

David's mind was miles away. Not sure what the man had said and wanting to avoid conversation, he faintly replied, "Indeed".

It did not matter to the dapper-man what reply if any David made; he was going to say what he wanted to say, anyway. Taking the pipe from his mouth he licked a stamp and precisely placed it on an envelope saying: "Never sent two no matter the importance of the communiqué. No siree, no never did!" Not looking at David, he went towards a post box.

Like a tap over a sink, David stood with his gold biro held motionless above the beige letter card. The legend of Cu Chulainn wormed into his mind as he looked at the bronze statue in the middle of the GPO depicting the dying warrior.

This was the favourite story of David's childhood, Ferdia, Queen Maeve and the brown bull of Cooley. Memory telescoped the years and he was once again held aloft by his father Tim Pat in the GPO. From the security of his father's arms he would stretch out a tentative finger and touch the head of the raven perched on the shoulders of the dying Cu Chulainn before recoiling into the sanctuary of his father's arms. Tim Pat O'Leary loved Irish mythology, the stuff boys' dreams are made of and some latter-day patriots. Emma, Tim Pat's wife, had herself become an expert having to listen to Davids' rambling retelling of those various myths.

David had been called after his paternal grandfather, Dave.

Dave and Helen O'Leary had raised eleven children on their middling sized farm in West Cork and blessed was their parish in having a headmaster Murphy who considered it his duty to advise, cajole or bully parents of his brightest to ensure their children continued their education though some could ill afford to do so. At school's closing in July, a summons from Master Murphy was feared by some and welcomed by others. The summons for Dave O'Leary to visit the Master had not arrived though Tim Pat was due to finish.

For generations the land had been farmed by the O'Learys and Dave had no doubt if he sold the land graves all over the globe would disgorge hoards of vengeful O'Leary ghosts to cart him off unceremoniously to the underworld. Desire was never satisfied in the O'Leary household, need was, the need for education. Nine were 'done-for' between them every letter in the alphabet had been exhausted in describing their qualifications. Dave and Helen had heeded Master Murphy's mantra "The pen will dig you out of the shit, the shovel won't". They were left with Tim Pat and the youngest Tom; one would have to stay on the land. It was a matter for serious consideration. Dave would discuss his predicament with Master Murphy when he called to his home in town to enquire about the absent summons.

Continuous ting-a-linging heralded the coming and going of Master Murphy's bike as, nonchalantly, he peddled the roads and bohareens of West Cork. Dave O'Leary and son Tom rested their forks and followed the journey of the ringing until it came to a stop outside the whitethorn hedge that hid them from the road. Tim Pat's fork went into overdrive on hearing the ringing and had hay flying in all directions. Dave sunk his fork into the meadow and strolled towards the bell's location, chewing on a sop of hay as he went. Noisily, a blackbird rattled from the hedge before scuttling low across the cut meadow frightened by the climbing Master Murphy. Tim Pat and Tom heard their first loud exchanges as their father drew closer to the Master now standing upright on the ditch. "God bless work and workers, Dave O'Leary. One glorious day for tossing the hay".

"Couldn't come better for the job. Whatever has the Master coming all the way out here in the roasting sun?"

Master nodded towards Tim Pat and Tom, "Two strapping honest workers you've got there."

"If they got feeding there'd be no stopping them. But the honest part I'd have my doubts about and I'd be thinking you have too, Master"

"Sun puts gizz into ageing bones, Dave. I was glad of the exercise."

"No shortage of the same gizz in you Master. Wasn't I saying to herself last night I'd have to call on the Master. Matters kind'a … bothering us."

"And how is Helen?"

"Great! Great altogether, thank God, great."

Dave was now standing directly in front Master Murphy. Though Tim Pat's and Tom's straining ears could no longer hear what was being said they focussed on the many gestures and the sometimes glances in their direction trying to interpret what was being discussed.

"Something's cooking, Tim Pat." whispered Tom.

"Tim Pat's what's cooking, Tom! The master gave me notes for Da and didn't I feck 'em!".

"Feck 'um? You … you'll be scalped, scalped!"

"My head's used to being scalped. Scalp or no scalp 'tis Skibbereen bound I am; that's what they're on about. I know 'tis."

"Didn't the rest survive the secondary in Skib?"

"Tim Pat's not the rest. Cocoa! Six years of cocoa. Cocoa! I hates cocoa, fucking jackasses' piss, cocoa. Sticking his hooky nose into my businesses, letting-on to be interested. If 'twasn't for the bike he wouldn't be here. His interest wouldn't have him walk out here: interest me arse."

"There's lovely girls in Skib. Tim Pat, lovely"

"Do you know what them Skib lovelies call our likes? "

"Culchies! Tim Pat, culchies!"

"My fecked notes have me hanged."

"Murph. mightn't have said nothing".

"Look at them, look at them. Do them two look as if they're on about nothing?"

"Da wouldn't stick you with the hay-fork would he?"

"Modern Daas are not to be trusted; they're all hen-pecked, hen-fecken-pecked".

"Ma talks and Da does, that doesn't make Da hen-pecked?"

"No! Makes her the boss though. Fuck sake, grow up."

"Give me time, Tim Pat, don't be rushing me, give me time!"

Meanwhile Dave and the Master had progressed their conversation from the merits of the harvest to current tragedies, celebrations, politics, immigration, market prices and had exhausted the more serious topic of Cork's prospects of an all Ireland double in football and hurling before Dave mentioned Tim Pat's future.

"For all its merits education could put paid to the O'Leary's owning this land, how would the world see me then? A traitor to my own clan. I'd be a traitor".

"That is not going to happen, Dave. Here is the scenario as I see it. Tim Pat will fly through Skibbereen, a call to teacher training is a definite, a definite he will have to refuse given his temperament…"

"Agreed, the parish can do without a parents' revolution".

"He will be offered a University scholarship, can't see him knuckling down, then he could prove me wrong. He will get a civil service offer which he should take, paid from the word go. That is how I see Tim Pat's future".

"Okay, the maverick is fixed up, Tom gets the land, is that it?"

"Not exactly, Dave. Tom must be given his crack at education same as the rest".

"But….?"

"Hear me out. I'd like nothing better than a son of yours to take over from me when I retire in nine years. A long time away, I know, but God is good. I'll see Tom gets the post".

"Now that, that would be something. Helen will be over the moon".

For another ten minutes they chatted before the Master climbed out of sight onto the road. The bell went ting-aling-alinging into the distance. Dave pulled his pike from the ground and began turning hay with his all too silent sons.

"Don't suppose you'd have any idea what the Master was on about, Tim Pat?

"Not an iota, Dad, not an iota!"

"Any chance 'twould have something to do with school, Dad?" asked Tom.

"Do you think Tom is right, Tim Pat?"

"All equal to Tim Pat whether Tom is or Tom isn't. Come to think of it, Dad, 'tis like a dream Murph. gave me notes to bring home, they must have blown away; nothing much in them anyhow, tiny they were, tiny!"

"No doubt they blew away, no doubt they did. We best get this meadow turned!"

" Rain is never far away from a meadow that's down, that's what they say, Dad."

"And Dad's boot is never far away from an arse that lies, Tim Pat."

11

CHAPTER 3

Tim Pat, having sat the Leaving certificate after five years at secondary school in Skibbereen was offered the three choices predicted by Master Murphy. He entered the civil service. It was his own decision based on the persuasive powers of money in the pocket straight away. Hand-outs from home not needed, his own boss, independence.

The novelty of his new life style in Dublin quickly wore off. Spending money hurt Tim Pat; he slept happier when he had lodged his wages in his Post Office Savings Account. Wanting to do something constructive, he studied for a BA degree at night in UCD.

Tom sat the Leaving Certificate the year after Tim Pat and had a choice of one, teacher training. Master Murphy was as good as his word, Tom replaced him when he retired. It was everything Dave and Helen had wished for.

The O'Learys had been brought up in a world of practicalities. Their father Dave would reel off names of successful farmers and, with satisfaction, include himself in their number and finish by saying: "Lasting beauty is in the pockets of people with like minds. Them kind of relationships weather storms. Fancy city notions of love in the eye fades rapidly with a poor or no bank balance and a couple of squawking children."

Dave O'Leary was a measured man, methodical, not given to approaching excesses, not even from a shouting distance, except for his political colour; this he would banner-wave. Tim Pat proudly placed his hand on the family political flagpole.

All the young men in Skibbereen had meat in their trouser pockets and the majority nothing else. Tom O'Leary was an exception with his pensionable-and-permanent teaching job and the land, but he had great difficulty harnessing his flagpole, it wasn't political.

Mary Boyle's parents were not half-happy when, crying, she blurted out the news that she was in the family way. Mary and Tom O'Leary had been walking-out together for six months, and no obstacle was put in their way by the Boyles for them to adopt whatever posture they chose to adopt.

When Mary broke the news to Tom, he, in a lather of sweat, got on the phone to Tim Pat in Dublin. "Tim Pat, I'm in a spot of bother."

"How big is the spot?"

"Big and getting bigger!"

"You've a boil in your arse?"

"It's a boil alright but 'tisn't my arse is the problem. Tim Pat I'm talking serious stuff here."

"Don't tell me you got the sack?"

"Could happen!"

"You didn't beat-up the Parish Priest?"

"I'm bad enough without beating him up".

"Nothing wrong at home?"

"Not yet. Jesus! Mary is on the way!"

Tim Pat knew the Boyle referred to, Mary.

"A boil. I was right. Don't suppose you two are married?"

"I can do without that shite; be serious will you!"

"Are you sure it's yours?"

"Will you ever fuck off!"

"Well, as I see it, you have a choice of two".

"Tell me?"

"You marry Boyle or make a bolt for England or America."

"I can't very well bolt, now can I? What with the teaching and the farm. I'm in a right pickle. Fucked!"

"Father will be looking for a heap of money, a heap!"

"The Boyles have money, enough to satisfy Dave if it comes to that." "Maybe they have. But the Boyles don't have to part now, do they?"

"You mean because of our situation they might …they'd never do that. No, no, things are bad enough."

"Her ould fella has a shop; our man, a farm; for them, marriage is a business, a business proposition. The passing of money makes for harmonious relations between one generation and the next. That's how it has been, always will be, otherwise the person who moves in without the shillings will be nothing other than a second class citizen and recognised by everyone as such; that's if they're left inside the gate at all at all."

" It's exactly because of what you say the money will come; they'd want none of that finger pointing at their daughter."

"If that's the case a problem doesn't exist, go ahead and marry her – fast!"

"I'm not sure I love her."

"Fuck off , donkey. I suppose you two are humping this past six months!"

"Shut up, you filthy hound; once, just the once, and look at what happened?"

"If you like a girl for six months you'll like her for the rest of your natural, provided you're allowed live that long."

"What will I do?"

"You'll make an honest woman out of Mary Boyle, that's what you'll do, and the quicker the better!"

"It's looking that way."

"That love business is for the birds; you like her, she likes you; you have teaching and the land, she has money. Christ man, you're away in a hack on your darling Mary's back!"

"Stop!Stop! Stop!. What will dad and mam say?"

"When you stand at the gate and heave the dowry in before you Mary   will be as welcome as the flowers in May."

"You make it sound awful simple. You wouldn't come down for a few days until this is sorted out; as stupid as you are, I could do with help?"

"Today is Tuesday, last train Friday night, pick me up."

"Perfect. I'm meeting her ould fella tonight."

"Tell him you are delighted to be marrying his beautiful daughter Mary with her heaps of money."

"I am too!"

"Sure don't I know you are too, that's why you rang me; it was obvious from the first time I clapped my eyes on the two of you rattling like rabbits in the hay-shed."

"Lying bastard!"

"What the hell do you want me to say? A shrewd Kerry shite working in the office with me, says, 'a judicious opening of the clothes pegs is better than all the education in the world.'"

"Shut, Tim Pat, shut!"

"There is one thing; you will have to build your own house. Mother wouldn't stand bringing a woman into her kitchen."

"There is that. I'll play that card first. I haven't slept a wink this past week, worrying."

"Well, you better get enough sleep for the next few months, sleepless nights ahead for chalk of teacher Tom."

"Do you think the parish priest will cause trouble?"

"My arse he will. Grease his paw; that will keep PP happy. Don't we all know of premature babies fit to plough born after six or seven months, sometimes six or seven weeks. Hurry, hurry, and they'll be no worry."

"Will I break the news at home before you come down?"

"Depends on your meeting tonight, doesn't it? If Boyle starts shouting you had better break the news before he does. Worry not, they'll be happy to welcome a farm and a pension into the family. Don't go cringing to them Boyles or anyone else; you are in love and you can't wait to marry the girl."

"That part is true anyway, I suppose."

"That's better. Toughen until Friday; we will break the good news together. Arrangements have to be made"

15

"Sound, sound as a bell; you're still an ignorant bollix!"

Tom's marriage got the blessing of both sets of parents. Mary had all the independence in the world when the Boyle's dowry preceded her in the road gate. They built their house beside the old home. Everything was hunky-dory; Tom and Mary discovered they loved each other, anyway

CHAPTER 4

Dave had written the commandments for his sons: when marrying time was upon them, a laying hen, a professional or a woman with a wagon of gold should be their target. 'Tis as easy pull a turnip as a mangel!' he would preach. As long as she looked likely to provide an heir, looks, dimensions, age or otherwise should not enter the equation. When Tim Pat returned with a wife to West Cork, she was going to be a woman of substance in her own right - by God, she surely would be.

One evening Tim Pat called to a garage in Ranelagh where his friend Finbar - from home - worked as a mechanic. He found Finbar with his head under the bonnet of a Morris Minor. Tim Pat muttered loud enough to be heard. "Never heard of one leaving a man down on the side of the road. No, sir, no whacking the Morris Minor. Can't be beaten!" Finbar, not looking or pausing from his work, replied: "Given half a chance this Minor wouldn't be down either – woman driver – you know the story, Tim Pat! "

"Explains everything. Would that be her white coat on the back seat?" asked Tim Pat.

A natural glutton for information, a nosy individual, his curiosity was flecked with interest. Finbar, knowing O'Leary thinking, volunteered:

"Doctor! Available! Calling shortly!"

Country people had a knack of saying things casually, giving the bare bones and leaving it to the listener to pack on the meat. Truly gifted they were with intuition or as be-grudgers would have it, survival techniques.

"Country?" asked Tim Pat dropping the important question casually.

"Finished!" said Finbar; straightening his back. Wiping his hands with a rag he answered, "Nope, couldn't be more city, Fitzwilliam Square!"

"Oh, oh, oh!" said a disappointed Tim Pat.

The white coat was in his eye as he traced the outline of the driver's window with his index finger. A country man's interest in a woman invariably waned with the declaration that she was 'city'. Too brittle, they made bad marriage partners. They could not cope with calloused hands, sweat, clothing and boots dirtied by hard work; language, minted over backs of heaving stubborn animals, over broken down machinery, over nature's destruction; the embellished 'meitheal' banter of bog and field where men toiled together and lightened their load with fanciful Herculean deeds of strength and sexual prowess. A rich vein of colourful harmless curses interlaced their language, and, when used properly, rendered potions and tablets redundant.

The city woman was better suited to the type of man who worked in the rarefied atmosphere of offices and the like. The say-it-with-flowers type, publicly genteel, who remembered birthdays, wedding days, mother's day, the tailored man, clock reliable, the 'I beg your pardon' and 'excuse me' man. Not in the least like free-range Tim Pat.

Finbar, peering with scanning eyes at the job just finished, said nonchalantly:

"I get a pile of these women in here; has to be my pit-side manner. I wouldn't rule this one out, Tim Pat; for a city girl, she's what I'd call 'different'."

Tim Pat filed away this piece of information. Nodding toward the Minor he guessed, "Carburettor?"

Finbar visited all women drivers with the same mechanical lack of savvy when he declared: "Why they leave their shagging tanks run out of petrol is beyond me; sucks up ever bit of muck. That carburettor I've cleaned at least six times. Let's see has surgeon Finbar performed his miracle of grease."

Finbar, half-sitting on the driver's seat, placed his left leg on the accelerator, his right earthing him to the garage floor before turning the key in the ignition. The car purred at first, orchestrated by his left foot, raced to a honeyed crescendo. Smiling his satisfaction, he winked at Tim Pat.

Tim Pat, crouched, left hand on the roof over Finbar's head, right elbow on the door, smiled. Sharing his friend's success he knowledgably declared, "Sweeter than mother's sewing machine. Beautiful, Finbar, beautiful!"

Finbar, leaving the engine running removed his tools from under the bonnet before deliberately closing it, hardly making a sound, saying, "The way some bang down these bonnets you'd swear 'twas a tractor they were dealing with."

While giving the bonnet a cursory rub of a rag Finbar looked up and beyond Tim Pat, "Ah! There you are, Emma, timing perfect, Inspector Tim Pat O'Leary from the department has certified Minor to be in ship shape."

Finbar liked his female clients; they were without exception, generous, friendly, and genuine. He was forever updated on the welfare of their cats, dogs, canaries, gold fish, ailments others suffered from but thankfully never their own. Traditional cures and piseogues were sought as were cures for ailing plants. His back lane garage was a confessional equipped with pumps, nuts, jacks, grease and spanners.

Emma's approach had not been heard above the garage noises by Tim Pat, who had been anticipating her arrival and now, because of its suddenness, he turned quickly and failed to conceal his appraisal. Emma, surprised at this blatant vetting, asked: "Does Inspector Tim Pat have to certify the driver is also in ship shape?"

Tim Pat visually digested the five foot three maybe four, late twenties early thirties, plump, plain looking, fair haired, well spoken doctor with bright laughing blue eyes. She looked lovely and comfortable to him. He replied quickly and he hoped humorously: "Start off being nervous of a woman; a man could spare himself a lot of trouble up ahead; that's my father's advice and father is a wise one fol-da-diddle-day-roe, he is a wise O'Leary, I tell you."

"Tim Pat is a chip off the same fol-da-diddle-day-roe, I caution you, Emma Dempsey!"

Emma, in no hurry, welcomed the idle chat with her mechanic and his friend. Her working days were tension filled. Finbar was obliging, friendly, courteous and reliable. The feeling of condescension was always in her when she stood on the garage floor talking to him. She did not like that in herself.

"Most definitely you are a neighbour of Finbar expressing caution before you say hello. Are all you men the same from that part of the world?"

The white coat put Tim Pat thinking. He wanted to sound interesting, different; "Calloused hands we have in common, in so many other ways we differ."

As Tim Pat had hoped, Emma asked for clarification. "Such as?"

" Some from West Cork are Hindu, some Jews, Muslim, with the very odd Christian thrown into the mix."

Finbar's tapping of one spanner off another enumerated, "Multiracial cows, donkeys, horses, goats, hens, even cultural O'Learys."

A believer in the influence of first impressions, Finbar had on purpose stitched in the 'cultural O' Learys'.

Not to be bested in describing West Cork, Tim Pat, despite not having a creative bone in his body but in deference to his family being described as 'cultural', gave poetry his best shake, "With furze, daffs, fuchsia, daisies and a stream that has so many trout, there's hardly room for water."

His assault on the medium elicited a laugh from Emma, he was pleased it did.

"Only for the first nine or ten years of courtship are we cautious in West Cork after that we are deadly altogether, but in Tim Pat's case his civil service background and university schooling doesn't help; a rule book has to be consulted before he makes the smallest decision."

Finbar knew Tim Pat would be pleased he had sketched in his academic experience and job location. That he did it in a cumbersome fashion would not matter. It told Doctor Emma Tim Pat was not a man of straw, he was a man with prospects – within the confines of the service. Finbar had no intention of hinting at the limiting factor Tim Pat's combustion would have on those same prospects.

Emma believing education pushed back boundaries of affront felt at ease to snipe at Tim Pat. "The pen and pencil in the top pocket certainly declared a rule book man. If I knew the make of car O'Leary drives, I could more accurately describe his personality."

"You'll not find any of his carburettors in here, Emma. Into the post office every week, there's one sound solid man for you." said Finbar, still tapping with his spanners knowing full-well Tim Pat would not pursue the post office aspect too far. Synonymous with the word 'tight' in West Cork was the name O'Leary.

"Time enough for cars - you have this one in great shape, Emma," Tim Pat hurriedly replied.

Emma praised, "Finbar takes credit for Minor's condition."

Finbar checked the clock standing on a shelf above the workbench: "Two quid, Emma. Yourself and himself can gossip for the rest of the night but I've another job on hand before pulling down the curtains."

"Daylight robbery, Emma." declared Tim Pat, discreetly going to the far side of the car not wishing to witness the passing of the two pounds, and, more importantly, the always appreciated tip. Emma and Finbar spoke together for a few minutes. The way they glanced in his direction, Tim Pat knew that he was the subject of discussion. He felt uncomfortable because he knew they knew he knew. Finbar walked smartly towards the car requiring his attention, saying:

"Emma will give you a lift, Minor is heading in your direction."

Tim Pat reckoned Finbar, on the strength of his performance that evening, had lost his vocation. He could swap jack and grease gun for match-making. He had not intended going back to his flat, but willingly allowed himself be carried by the current of the evening's prospects.

"Sure it isn't a bother?" asked Tim Pat, as he sat into the car, certain Emma wasn't going to say it was.

"Sure, it is a bother. But I can hardly jeopardise Finbar's preferential treatment by refusing his friend, can I?"

Emma fixed herself behind the steering wheel and carefully adjusted the rear mirror. She was busy; so busy she clipped Tim Pat's face with her hand as she placed it behind the passenger seat while reversing out of the garage.

"Nearly missed!"

Rubbing his face Tim Pat said, "I'm not getting out!"

As Emma weaved her way through traffic, Tim Pat took the precaution of placing his hands on the dashboard. This lack of trust irritated Emma. "Will you take your hands off the dash, you are making me nervous!"

Against his better judgment Tim Pat removed his hands.

"No shortage of zip in this one!" said Tim Pat, wanting to bring to her attention the speed at which she was travelling. Emma knew what he was attempting.

"O'Leary, shut! Do you like living in Dublin?" enquired Emma glancing sideways at the West Cork man. The craggy jaggedness of his bone structure stated the O'Learys forever had those lean looks. There was a statement of sinew, of the wild and its space, of freedom, about Tim Pat O'Leary. Interesting! A fish out of water condemned to a civil service job that had more rigidity in its rules than a maximum security prison had steel bars. She knew this man beside her would regularly need to walk and work in his origins or explode.

"He did not answer her question but without questioning, she brought the Minor to a stop outside a chip shop when Tim Pat pointed and directed:

"Stop there!"

"But of course, master."

Getting out of the car Tim Pat said,

"I didn't mean it like that. What's yours?"

"Smoked cod and chips, please."

"Salt, vinegar?"

"But of course. "

Emma's condition of portliness was not helped by her indulgence in everything she counselled patients of similar proportions to avoid. Reprehensible editors who insinuated into the public mind that small fattish ladies should not be seen bouncing on horseback or dipping themselves in the sea, she would have their editorial lives terminated. These persons promulgated the theory that ladies who stood at the other end of the cat-walk from skinny emaciated felines were neither fun to be with nor around.

Emma's tactful mother Heather approved her choice of motor car by referring to an article she had read to the effect that the Minor was constructed with heavy loads in mind. Emma enjoyed all outdoor activities and participated where possible. She knew her natural presentation attracted the attention of middle-aged if not senior suitors and rarely males of her own age. Obviously weight was not considered a problem in West Cork, maybe fat was a virtue. If so that would be a welcome change. She reached across and opened the door to allow Tim Pat in with his steaming bundles.

Tim Pat advised as he handed Emma her cargo, "Thoroughbred chips must have their flanks massaged with salt and vinegar to bring out their natural juices."

"Do you have horses in West Cork?"

"Elephants are scarce enough but horses we have in plenty.
Do you ride?"

"Yes I do. Where are we going to eat these?" asked Emma, seriously

"What's wrong with here? No better place to watch the parade of envious people passing!"

"Why not, indeed!" Emma opened back the layers of paper to get at the steaming treasure.

"Lovely" said Tim Pat, wolfing his purchase.

"Gorgeous! I haven't had these in ages." Emma got locked into the rhythm of Tim Pat's fingers as they went laden from paper to mouth. Not far behind him did she finish.

"Show me!" said Tim Pat. Taking the empty papers from Emma, he went back into the chipper and returned without them.

"Now for a pint. I'll see you home then." said Tim Pat, his hands back on the dash. Emma wondered at his reference to seeing her home, particularly as it was her car.

She was savouring the experience of their impromptu relationship and had no intention of ending it in a hurry.

"Where to?" she asked as she started the engine.

"Well, I live in Rathmines and I suppose it will be handier for both of us if we have the pint there, my local."

How O'Leary supposed it would be handier in Rathmines was a mystery, but she went along with it.

"Rathmines it is. Take those greasy hands off my dash or I will chop them off!" Emma commanded in the certainty that if it was a man that was driving, Tim Pat would not be holding on for dear life.

"Only drying the vinegar off of my fingers. It isn't how I don't trust you. I'm great at everything, anticipating crashes is a speciality. Crashes do happen you know."

"Which pub is your local? And I assure you O'Leary there will be no crash while Emma Dempsey is driving."

"Martin B. Slattery's; near the junction of Castlewood Avenue with Rathmines Road."

"Haven't been to that establishment!"

"Soon to be corrected."

Emma had been to pubs with her own class of people, to their own class of pubs. When they got near the pub Tim Pat directed: "Park here, perfect."

She had hardly stopped when he was gone out of the car, ordering: "Come on!"

Tim Pat skipped across the road and stood on the pavement looking across at Emma still sitting in the car. Looking out through the window,

24

she lingered a moment. She saw the world, the real world, the street with its teeth and lips, people of every hue and description, of fish and chips and pints. Her place in life's choir would rarely occasion her associating with the likes of Tim Pat. If one of her kind took unto themselves a spouse from the 'common herd', as her mother would describe them, they effected their own social exclusion.

Emma was disenchanted with her designer grouping; they were claustrophobic in association, location and discourse. What nonsense she thought at her age not doing what she wanted to do. Getting out of the car, she crossed the road.

Tim Pat pushed open the pub door and was half way in when he checked, stepping back he allowed Emma in before him. His correction registered with Emma. Tim Pat was rarely in female company or else Martin B's was a pub frequented by males and avoided by females, she surmised.

It was unusual for Tim Pat to be in the bar that early prompting the barman to remark;

"On the early shift, Tim Pat? … Usual?"

It was the first time Tim Pat had taken a date into Martin B's. He had no intention of engaging Danny, the barman, in their conversation.

"Yeah! Emma, what'll you have?"

"Oh! Glass of Guinness, please, Tim Pat." replied Emma, looking at the ebony décor: everything, in particular the ceiling, ennobled by years of cigarette smoke and a strict avoidance of the paint brush family.

"Make that two pints, Danny!" Tim Pat ordered.

"I said a glass, Tim Pat."

"Tim Pat would be looking at it from a financial angle, Miss. You see, a pint is cheaper than two glasses"

"How you robbers justify what you charge for a glass against the price of a pint whips shit!" replied Tim Pat.

"In that case you had better make mine a pint also, Danny!" Not having drunk from a pint glass Emma quite fancied gripping one.

Danny advised, "O'Leary can be approached from any side except his pocket."

Two-way banter flowed freely between barmen and customers in Martin B's. Never offence taken or intended.

"Shag off and pull them pints". Tim Pat threw the words after Danny, who had moved up the bar to the Guinness tap.

"Your language is shocking, Tim Pat." said Emma as she opened the snug door, took a quick glance inside before closing it again.

"In here no one understands any other language. There's a larger snug down below. Take a peep."

"Finbar obviously doesn't frequent this bar; he doesn't use bad language. I will take that 'peep.'

Tim Pat took account of Emma's correction; she was not the first to protest at his expletive ridden tongue. Previously, he reacted by thickening the dose, but not with Emma. Emma had the white coat.

Emma's inspection took a few minutes. Tim Pat knew she was returning when he heard Danny tell her,

"That's the dining area. Is he buying you a meal? Half portions, half prices, not like the drink, should appeal to O'Leary."

"We have eaten already, thank you", replied Emma respectfully. "Is that a fact now?" said Danny.

Tim Pat knew this juicy snippet of information would be broadcast to his friends.

"Bring down them pints!" barked Tim Pat, afraid Danny would wheedle further information from Emma, and knowing well whatever she did say would be well and truly contorted in its retelling.

Emma arrived back from her 'peep' at the same time as Danny arrived with the pints. Placing them on the counter in front of Tim Pat, he said in a cautionary fashion, "We have to be careful of the indigestion, Miss. Those Shelbourne dinners need time to settle."

"You'd know all about the settling of Shelbourne dinners; the brother peeling spuds in there!" declared Tim Pat motivated by envy.

"Cheffing it is called Tim Pat, cheffing!"

"That's what I said, peeling spuds!"

"All the fuckin' one to you what he's peeling; you'll not be eating in there anyhow."

"He'd want to be better at peeling spuds than you are at pulling pints, that's for sure."

Before leaving them, Danny advised Emma,

"Miss, if you have any spatter of sense, you'll run a mile from this fella - daft, daft as a brush without bristle or handle."

Emma asked Tim Pat, "Do they really serve meals in here?"

"The rats are on liquids in this gaff; what does that tell you?"

"In this gaff there is absolutely no difference between rats and men."

From that first pint, Emma was a regular with Tim Pat in Martin B's'.

CHAPTER 5

Emma Dempsey was the youngest of three plain plump daughters whose parents, George and Heather, were medical consultants and had their rooms in the family home in Dublin's Fitzwilliam Square.

Heather feared for the future of society when viewing laden clothes lines in poor and lower middle class areas. The rabbit syndrome could only lead to disastrous consequences she opined to her friends when first married.What Heather Dempsey said had to be considered with gravitas, and she was at her definite best when postulating that the size of a family, if not to be rude and common, should not exceed one. Except that if by some misfortune that one should be a girl, then and only then should a woman be allowed stretch-marks to two.

So it came to pass that, when Heather decided herself and George should have a son, George was called into active service. Heather didn't much like sex, for a meek man George was messy. For eight and a half months a room decorated in blue was prepared. Knitting needles of her dear friends turned red in their frenzied knitting of blues. Staff in the house doubled from one to two. A cook-cum-housekeeper was already in service. A month before the child's arrival a nanny was employed so she could familiarise herself with procedures. To Heather's dismay, a dismay sympathetically shared by her dear friends, the child Florence arrived without balls. No one could understand what went wrong; their collective heads were scratched in wonderment. George was again cranked into service. The mistake would be righted this time; but, lo and behold, the child Stephanie arrived. Her doctor parents looked under the child's armpits, into her eardrums, up her arse, but balls were not to be found. The clothes line was getting heavier. Heather Dempsey reluctantly decided on one last trick from George's procreative dick.

While Doctor Meek was astride, she placed her hands round his neck and pressing on his Adam's apple threatened: "You better get this one right Georgie Porgie or dick is dead!"

The way the pressure from Porgie's neck came and went off her hands told her he had managed one affirmative nod. Obviously Georgie got his affirmatives awry because now the family Dempsey had baby Emma. Several times their clothes line broke.

Snobbery and pure unwantedness saw each of the three children terrified in turn; incarcerated into the privilege of an English public school at six years of age. The crude hacking at home's umbilical cord by distance, and association with similarly distraught lambs did not diminish their sense of abandonment or prevent pillows being drenched with bitter tears. Emma, the last to be jettisoned from Fitzwilliam, had found isolation in Florence and Stephanie's going as distressing as the predicament they themselves found in being deported.

The tick-pause-tock-pause-tick of the grandfather clock in the hallway in Fitzwilliam Square drowned in unbridled children's joy on days of holiday homecoming only. At all other times, the basement entrance was used by children, cook, and nanny.

A basement which incorporated the kitchen, housekeeper's room and unused wine cellar, and in the long ago the servants had to climb the eighty-seven steps to their quarters at the top of the house. Nanny was not at all impressed by those eight-seven steps or her quarters.

"Hush please. Be quiet, please. Don't do that, please. Leave it alone, please. Stop, please." were the monotonous directives by cook and nanny struggling to keep the children's noise levels to zero in the basement and upper floors of the house, the only areas they were allowed access while at home. Silence ruled the ground floor that had been converted into two separate consulting rooms and the first floor, the principal floor of the house, with it's front and back drawing rooms that had pristine period furniture, works of art, silverware etc etc etc, and were used only for entertaining. A home of restrictions.

Rebellious first feathers quickly manifested themselves through

Emma's child-down when she joined Stephanie and Florence at boarding school. She hated being away from home and her disruptive behaviour caused the Principal to issue a stern warning to the three, supported with an equally stern letter to their parents that expulsion would follow if Emma did not behave.

Admonishing letters to the three daughters and a suitably contrite letter of apology to the Principal were hastily dispatched across the Irish Sea from Fitzwilliam.

During school term, a father was sometime seen driving up to the main door to collect an expelled child. The way cases were flung into the boot and the quick opening and slamming of the rear door before the car screeched off through the big wrought iron gate entrance with its never to be seen again little captive sitting in the back seat confirmed the Principal's ruthlessness in matters disciplinary. Neither Principal, janitor or gardener stood on the granite steps waving goodbye to a parting father and daughter. Mothers never ever came to pick up their fallen swans.

Stephanie and Florence, realising ejection for one was escape for all, prompted Emma to commit the cardinal sin of bed wetting, but not before they had misdemeanours recorded against themselves to ensure a family ejection. A peremptory, "Come and get them!" was shafted into Doctor Heather's eardrum when she answered an eight-thirty phone call from the Principal, a morning that heralded Emma's third glorious piss in a row. The doctors Dempsey had no trouble placing their daughters in a boarding school that allowed weekend home visits, if sought. The understanding Principal thought it an eminently wise decision on their parents part to bring the children back to Dublin in view of the polio scare which they lied had beset the shire in which their former school was located.

Fitzwilliam Square is but a leisurely stroll to fashionable Grafton Street. Late eighteenth century Georgian, designed by Luke Gardiner and called after King George of England; stretched from Parnell Square on the north side of the Liffey across to Fitzwilliam Square on the south side. Red bricked four storey over basement houses that were at a time home to Lords, MP's, army generals, judges and merchants. By the twentieth century Fitzwilliam was still home to some merchants but the others had packed their traps and fled back across the Irish sea. Fitzwilliam was now home to middle class families, to board rooms, offices awake from nine to five, Monday to Friday, with chattering typewriters, telephones, teleprinters; home to soft voiced, soft handed consultants dealing with esoteric illnesses complained of by clients looking for a cure for old age but was neighbourless and friendless for the sisters Emma, Stephanie and Florence.

The three sisters having finished secondary school went on to University and it was there friendships were forged for the first time. Homes were visited where parents welcomed their children's friends without vetting or fuss. Homes where furniture and fittings spoke with squeaks and creaks, lived in homes where pristine furniture, oil paintings, ornaments, if present, had their own live role to play and were enjoyed. Homes where fridges' bellies welcomed probing hungry scholars' fingers and, if empty, an imaginative menu could be hastily constructed round a tin of beans.

No hush, no stop, no restrictions in these homes.

Battles were waged against mother's rules; entrenched positions yielded until at last they could, without embarrassment, invite friends to Fitzwilliam Square. A home took shape against a backdrop of reluctance rather than approval on their mother's part. The basement entrance was no longer insisted on. Entry and exit became a matter of choice.

Stephanie and Florence did not disappoint their mother in their choice of husbands. Emma's arrival on the doorstep with Tim Pat in tow was the subject of nervous hilarity. Could Emma possibly be serious about this rustic, wondered and worried mother Heather.

Emma was headstrong. Heather Dempsey could not mask her disgust as she repeated at every opportunity her boyfriend's name, in full, in a tone most supercilious. Emma had always been rebellious, the only one to best her in arguments, who challenged her authority. Emma chose to disregard this name-goading hoping it would pass but mother did not let up.

After what was for Heather Dempsey her first nauseating encounter with Tim Pat O'Leary, she made her feelings clear to Emma; she did not want him calling to the house, she did not want her daughter to have anything to do with him.

In the first two weeks of the couple's friendship she answered the front door three times to Tim Pat's ringing. Twice she discourteously did not speak to him but went and told Emma she was required by 'something or other' on the doorstep. The third time she glared at Tim Pat and pointing at the stairway to the basement shafted her festering abhorrence, "Those steps are to accommodate you and your likes, do you understand that, Pat Tim O'Leary or Tim Pat O'Leary or whatever Tim you think you are, you clown?"

Emma had been profuse in her apologies for her mother's insulting behaviour and had asked Tim Pat to be patient, not to heed her. Tim Pat was not very good at being patient and welcomed the opportunity to do a bit of equalising in the insult stakes.

"And God made darkness so that ignorant crones like you could answer doors at night to quality like me, a West Cork O'Leary."

"How dare you, you-you-you blasted country yokel!" she choked back at him.

On hearing the raised voices, Emma hurriedly finished her titivating and ran to the front door. Tim Pat had left and was making his way towards Leeson Street where she caught up with him.

"It is Emma you have the date with, Tim Pat, not Emma's mother. And I would love a glass of Martin B's Guinness, I've had an exhausting day."

" You'll have a pint!"

" But of course a pint!"

Such as it was, that spat was the only dialogue of any significance Tim Pat had with Emma's mother, Heather.

Neither Emma nor her sisters ever knew where their father George stood on matters espoused by their mother. They pitied him being married to her and never ever contemplated hauling him into arguments where they knew he was certain to vaporise. George, the essential pacifist, regretted Emma's involvement with Tim Pat for no other reason than it distressed his wife, therefore distressing himself.

The fermenting of Tim Pat's and Emma's relationship was given an accelerant after ten months when one evening Emma, in a happy mood, was leaving home with a pair of wellington boots under her arm. She and Tim Pat were going for a walk to the Featherbeds near Glencree in Wicklow, their favourite walk.

Mother, observing her going and the boots remarked,

"Meeting Timothy Patrick O'Leary again, are we?"

Pointing at the rubber boots she continued, feigning concentration: "Venue? His office or his bed-sit, which peasant patch, Emma?" and laughed heartily if derisively.

"Oh Mummy, how remiss of me, I should have asked what boots you were wearing when you told Daddy he had to marry you!" replied Emma. Innocence written all over her face. Emma placed emphasis on the 'had to marry'. She saw pale take over the face of her mother, now standing bold upright: "How dare you do this to the family" she hissed. "You dare not marry that disgusting grub O'Leary."

"Mother, I am marrying Tim Pat O Leary."

"He will never come inside my door."

"Mother, be assured, Tim Pat never will!"

There was no truth in Emma's insinuation but having said it the idea appealed to her. Tim Pat and herself were tailor-made for each other when the false Fitzwilliam aspect and her mother's ridiculous snobbery were removed. A woman ignored a rare-one like Tim Pat at her peril. Emma wanted Tim Pat O' Leary and she did not want Tim Pat to change.

"Something cooking in that medical head of yours?" Tim Pat enquired as they drove towards the mountains that evening.

"Could be!" replied a meditating Emma. She had made the statement of intent to shock her mother. The effect had been immediate – just stopping short of a coronary. She was cogitating on her statement's content.

She glanced sideways at her companion of the previous ten months. Her husband would have to be like this man sitting beside her: strong, independent, intelligent with an acceptable disorder attaching to him. There was freedom in his company and what pleased her immensely was the obvious sexual attraction he had for her. This was an area most sensitive. Previous escorts who attempted sexual overtures required alcohol before ignition. Those who didn't have alcohol didn't try. Both groupings insulted her womanhood.

As they drove through Rathfarnham village going towards Glencree and the Featherbeds she recalled reading her mail at supper one evening as it had not arrived prior to her leaving for work. Her mother had, without warning, launched into a vehement dissertation on the negatives of Timothy Patrick O'Leary. To her mother's fury, she had not batted an eyelid.

"That peasant of yours is beyond social redemption; you will never dislodge him from his bog origins; that voice of his, God! His unwillingness even to make an attempt. It would be asking miracles of elocution lessons but get him to take some!" When Emma did not defend or agree or react in any way it caused her mother to scream.

"Have you not heard one word of what I've said?"

"Pardon, Mummy?" Emma had replied politely, not taking her eyes off her correspondence.

"For God's sake Father will you say something, do something, anything, before disaster befalls our family."

Father meekly complied with his wife's instruction. "Of course, Mother; please listen to your Mother, Emma."

Then George, true to form, clamped-up.

Now laughing out loud at the memory, she looked at Tim Pat who, not surprisingly, looked peculiarly at her.

"Never mind, Tim Pat, there are tablets for everything these days".

"If there is, don't take them." Tim Pat dropped his few words, never a hint of romance, that was his way.

She felt confident she could have him. He was with her because he wanted to be. Not even a contrary reason could she think of as to why they would not be happy together.

Fostered by Master Murphy in his school going days, Tim Pat's knowledge of and interest in flora and fauna was of encyclopaedic proportions. It was important for him to identify the different plants and species wanting to expand Emma's education in these matters. Master Murphy would expect that of him. Emma's external expression of interest was not matched by her digesting the information imparted. She liked to listen to Tim Pat but had no real interest in either flora or fauna. As they walked, Tim Pat crouched beside a clump of grass bedecked with tiny flowers, tangled weeds and billions of different insects. As he intently studied the clump, Emma asked softly but deliberately while her hand slowly brushed back and forth, back and forth across the top of his head barely touching his mop of jet black hair.

"I believe you have an important question to ask me, O' Leary."

Tim Pat continued teasing the clump for a few seconds, stopped, looked across the valley at the mountain opposite with its myriad colours, shades and gently moving eastwards lazy clouds; rising, without looking round he asked in a serious but calm voice:

"Are you sure, Emma?"

"I'm not a child, of course Emma is sure."

"You have considered your mother's attitude?"

"It's a gentleman's prerogative to ask a lady. Now are you or are you not going to beg?"

Tim Pat, turning, circled Emma's waist and wheeled her off her feet, round and round and round crashing them both into dizzy dizzy.

As a child, Emma had been wheeled dizzy by her nanny in the basement. She was happier there in the Featherbeds in the arms of West Cork's Tim Pat O'Leary than she had ever been.

CHAPTER 6

Tim Pat and Emma set their wedding day. Doctor Heather was devastated when told and bitterly informed Emma she would not be insulting any of her friends by inviting them but would discharge her responsibilities as the bride's mother.

It didn't bother Emma in the least. She had plenty friends of her own and there were sisters Stephanie and Florence and their families to invite.

Heather Dempsey's openness about her own affairs and the incisiveness with which she dealt with problems had the effect of casting her as counsellor to her friends - friends who refused to be derailed by her caustic remarks. She was particularly good and keen to advise on their marital difficulties. She was their trusted confidante. If her counselling necessitated the fitting of a jackboot, she provided the psychological backup to ensure comfort in trampling. Her role gave her enormous power and she thrived on it. She was the bane of her friends' husbands who saw her as the repository of the intimacies of their marital relationships. Her arched eyebrow would brazenly acknowledge their discomfort. Her jackboots kneaded cobblestones of male privilege and transformed them into smooth gender-equity surfaces.

Her patients were similarly treated. If they did not have the palate for direct medicine, they were told to go elsewhere. She whipped them into shape with maximum discipline and minimum drugs having discovered early in her career that people operated better when choice was removed. She apologised to her friends for her failure to put an end to the relationship between West Cork's Tim Pat O'Leary and Emma. She said she had foreseen something like this would happen to

Emma who had been a magnet for lame ducks and a champion of lost causes. Not being familiar with peasantry's pecking order she was at pains trying to locate him on that particular scale but Tim Pat was definitely way down there, somewhere. She expected her friends to understand; she was not being evasive.

Given daughter Emma's social treachery, Heather's friends marvelled at her buoyancy. Heather told her friends she did not intend to test the elasticity of their loyalty to the point of inviting them to the wedding and therefore they would not be in receipt of invitations. She did however promise a party in Fitzwilliam Square at which she would give a full and complete account of the day's happenings. She assured them they would miss nothing other than the pain of attendance.

Heather had surveyed the wedding and the South West primates with two jaundiced eyes above a jaw she had fashioned into a jib for the occassion. At the promised party afterwards she stood in front of the Adam's fireplace in the drawing room dabbing gently her upper lip with a scented handkerchief emphasising her nausea at her selective telling of that most disgusting of days. All tales were duly greeted by a chorus of 'oh no's', 'Great Gods!', many many 'terribles', interlaced with a myriad of the least colourful exclamations one was likely to hear at any gathering outside the walls of the Vatican.

George, smiling, standing beside but in deference slightly behind his wife, clockwise nodded to each of his wife's entranced semi-circled retinue. In the vernacular of head nodding, he was confirming, 'true', 'true', 'true' at every word Heather uttered.

Heather began her tail of woe by describing the controlled half stumble and push of Tim Pat's brigade as they went sideways from incomplete genuflections into their pews. Their servitude in greeting the priest's arrival on the altar belied the laughing giggling and coarse talk that went on before hand in that same house of God.

She related how at the moment the wedding ring should have been placed on Emma's finger, Tim Pat's brother Gerard, the best man, when handing the ring to Tim Pat fumbled clumsily; between them the ring dropped, hitting the altar rail's marble step, its high pinging note heard in the remotest shadows, before bouncing onto the tiled floor where it began it's golden roll. Like a veritable cobra the groom's shoe stamped to a halt the rolling band. The collective cillary muscles of all pinched in the poor light as Gerard bent, standing he held aloft what appeared to be two fused golden matchsticks. The celebrant joked, "Knowing Tim Pat, this ring has to be a barmbrack job". Emma's laughter placed the ring's crushing not in disaster but hilarity and she was joined by all with the predictables abstaining. Tim Pat had placed his own mother's proffered wedding ring on Emma's finger before the laughter had abated.

George interjected with a snippet of information he thought valuable and his wife wished the same information had stuck in his throat. 'Timothy Patrick's brother Gerard is an orthopaedic surgeon in the Mayo Clinic. He was best man and another brother was the celebrant'.

George visibly shrivelled under the withering gaze of his wife. Smartly, he took off his glasses and began feverishly polishing the already over polished glasses.

No one in the room blinked or enquired further. No credence given. Like an idle moment, George's snippet of information passed unregistered. The gathering were told about the pale-necked men and permed women devoutly receiving Holy Communion and how this meek flock morphed into a boisterous, back slapping, unhygienic, whiskey-bottle-sharing mob having stepped from the Church, jigged and reeled though still on consecrated ground.

Immediately after the wedding breakfast, Heather and George departed – or, 'escaped as she later termed it - from proceedings and parish, swearing never ever to return.

The tea party in Fitzwilliam petered out as it had petered in.

Life with Tim Pat highlighted the clogged arteries of family life in Fitzwilliam Square. Emma knew her mother to be a thundering bitch and deserved the great chunks of Tim Pat dialect hurtled at her that night on the doorstep. For Tim Pat there was no easy side or difficult side to trouble, he went straight for the jugular.

Heather Dempsey, as time went on, changed tactics. She wasn't as confrontational; she adopted a more insidious style of baiting, foxing Emma into making choices. She became more of a schemer, a viper. She hated Emma for the heinous imposition of Tim Pat on the family and saw him as a stain on their respectability.

Florence's and Stephanie's procreative eggs, within their respective marriages, ensured their mother's stock of thirty-year-old blue knits were long exhausted before Emma gave birth to a baby boy.

A bouquet of flowers preceded their holder into the private ward of the maternity hospital. George Dempsey placed them at the end of the bed before kissing Emma, issuing suitable congratulatory words interspersed with questions of concern for mother and baby.

"Thank you Daddy, these are beautiful. Where is Mummy?"

"She should be along any moment, my dear." replied George as he positioned a chair at either side of the bed anticipating his wife's arrival.

Emma saw her Mother's eye scan the room through the small glass window in the door before entering. "You're fine!" she remarked without emotion as she sat on George's positioned chair.

Emma was hurt, her mother had not mentioned her grandchild.

"I must send for your grandson!" said Emma, looking from one parent to the other for approval.

"No, no! We can wait for a more suitable time," objected Heather.

George, taken aback by his wife's rejection, asked, "Emma, please, if it isn't too inconvenient."

"We shall see, Daddy!" said Emma, pressing on a bell.

"Proud grandparents I expect." said nurse when she came into the room.

"Grandparents, indeed, Nurse!" Emma confirmed.

Heather's face twitched in what passed for a smile while George acknowledged the nurse's pleasantness; "Good evening, Nurse, I hope Emma is a good patient, not too demanding?"

"Mothers like Emma make coming to work a pleasure; you can't wait to see baby O'Leary, right?"

Heather snootily corrected, "Doctor Emma to you!"

Taken aback by the sudden formality the nurse stood corrected, "Doctor Emma!"

"Rubbish, Mother, rubbish! If it isn't too inconvenient, Nurse, please bring my baby, and my name is Emma O Leary and I would thank you to address me as Emma."

"Certainly, Emma."

Nurse returning to the room and assuming the answer would be in the affirmative moved with her bundle towards Mrs. Dempsey, saying, "Gran would like to hold baby O'Leary?"

Emma had hoped her mother's aversion to Tim Pat would not extend to her child but Mother's recoiling shattered that hope. Not pretending she noticed, Emma extended her arms, "I will take Baby O'Leary, Nurse, grandmother is much too excited."

Not in a month of Sundays would George ask to hold a baby, newborn or otherwise, but attempting to redress his wife's rudeness he put out his arms, insisting,

"Grandfather, please Nurse!"

Standing, he silently studied and admired the pink wrinkled face and the black matted hair of his sleeping grandchild.

"Beautiful, Emma, beautiful. A boy, a boy!" said George, nothing more.

At that moment Emma glimpsed the measure of disappointment her mother must have experienced when she so needed a boy and three females arrived. George carefully handed the baby to Emma.

"Emma, ring when you need me." said nurse before leaving the room.

Emma moved the clothing from around baby's head allowing her mother to see its face from where she sat. Heather had hoped infidelity or the Holy Ghost would have come to the rescue but unmistakeably here was Timothy Patrick the Second, their first child a boy. The years of bitterness welled up in her. Of her three daughters she liked Emma the least and of their husbands she hated Tim Pat the most.

Heather, pretending to be contemplative, murmured, "Striking resemblance to us Dempseys, striking."

Emma had no intention of correcting the glaring lie.

'Tim Pat must be delighted?" said George.

His wife hated hearing the name but George considered it would be nothing short of ignorance if baby's father was not mentioned. He had never found anything wrong with Tim Pat other than that they had absolutely nothing in common, which, under the circumstances, was not at all bad.

"Tim Pat should be along shortly." said Emma casually, pleased to mention her husband's name knowing mother Heather would scamper at the information. George, barely audible, for many reasons, not least of which was his terror of wife Heather, requested, "Please give Tim Pat my congratulations, Emma."

"Father, I already have!"

Heather took the flowers from the bed and placed them on a table well out of Emma's reach. Emma saw her place an envelope among the flowers and believed a decent gift lay within. She did not check but left it there to surprise Tim Pat.

"Thank you for calling. Tim Pat will be sorry he missed you."

"No doubt celebrating with his public house friends. Meeting him would have produced a multitude of false pleasantries. Come along, George."

What her mother had said before leaving had Emma looking askance at the envelope just before Tim Pat's gentle knock and entry. Emma was relieved her mother and Tim Pat had not met. A disturbance of some sort would have been guaranteed: its proportion, great or greater, the only variable.

"How's my family?" asked Tim Pat as he kissed Emma but looking at his son,

"An O'Leary, by God! An O'Leary out and out. Has he a Cork accent?"

"He drinks like one! That's quite enough for his mother and him to be getting on with."

Moving towards the flowers Tim Pat turned his head to read the envelope.

"Mother brought those." said Emma, pleased to suggest to Tim Pat that her mother had undergone a change of heart with the arrival of a grandson.

Tim Pat liked money. Emma hoped her Mother had been generous.

"The bitch brought them to the wrong fucking ward if she did!"

Emma, shocked at Tim Pat's reaction, asked, "I beg your pardon, Tim Pat?"

Tim Pat, tossed the card to Emma, saying. "Reginald George fucking Ignatius my arse, Reginald George Ignatius!"

From the folds of the swathing clothes a gurgle emanated as Emma read the card out loud,

"To E. Dempsey on the arrival of Reginald George Ignatius". Slowly Emma's head nodded from side to side as her fingers deftly touched clothing from their baby's face.

"That is why she left the flowers out of my reach; she took a chance on you reading it first and won. What she would not give to see your face right then. Father's name in full, Reginald George Ignatius."

Tim Pat spat with vehemence, "All due respect to your father but Tim Pat wouldn't abuse the handle on a chamber-pot by calling it Reginald George Ignatius. You hadn't anything to do with this?"

"Don't be ridiculous, of course I had not. Even baby gurgled his protest on hearing that name."

Tim Pat sat sideways on the bed, glanced towards the door before planting a kiss on Emma's lips.

"She's a banshee that one, a hoor of a banshee!"

Emma's laughter blended with his. "Mother-mine certainly knows how to get Tim Pat hopping. Have pints with your friends in Martin B's, celebrate!"

"Meeting Finbar and a few of the boys; sends his regards to Mother and Dave minor."

Emma had assailed the heavens with fervent prayers her husband would not insist on lumbering their son with one of those West Cork monikers like Dinny Pat, Tom Joe Micky, Willie Joe, Tim Ger, Pat Tim or even a Tim Pat. To her relief her fervent prayers had been answered.

Says Finbar in the garage, "Tim Pat, child's name has to be Dave, the ould fella will be proud you called him Dave; means the world you know. Could translate into shillings down the line.' Emma, there are Dave O Leary's strewn all over the world but our Dave is the genuine article, the one true Irish Dave. Up the rebels, Dave boy, up the Rebels!"

Not being a hospital type, Tim Pat wanted to escape. He regretted not having consulted a paternity hand-book to find out what constituted an acceptable period of time a father was expected to spend with his wife and new child. He had enough, he was getting out of there.

"I'm gone! And I don't want to hear any more bad language out of you either, Dave O' Leary or across my knee you'll be put!"

CHAPTER 7

Authority in the Civil Service could not stomach Tim Pat O'Leary's arrogance and stubbornness. There was no doubting his ability but his bad language, bellowing, lack of respect, ensured he went so far and no further in the promotion stakes. Propounding department heresies, disturbing cobwebs of established procedure, disrespect for authority, guaranteed Tim Pat a lonesome burden. He made the balls, ran with the balls and wound up on his arse with his balls in the 'To be overlooked department'. A firm believer in pen and paper and remembering Master Murphy's maxim, 'the pen would dig you out of the shit', he tried, at all times unsuccessfully, to dig authority into it. With Tim Pat that which invariably started out as a simple memo wound up as an objectionable weight for the porter who had to lift an ever-increasing file from Tim Pat's office to the next and back again. Never any further. Eventually every one of his files died a death when Tim Pat would confront an available superior or a gathering of superiors and fuck the lot up hill and down dale leaving himself heaving like a breathless bull and them pissing themselves with laughter up their collective sleeves.

Tim Pat settled for these conclusions satisfied that his dignity was intact. He would have a few pints on his way home from these skirmishes and filling or not filling in the details would say to Emma – and in later years to Emma and David-

"I peppered them fucks with West Cork logic; craw-thumping, arse-licking shower of mangy hoors, the seed and breed of informers. Up the rebels, Up the rebels!"

Sporadic outbursts of table thumping, leaping and fist waving signalled his colourful regurgitating of these encounters.

Tim Pat was blessed with an incisive brain, the product of which was never placed on conditioning scales but belted out verbally or on paper. Novel interpretations, buck passing, side tracking were the rubber tools of arse-lickers according to Tim Pat. His juniors in the department loved West Cork O'Leary at work or socially. They were the beneficiaries of his gravel psychology, wit and abuse. He elicited similar responses, the cut and thrust of debate, gender made no difference. They knew this and blossomed in his refreshing attitude but hauled back from outgunning him. Respect! His ambition in the department had an inbuilt ambivalence expressed in his hostile attitude towards authority. Those civil servants whom he referred to as having a devotion to advancement and a yellow cunning, he foxed into refusing him the promotion that would assuredly have drawn some of his teeth.

For Emma, Tim Pat was a breath of fresh air. Emma was being shouted at from every page in every publication that she did not have the shape of a modern woman. Living and lying with Tim Pat taught her otherwise; she was beautiful, her own best friend. Emma enjoyed his coming home with a few pints on board, and, certain of his reaction, she would, the odd time, leave a magazine she had been given by a patient, open at a page showing photographs of English royalty. This guaranteed launching Tim Pat, gesticulating and shouting into the emancipation of Ireland by the spilt red blood of West Cork rebels. Men, he would declare, hundreds of whom were revealed to their deaths by the trigger of an informer's tongue. He would reproach Emma for bringing such tripe into the home of a West Cork man. Merciful hour, he would declare, what would his friends think if they came into his home and saw them shower of Royal hoors revered there, their photographs in every book in the house; he would never again be able to show his face in Croke Park, or worse still, West Cork.

Before meeting Tim Pat, Emma had not heard of political affiliations referred to in a colour context. According to Tim Pat, one was either the right colour or the wrong colour. She would tease Tim

45

Pat about his colour, about his relations running up and down the hills in West Cork shooting the other colour, the ambushes, the Black and Tans - worse than General Custer and the Indians she would tease. Tim Pat always closed proceedings with a cut at Fitzwilliam Square, "No doubt Fitzwilliam's sycophants were sorry to see their betters driven from our shores by my crowd. A wonder now that that mother of yours didn't tag along on their coat tails."

Emma could judge to the second the expected duration of the tirade and would leave for the kitchen. As the smell of frying rashers, sausages, black and white pudding got stronger, Tim Pat's speech fizzled out in inverse proportion. After his heart being patriotic his belly became decidedly peckish.

If the oration was being delivered at a reasonable hour, young David was got out of bed. Emma wanted him to see and hear his father in full verbal flight. David would equip himself with a toy gun and racing round the furniture would repeat some of his father's phrases: "Which colour today, Dad, which colour today? We're going on the run, get the picnic basket, the picnic basket; don't forget the rug when going on the run. The bastards will be watching the masses, forget the rug and picnic; we will go to the pub instead".

Attention would quickly focus on David who didn't have to strive too hard to make his adoring parents laugh.

All three would partake of the frying-pan feast. From his perch on his father's knee David, while engaging a sausage, would ask a million curious questions as his greasy fingers would, skim his father's stubble of beard, wipe off his shirt, dirty his trousers, never a 'stop' being uttered or 'be quiet' or ' don't do that', not even with a 'please' prefacing or added. A home of no restrictions.

Emma envied Tim Pat his roots and understood why he had to return regularly to his place of birth among the fields and streams of his youth. Fields, hills and streams that had his heart in their bind and at no time more so than when Zeus forked asunder Dublin's sky turning loose it's roaring heaven's deluge. Violence, Emma had heard Tim Pat's god-fearing parents refer to, as 'the provoked tears and breath of God'. Tim Pat's concern would not be for his Dublin home but his paternal home, its outhouses, orchard, haggard, each field, the flooding, levelling of crops, dung-wet turf in the bog, the animals. Returning home to West Cork sleeves of union he rolled up and the labour of birthright tackled with his kinfolk.

After a sojourn home, it took Tim Pat days often weeks to acclimatise to city life. His roots were as firmly implanted as the veins in his body.

As the years passed, together with education's days and nights of ink and chalk in Dublin, David grew a man in West Cork. Standing side by side with seasoned men, he, with undeclared blistered hands, cleared the top sod, opened turf banks before cutting and spreading its soft heavy brown belly. Schooling decided his availability for all aspects of turf's harvesting, but July's high sun saw him help with the drawing home and his eventual graduation to clamping in the haggard.

The meadow was David's true romance with the country. The brought-in-gallons meadow tea was warmer and sweeter than the wilder bog stuff. Bog weather could be anything, but meadow blue skies sang and droned and lowed and barked, the whole orchestra entered David's head as serenity.

The slow lurching on steel rimmed wheels of the hay-cart from meadow to hay shed was pure magic for David. Sitting on the back, facing from where they had journeyed, bare feet brushing the bohareen's central grass mane, rutted grey white dust tracks flanked by ditches of confused harmony, briar, wild flower, weeds, all fighting for space and light; he smelled and saw it all, the thorn grasping fractured golden hay sops from their passing load. All of life from, badger to field mouse, rabbit to rat, pheasant to ladybird, hare to hedgehog, corncrake to finch, bumble bee to doctor fly, crossed his path. He rode that hay cart in wonderment at the vastness of plant and animal life in that nowhere path through nowhere fields.

CHAPTER 8

A rash of burglaries in the Fitzwilliam Square area prior to David's sitting his Leaving Certificate had Emma concerned, in particular, for her father's safety.

Emma, without thinking or consulting suggested to her father, that David would stay with them in Fitzwilliam when he had finished his exams. George consulted with mother Heather and she was at George's elbow when he rang Emma to confirm their acceptance of the offer. Heather was chuffed; David would be living under her influence. Emma had handed her a glorious opportunity to sunder the O'Leary household.

When George said to Heather, "They are so kind, so considerate, the O'Learys."

Heather answered, "The relationship between David and his father has to be strained. Emma used the excuse of the burglaries to suggest David should stay with us; kind and considerate my foot!"

Too late, Emma realised that by this one act she had changed forever their family plan that had been firmly in place since David's birth. When Emma told Tim Pat what she had done, she knew by his demeanour that his agreement would be a painful extraction rather than willingly given. He had said, "They're your parents, I would do the same for my parents but not without first asking for your approval and David's."

Tim Pat's brow furrowed with torment as he contemplated David's young mind in the clutches of his grandmother. Tim Pat knew David had arrived at the sparking age when meadow, bog and briar would be no match for Dublin's skirts and tits. He had been hoping for one last summer with his son. Christ, how he loved David.

"Thank you, Tim Pat, you are a big big man!" said Emma, slowly and expressively making sure he knew she acknowledged the sacrifice he had made on her behalf.

"A big, big idiot that's what I am. If it wasn't for your father he wouldn't be going there."

"I know!"

When Emma asked David, his reply was what she expected,

"Mam, I will have to discuss it with Daddy, first."

Emma did not make David aware that the matter had already been discussed. She let the play take its course.

When David asked his father what he thought of the proposal, Tim Pat replied, "Son, you don't have a choice. Grandparents have to be looked after, that's how it is, that's how it should be. David, you look after them. Myself and Tom will manage the harvest. "

"Thanks, Dad!"

David's quick 'Thanks, Dad!' left Tim Pat in no doubt that the West Cork chapter had closed for David.

David had enjoyed West Cork; it had been fun, carefree, but the past year had seen a workload prepared for him. The relaxed holiday atmosphere had faded. His father was committed to getting the different jobs done before returning to Dublin and he and Tom had a schedule worked out; he was part of that schedule, work expected. Now that he was not returning, the relief he felt surprised him.

His grandmother's request had pre-empted him giving expression to his disenchantment to his father. The ending at this time ensured memories stayed sweet and no feelings hurt.

When George told Heather, "Emma rang me, David is moving in with us today."

It did not at all surprise Heather that Emma chose to ring when she knew she would not be in the house. Heather snidely remarked, "Moving in! Grandparent's do have responsibilities."

"I thought you were delighted when Emma offered?"

"She knew her father would not refuse. Can you not see that is why she rang you, not me?"

"I hope David's moving here has not caused a falling out with his father?"

"A falling out may or may not have taken place but one inevitably will."

"What a terrible thing to say, Heather."

"I find it incomprehensible that Emma waited until now to separate her son from that ignorant man. Stupid pride has to be the blame."

"They are a very happy family; Emma is certainly happy."

"Puts on a brave face, does Emma have a choice?"

"What are you suggesting?"

"Married to that fellow – how could she now admit to having made such a mess of her life after all these years?"

"She has never intimated to me that she was anything other than happy."

"You don't listen, George, you don't listen."

"I may not be forthright in my comments – but I do listen, Heather"

"I mean you don't listen in an intuitive way."

"There are those who listen too much!"

"Are you suggesting?"

"No, Heather, I am not suggesting. I don't want you getting upset. Those burglaries are disquieting. Emma's suggestion was most thoughtful."

"I said those burglaries were a lame excuse, George?"

"Indeed, indeed! Every effort must be made to ensure his happiness. Youth in the house again, pleasant change, pleasant."

"It's O'Leary's obduracy, his ignorance, lack of culture, that has deprived us of our daughter's love and the love of our grandchild."

"A very refined boy, difficult to believe he is the son of Tim Pat though the physical similarities are obvious."

"Don't mention that name! Do … not … mention that name, induces migraine!"

"Sorry, sorry, - do you think his coming here has his father's blessing?"

"David's coming would not be without his knowledge whatever about his blessing!"

"I would not want it otherwise."

"George, Heather will deal with the matter."

"Of course – but there does seem undue haste – no consultation."

"What is there to consult about? Emma said she will rest easier if David stays here while she is on holiday. The real reason – well, we can only surmise"

"Considerate of Emma, very considerate."

"Convenient more like. David must have refused to go to that West Cork bog with them."

"He hopes to do medicine, that is what his parents … Emma wants."

"I'm sure I will make the right decision with his best interest at heart."

"But it will be medicine?"

"You heard what I said, let that be the end of it."

"A cup of tea would be nice!"

"Make mine coffee!"

CHAPTER 9

'Divide and Conquer!' Heather had been gifted the 'divide' part of the equation when David moved to Fitzwilliam Square after his exams. To ensure the move's effectiveness she contrived David's visits home, while his parents were there, had to be ended. The 'conquering' process would take time. To keep David occupied, it was difficult but necessary for Heather to plan a full schedule of engagements for each night of the week and particularly at weekends. The last fortnight in July and the first fortnight in August would be a welcome respite from those engagements as Tim Pat and Emma would be away on holiday in West Cork.

This new schedule of social activities which Heather undertook, accompanied by an exhausted George and an enthusiastic David, was the subject of complimentary discussion among her social group.

Discretion on the part of Heather's friends had guillotined conversations regarding Emma since the day she socially wounded mother Heather by becoming engaged to Tim Pat. Heather's friends were pleased at the parading of David; whether the parading meant harmony between the two households they did not know, nor would they have the effrontery to ask.

Heather attributed her re-energising to sound sleep experienced because of David's arrival in Fitzwilliam Square: burglars beware!

She would fawn over him in company, placing public emphasis on her dependence on him for her continued good health.

David warmed in the vestments of protector; it imposed manhood status. At these visited houses he met and looked forward to meeting beautifully groomed young ladies. Puberty's muscle was well in David's hand.

David had practised driving in his Uncle Tom's car on the farm in West Cork but had not been allowed onto the public road, though considered an expert by Tom. When he made his grandmother aware of this restriction she was pleased and when he added that his father would not allow him drive until he reached the age of twenty, she was more pleased. David lamely protested his father's objection but gladly went and got a driving licence at grandmother's insistence. Grandmother, elated at her success, tested David's attitude towards his father, "Your father is a country boy, David, old fashioned in his ways, please do not expect too much from him!"

David did not object to his grandmother's criticism, he had too much to thank her for.

By his not defending his father, Heather had put in place the first stitch in David's allegiance to her. Heather appraised with satisfaction her unravelling of parental control and David's growing dependence on her.

Six nights on the trot Heather, George, and David visited the homes of Heather's friends. Each night saw Heather's humorously delivered criticism of David's father became more forceful and pointed. All knew the sharpness of her tongue and thought her wittier than ever. David had listened in embarrassment at his father's denigration by her in those homes visited and because he did not protest she believed he had conceded the veracity of her statements.

On the sixth night Heather went too far, "Maturity in adults should not surprise, but there are those adults who masquerade as free spirits, irresponsible people, bohemian types, artists employed and otherwise artists, civil servants of no background, too stubborn, too pig-headed to let go of their parish pump rags and indecipherable peasant tongues. It would pain them to let go; they refuse to consider the greater pain of holding on, pain that has to be endured by their families that renders decent friendships impossible."

As they drove home David waited his opportunity to express his feelings. The opportunity came when his grandmother said:

"Another pleasant night, David!"

"Not for me it wasn't!" replied David, rushing his words.

"Oh, Grandmother is sorry to hear that, something you ate?"

"It's what you said about my father."

"Your father's name was not mentioned, David!"

"You didn't have to mention his name, everyone knew who the civil servant of no background was meant to be. You hurt me, the horrible way they laughed!"

"David, these are fun evenings, not evenings when one expects their every syllable to be dissected."

"Whatever faults you think my father has I don't want to hear you air them in public or air them to me either. I mean that Grandmother, if you want me to stay in Fitzwilliam while you and Grandfather socialize I will be happy to do so. It will give me a chance to visit Mum and Dad; haven't seen them in ages, they are at work when I call, the only time I can call."

Heather encouraged David to visit his home in the afternoons knowing his parents would not be there. Allowing David a night off from her social whirl was not an option, though the same whirl had George exhausted.

"Staying in Fitzwilliam will not be necessary, David. I did not think we were that sensitive, it was not my intention to offend. I'm surprised you think so little of me."

"It's the least my parents should expect that I defend their good name in public and not stand there and, and, and…."

"And what David?"

"Listen to people laughing at them."

"And you would be right, David! But it is most hurtful – most hurtful – to suggest I intended that to happen. None of us are without our sensitivities; I am distressed by what you suggest! – Most hurtful!"

"I don't mean to be hurtful but I had to tell you how I feel".

"This accusation is a bolt from the blue. I had no idea you were personalising my statements, you should have informed me earlier and

I would have explained the error of your thinking. Isn't that so, George?".

George, sitting in the rear of the car wished he wasn't a witness to the conversation, replied, "George has not been paying attention. What is your question, my Dear?"

Heather, as ever, ignored George, which, as always, suited George.

"Really, David, I though we were friends"

"I'm sorry Gran, but put yourself in my place, what would you have done?"

In the certainty of David's response, Heather tested, "Maybe you are tired of my socialising, David; a rest might do you good; George and I will visit on our own though I must admit Grandmother has become reliant on you to do the driving".

"No, Grandmother, no. I'm fine, honestly, I must have picked you up wrong".

"I assure you David you did pick me up wrong and I find it exceedingly hurtful you thought so little of me."

"I'm sorry".

"Thank you, David; whatever would your Grandparents do without you ... those dreadful dreadful burglaries".

"I'm happy being with you".

"Would you prefer to return home ... to go on holidays ... to West Cork ... perhaps?"

"Oh, no, no no. I'm fine, just fine, my imagination".

"In future, if there is anything, anything at all troubling you, I want you to discuss it immediately with Grandmother. No delay, mind. Discussion avoids misunderstanding; isn't that so, George?"

"Yes!"

"Grandfather isn't given to long-winded statements but what grandfather does say is well thought out, David".

"Yes! Grandmother, if I had not said what I said it would have bothered me – I'm glad I said it though I now know what I said was wrong"

"Always clear the air, David, causes stress if you don't."

"Indeed!" contributed George.

Such was his wife Heather's voracious appetite for this stuff called stress, not alone could she effortlessly absorb the Dempsey quota, but she encouraged her friends to unload their quotas onto her more-than-capable stress digestive system. To her friends, Heather Dempsey was a godsend. In turn, Heather was the repository of their innermost thoughts. Heather had the power, the power of knowledge.

Three weeks had elapsed since David moved to Fitzwilliam. Tim Pat, returning home early from work one afternoon found Dempsey's car parked outside. Unusual, he thought, she never visited, knew she was not welcome. She had to have David along with her; how else could she have gained entry. Tim Pat did not want to meet her and was about to walk away when David came from the house. The mutual delight at father and son meeting was apparent. Tim Pat shook David's hand and gave him a big hug. Chatting, they went back into the house.

"Thought you had left the shagging country. How is that one treating my favourite son?" asked Tim Pat as he sat at the kitchen table. Before David could reply he was ordered, "Stick the kettle on, Dave."

Tim Pat appraised the new suit on his son's back. Knowing who had paid for the suit he passed no remark.

Grandmother, moving David away from attitudes and customs paternally inherited insisted casual dress was not acceptable in Fitzwilliam no more than casual was acceptable in the homes of her friends.

Dress had never bothered Tim Pat and it certainly wasn't bothering him now; sitting at the table in his sports jacket, trousers showing more than the slightest signs of wear at the knees, top shirt button open, loose tie. Contented, he would work in his garden and go to work without changing a stitch.

Tim Pat scrutinised David with eye and mind searching for change. Realising David was on his own he knew their authority had been subverted. David was driving the Dempsey car. Tim Pat hid his fury. It would be at the peril of losing David if he attempted to take the wheels from under him. They had been outfoxed by Heather. He was not going to chastise David for the breach of a rule which he knew would cause Emma great anxiety when she found out.

Rules were rare in the O'Leary household. Family life was a charm and David was the gold thread in his parent's union They had discussed the buying of a car for David and its purchase was being delayed for the good reason of allowing him to mature. Emma was all too familiar with death and serious injury on the roads occasioned by teenage drivers. It was decided David would not be allowed drive on the public road before the age of twenty. David had been informed of their decision and he had accepted their decision without argument.

David was as taken aback as his father was when they met. He would not have had the effrontery to drive up to the house if he had known either of his parents were there. He was caught red-handed. He knew his mother would be distressed when she heard about his driving and his father would be furious at Grandmother's abrogation of their authority.

Grandmother had said, with emphasis, as she handed David the car keys before he left Fitzwilliam to visit what she expected would be an empty house the same as it was every other working day of the week, "David, a young man will remain a boy while living with his parents. You are responsible, intelligent. There is your keys, drive to your heart's content."

Heather's smug smile had said it all, 'Over to you Tim Pat O' Leary, I dare you to take a steering wheel out of your son's hands.'

As David filled the kettle, he said, "I'm here most days, Dad, I always leave a note; the one I left today is there at your elbow."

Tim Pat picked up the note for no other reason than to please David. A glance told all that was in it, the same every week day. "I'm fine, love David."

David sat at the table opposite his father, who dismissively tossed the note sideways. When Tim Pat stretched out his hand, David felt it's sincerity. He knew exactly what his father was going to say.

"You have to feel the flesh, son!"

He was being told the note was not good enough. The calling when his father and mother were not there was no damn good. He would have to call after work or at weekends when they were at home. A jumble of emotions went through David's mind as his father gripped his hand. Statements expressed by his grandmother were forcing their way from what should be vague recollection to full blown study. His mind challenged his heart to consider her insinuated deficiencies in his father, and the unlikely relationship between his parents given their different backgrounds.

He listened with criticism's ear to the accent and language he had considered colourful and lilting. There was room for its distinctiveness in the cacophony of Dublin's throngs but definitely not acceptable in the social plateau he was privy to because of his maternal relations. Its owner would be rejected and acceptance of the owner's son at the very least impeded.

David knowing an explanation was expected of his father's remark: 'You have to feel the flesh' gave an unguarded answer. "Grandmother is so busy each night visiting, and especially at weekends, I just cannot make it home when I know you and mammy are here. I wish I could but I just can't."

He regretted mentioning his grandmother. His father would explode, they hated each other. Beads of sweat formed under his armpits and ran quickly down his rib cage as he held his father's gaze, their hands still locked on the table. He saw nothing in the dark orbs. He had never seen them so silent, so cold. He felt bared and wished his father would activate in some way. It was out of character for him not to immediately climax situations like this. He must have seen the car outside and yet had made no reference to the fact. He expected to be fucked in all directions in his father's inimitable style but it had not happened. Maybe they had spotted him driving or had been told of his driving. His driving must have been already discussed between them and Mother's balming influence was now stifling the honesty of his response. That had to be it, he concluded. His father, never temperate in language or action would have skinned him by now but for mother Emma's influence. David, though quiet in his ways, had spunk. Spunk was bred into him and Tim Pat baulked at posing an allegiance ultimatum.

It was not the time for Tim Pat to be foolhardy; he could drive David permanently into the clutches of his grandmother. He was uncertain of his son's response if tackled hard. That conniving strap Heather would gloat in his insecurity if she could see him now. Tim Pat's dilemma was reproaching David for not visiting and his driving against their wishes, but feared driving a wedge between himself and his son. Heather had out-manoeuvred him by giving David that which any youth would swap his soul for – car keys. Tim Pat was not accustomed to the small stepping-stones of diplomacy. They were never part of his vocabulary no more than he ever pussyfooted his opinions, but he would have to play by Heather's rules if he was to hold his share in his own flesh and blood.

"What does this heavy schedule entail that that 'one' has you pegged to all of a sudden?" asked Tim Pat, placing emphasis on 'one'. He knew grandfather George's input into the same schedule was nil but could not bring himself to say Mrs. Dempsey, and definitely not grandmother.

David interpreted a change of heart on his father's part when the expected reaction did not materialise at his mention of Grandmother. Tim Pat's attitude might be softening towards her. Wanting to believe, his good sense clouded and he answered, "Grandmother has an amazing amount of friends, really beautiful people." before going on to list at least a dozen giving the beautiful roads these beautiful people were living on.

Tim Pat's mug rattled as he placed it on a side plate. He had looked into his son's eyes over the rim as he sipped and wondered what kind of a fool he had reared. The sarcasm that crept into his voice did not register with David as he said while feeling the collar of David's new suit, "Nice piece of clobber, no doubt fits in with the addresses."

Nervously David blurted out, "Hand made, myself and Gran picked out the material, I know Mammy will like it."

"So seldom you call to your Mammy your arse will be out through your handmade before she sees it!"

The sour note struck was all too obvious to David. He knew the question of not calling would keep cropping up. He was conscious of becoming defensive in his answers. No matter what he said his father would insinuate shades and colours just as he had linked the suit to the addresses. He knew the kind of mind his father had, the way it worked. He wished his father would look inside those doors he had spoken about and allow the very eye and ear of objectivity to fashion what he was certain would be a new and pleasant experience.

Grandmother's listed imperfections were there within arms' reach screaming at him. Forgetting about his accent, how in the name of God could his father's tongue be harnessed? The loose un-matching jacket, shirt, and tie, sartorial vulgarity. His father was socially checkmated and worse still he gloried in his being checkmated.

The beginnings of a wry smile died at the corner of David's mouth as he beheld his father. Fathers could see through their sons, knew what went on in their heads. His father might choose not to let on he knew, but he knew. The notion that his father was mellowing towards Gran was withering rapidly. David believed his father would think more of him if he spoke his mind. His grandmother was not present to make her case or defend herself. No more than the night he had spoken in his father's defence when grandmother went over the top. His father, sitting across the table from him, had counselled, 'Treat people as you find them'. Grandmother had been good to him.

In the situation in which he now found himself, he arrogantly thought, damn the consequences; he was going to take up the cudgel on grandmother's behalf and said in a measured tone,

'Dad, you have never concealed your animosity towards Gran and

I had no trouble supporting your fixation, but, like me, I am sure you would change your mind if you gave her half a chance. It is at her insistence I call everyday. I know I don't make it at the weekends but we are very busy at weekends". David paused, his expressive face declaring honesty, but mostly innocence.

Not wanting David to see the fire and hurt in his heart, Tim Pat kept looking down at the table as he spoke, every syllable saturated in venom. "So, you have changed your mind, have you? By God, Tim Pat must be pure stupid not to see that all the time that bitch was a staunch ally of mine. Whips shit!"

"You know that is not what I am saying; don't wrong me, Dad. I'm saying she has been extremely good to your son and I'm sure Gran would like to be on good terms with you".

David tried to interpret a message in the greying spiky hair on top of his father's head. That is all he could see of the bowed head as his father appeared to study the bottom of the now empty mug. If the head had been bald he would have seen the swollen veins, blood pressure at boiling point.

"She definitely has pressed all the right buttons for you."

Tim Pat had the car driving aspect foremost in his mind.

The same was true of David, who asked, "Will I tell mummy I'm driving?"

"Like fuck you'll tell her! Your mother and myself are going to West Cork, Saturday. I don't want her worried to death over you flying around Dublin – things are bad enough!" charged Tim Pat dourly. David knew the way the last few words were spoken implied discord in his home. His going to Fitzwilliam was the cause, that, he knew.

Silence followed as Tim Pat seemed to brood on what had been said, "What do you mean things are bad enough, Dad?" asked David in a low concerned voice.

"Your going to Fitzwilliam Square has not helped one little bit," said Tim Pat as the back of his hand swept imaginary crumbs from the table. Attempting to defuse the implication of the word 'helped' David choose to slot it into a different context. "Uncle Tom will get all the help he wants; he won't be short without me"

"Jesus Christ, I'm not talking about a few cocks of shagging hay or a bank of shagging turf or the scouring of shagging dikes!" barked Tim Pat straight into the face of David.

"Sorry, Dad, honestly I thought that is what you meant." lied David, knowing his expressed naivety exposed him to this attack with the real live prospect of more to follow. In his armpits the odd drop of sweat had increased to a trickle.

"Fuck me, do I have to spell everything out for you?" shouted Tim Pat his temper-lid hopping.

"Don't shout at me, Dad, all I'm asking is what do you want me to do?" asked a frightened David.

"What do I fucking want you to do, what do I want you to do?" came the reply in a voice that abated from shouting to a scornful droll all in the one sentence.

Tim Pat could see no solution to his plight. He refused to discuss David's leaving with Emma and here he was gushing venom on one of the two people in the world for whom he would willingly lay down his life. David had done nothing wrong other than what his mother had asked him to do and he himself had consented to.

His father wasn't likely to blow-out of steam this time. David, familiar with his father's mannerisms beheld him screwing up his face as if looking down the sights of a gun barrel. From previous experience a clear indicator his father had arrived at the eye of his storm.

"I suppose you see your future development away from this house and all that is in it."

David had told grandmother of his deliberations with his father and mother regarding his choice of career, the result of which had medicine as first choice. But when told Grandmother counselled 'No haste'; she had close friends who would advise on the basis of knowledge and not be swayed by personal bias, mind over heart. Her friends, she informed David later, had recommended accountancy. Less stressful, control over working hours, more job satisfaction, more money to be made, not one negative produced. The best grandmother in the world easily convinced David of the grave mistake he would make if he choose to do medicine. If he were to tell his father of the enlightened switch at this time he could expect a fate worse than death.

In the full knowledge that what he was about to suggest would not happen, he stated forcibly, "Just say the word, Dad, and I will be back here in one hour. This is my home, yourself and mam are the only ones I want to help me make my decisions. What decisions are there to be made anyway?" As he said it, David regretted adding the last sentence but luckily Tim Pat chose not to latch onto it.

Tim Pat remembered his own counsel regarding pushing David too hard, but he now had a problem, letting go of a bone was against his nature which triggered him into saying, "That grandmother of yours is one thundering bitch. Tim Pat is an inferior animal according to her. The only reason she put a steering wheel in your hand is she knew we didn't want you to drive. Bitch!"

David judiciously abandoned the mantle of Gran's advocacy. His immediate objective was to get out of the house. With a quick straightening of his back and the slightest shake of his shoulders, he said glibly and hurriedly while looking at the wall clock, "Got to be going, Dad; traffic gets heavy at this hour, nearly six; how time flies. "Tim Pat, with an eye very much on tomorrow, said jocosely,

"Only when one is happy does time fly, Son."

"Great to come home, Dad."

Pushing back his chair, he was up on his feet.

A more blatant lie David had never told his knowing father, who let it pass. Every second in his father's company had been hell. All those fragrant memories of his youth had been obliterated in that one long hour.

Tim Pat said in a more conciliatory tone as David was leaving the house, "Remember, David, every time she puts a lump of sugar in your mouth she lays the whip across my rump and your mother's. Good luck, Son, keep in touch and I'm not talking phone."

Tim Pat put out his hand and crushed David's as he bade him farewell, reminding David, "You have to feel the flesh, Son, you have to feel the flesh."

David, his feelings in a mess, shed tears all the way to Fitzwilliam.

Before entering Fitzwilliam David stayed a while in the car hoping to gain composure. When he did enter, his distress was obvious, even grandfather enquired. "Something wrong, David?"

Grandfather liked David. They had little chats together. David listened.

If grandmother's reading of the signals that evening were correct David had been involved in an altercation with his father. He wasn't packing his cases; she was as chuffed as she had ever been in her whole life. To have bested uncouth Tim Pat and her stupid daughter Emma was no mean achievement. David had returned to Fitzwilliam and her. She lusted for knowledge of what had taken place and with great difficulty controlled her impatience. To gain her prize she would have no distractions that night and cancelled her arranged visit to her dear friend Constance Newman. Fitzwilliam was always quiet. Heather would not allow a television inside her door. The O'Leary's had one, suited those types, she said. Normally she would have the radio unobtrusively on as she read, but not this evening.

She saw David's fractured attention take up and leave down newspapers scarcely taking time to read the headlines. She dare not say a word against his father. David's defence of him was all too fresh in her mind.

George retired early to bed; he always did given the opportunity. He was relieved Heather's engagement that Wednesday night to the Newmans had been cancelled.

Grandmother put her book aside at ten thirty and placing a comforting hand on David's slouched shoulders said with enveloping warmth, "I'm going to make a nice cup of tea for both of us, David. Then, we will call it a day."

Youth's illiteracy did not allow David read his grandmother's baleful eye. She handed David a cup of tea and placed a plate of biscuits between them on the sofa.

"Well now, did you have a nice day, David?" she asked in an intimate, confessional whisper. David took his time in answering, but when he did there was no whisper about it. It was a hard nosed, "Met Daddy today!"

Gran knew he was ready to spill; coaxing not needed.

In recounting his afternoon David diluted the odiously described opinion of grandmother given by his father to a mere, "He does not like you, Gran!"

Having watched David mope about the house presenting a definite air of martyrdom Gran expected he had been visited by violence but no, Tim Pat had done nothing more than hurl bad language thereby rendering David pathetic. So much she thought for Tim Pat's choice of schools and holidays in West Cork. They had fashioned a gutless product. Hiding her disappointment she concluded the intimacy of their conversation: "I admire your forbearance, David, in face of such lowly conduct. You must avoid those meetings in future and thank God you are not going to that West Cork place; you have absolutely nothing in common with those types."

Bright and early, David was out of bed on the Thursday morning, West Cork wasn't even a memory. He was busy doing bits and pieces when the doorbell rang. When David opened the door a cockalorum of a postman extended a registered letter to David. He spoke with the thickest Cork accent David had ever heard.

"Will you ever sign there, boy."

"Are you from Cork?"

"Sure, sure, bloody sure I'm from Cork. West Cork!"

"I spent all my holidays in West Cork".

"What part of it?"

"Clonakilty. Six miles west of Clon to be exact".

"Jesus is that a fact. I'm from Clon, God's own country".

"You're not long in Dublin?" observed David.

"Not long in Dublin? Sixteen shagging years, boy.

65

Would you call that 'not long'?'

"You haven't lost your accent!"

"'I Can't believe it, like yesterday. The ould fella was in the guards. They made a sergeant out of him and sent him to Dublin. He thought he'd be promoted again if he did what he was told – a Neddy fuckin' Donkey that's what he was. Delighted altogether to get rid of him out of Clon, they were."

Pushing a form at David he said, "Sign there before I forgets. Yourself now, what has you here?"

"Born in Dublin, educated in Dublin but I've spent every holiday in my father's place in West Cork".

"Sure I must know them... you've a touch of a posh accent yourself, what's their names?"

"O'Learys"

"Not Dave O'Leary's outfit?"

"Yes, Dave O'Leary's outfit. I'm called after him, he's my grandfather".

"Well, that whips shit. Dave O'Leary's outfit. There was a right clatter of them O' Learys. Legends in Clon; temper, mean as shite, full of brains, priests, shagging doctors and whatever else you're having yourself. They'd be older than me now, but I heard the ould fella talking about them. Course he knew everything, guard, you know what I mean, everything?"

"That's the family, small world"

"Tis, when you aren't a postman humping a ton of shagging letters on your back looking for an address. Dave O'Leary- one of them crowd, by God. By the way, when I started this round, that would be a few years ago, now, I ran into a right ould rip in this very house. A fierce accent altogether, the plaque said she was a doctor – look, it's still there – look! – I wouldn't take a sick black pudding to that ould bitch."

Pointing to the brass wall-plate postman continued reading, "MD.FRCPI"

David enlightened "MD. FRCPI is my maternal grandmother, she's alive and well."

66

"Probably kicking as well. 'Tis the poison that's keeping that ould bag alive. Don't God have a great sense of humour too and the people he whips and the ones he leaves behind!"

"What happened between you?"

"Well, I'll tell you, she nearly asked me the same questions as you did and when I told her about the O'Learys, Jesus, she nearly flung that front door out into the middle of the road with the slam. I swear that railing went rattling and rattling all the way down to shagging Baggot Street. Never seen or heard the likes of the rattling since. Says volumes for the hinges they made back then, German, had to be German."

"Sorry about the rattling railing."

"Well, as the saying goes, you can't blame the dog for the bite of the pup. What's this again, you said your ould fella's name was."

"Tim Pat." answered David, chest out.

"Answer me this, how did Tim Pat, a pup off Dave O'Leary, wind up marrying a daughter of a posh house like this, must be a story."

"No story, they didn't have to get married either".

"Has to be a story all the same, like. Like the rest from our part we could be Catholics when we wanted, which never came in the way of making a woman happy. Wink wink, nod nod. As long as you give unto one of these little ones….you know the story yourself O'Leary".

"The gospel according to West Cork."

"You're an O'Leary alright. You must have a rake of brothers and sisters?"

"Only son I'm afraid, no rake!"

Postman hit the wall-plate with his cap, "That rip must have had Tim Pat squeezed. All the O'Learys gave a good account of themselves in the breeding stakes; well hung were the O'Learys, well hung."

"You married?".

"My bollix married! My mother had a rough time with that lump of a fool she was buckled to. Bald Tyres would turn the nation not to mind me off marriage".

"Your bag would be very attractive to some".

"That grandmother of yours, is she a widow yet?"

"Not yet".

"There goes Donovan's last chance. You tell Tim Pat you met Dinny, son of Bald Tyres Donovan. Bet he heard of him. Deadly on the bald tyres, you'd swear we had shares in Dunlops."

"Of course I will, Dinny."

As Dinny went down the steps his parting words came crystal clear to David's ears: "She never heard of fucking Daddy Christmas either the ould bitch. Never answered the door since, she must see me through the window. A kind of a quiet man answers – whatever, good luck. No class you know – not like us West Cork people, ha ha, no fuckin' way boy, no way. Up Cork."

David studied Dinny's swagger as he stepped out smartly with his bag over his shoulder. Dinny, already two doors away could be heard by David singing, "MD. FR. FAI. GAA. RFU. – ha, ha, hah! Fuck the lot of them, ha, ha, hah! Bury 'em Christy, bury 'em, the butt of the net, bury 'em Ringy boy, bury 'em. Up the Rebels! Up the shagg'en Rebels!"

CHAPTER 10

Heather Dempsey's cancelled appointment, on the Wednesday of David's unhappy meeting with his father, had been a visit to her dear friend Constance Newman.

Constance Newman, late seventies, and widowed fifteen years, lived all her married life in a large two-storied house on its own grounds in Dalkey with her husband Leslie. When accountant husband Leslie died, her son James, living in Howth, advised selling and moving in with him, his wife Ann and their three children, Norma, Leslie and Trish. Refusing to move, she convinced James they should move in with her instead. Constance did not regret making that decision having first consulted Heather Dempsey on its wisdom.

Constance Newman loved her home; her roof covered a veritable museum of memorabilia, a library of memories; its colours, smells, sounds, views, its feel. The smallest detail in the house made a cover for its own complete story. Her life with Leslie had been a happy one.

Constance and Heather had met while students in Trinity College and had remained firm friends ever since. A friendship that had survived honesty when she, Constance, had the temerity to question Heather on the suitability of George as her choice of husband. Theirs was not a fine weather loyalty nor silence a comfortable lie. Nature did not conceal their gender, and those same attributes ensured the jettisoning of males who saw women as nothing other than flesh.

The Newmans were of Church of Ireland persuasion. James had married Ann, a Catholic. This union had never created a problem in a religious sense but Constance could not find it in her heart to accept Ann, whom she saw as nothing more than a good wife to her son and a good mother to her grandchildren. Heather Dempsey had identified the absence of determination in Ann, and Constance regretted not heeding her friend's advice and not putting an end to their relationship. Believing nothing that had been done could not be undone, neither Heather nor Constance ever resorted to the finger admonishing, 'I told you so!' but got on with the business of identifying remedies.

Ann's good-mother business had its place, but James, who was not without ambition, lacked the steel to successfully prosecute assassinations when hard work failed to deliver promotion. While Ann believed God had decided each person's destiny, Constance held no such belief. Relentless was her badgering of James to gain promotion at any cost in Cavendish's accountancy firm where he was employed. Norma, being the eldest of the three children, had been privy to this badgering of her father by her grandmother Constance, who was in turn supported in her badgering by her friend Dr. Heather Dempsey. Norma's ear had also become accustomed to hearing the tragic story of Dr. Heather's daughter Emma marrying an uncouth Baluba named Tim Pat from the wilds of West Cork, who was definitely no relation of Rudolf Valentino no more than Emma herself could be mistaken for Goldilocks. From an early age Norma had learned from these two sabred sages, not her mother Ann nor father James, that achieving depended on wanting; nothing more, nothing less.

James hoped his son Leslie would follow him into Cavendish's but Leslie's dedication to golf ensured he would not gain the honours degree necessary. James was in a position to wield influence but Leslie wasn't doing the business. Grandmother Constance was furious with Leslie.

Cavendish's head office was in London and boss-man Bartholomew Cavendish visited his Dublin office on a regular basis. Bartholomew did not have the management structures in place found in the top firms, of manager, director and partner. It was his company, he had his own tidy pyramid in place with himself hovering over all.

Because of her son James's lack of promotion and her grandson's lack of ability, Constance worried. As always these anxieties were shared with her dear friend Heather.

So engrossed had Heather become in wreaking vengeance on Emma and Tim Pat, she had not thought through her plans for David other than ensuring he did not do medicine - which his parents had wanted him to do.

While listening to Constance, Heather was doing her own plotting. The higher James Newman climbed in the Cavendish pyramid, the easier it would be to have David accepted into that company. Heather knew there would be no victory for her if David did not succeed in accountancy.

Norma, owned her own boutique in Dawson Street. A woman blessed with beauty's abundance, who had refused to go beyond secondary school. Norma wanted the boutique, Norma was going to get her boutique. It was her father's heart not his accountant's head that had him back his daughter's enterprise. Ruthless, Norma had no qualms about her body aiding and abetting her ambition. Her reasons for insisting on living at home, while baffling, was not questioned by her parents. Grandmother Constance saw Norma as a winner, an achiever. Eighteen year old Trish had finished secondary school and intended to study law.

Bartholomew Cavendish had the name of being eccentric, which made what appeared to be bizarre promotions palatable to those who considered themselves disenfranchised. When he visited his Dublin office staff-tongues developed spasms of arse-licking to which his cheeks were most receptive. Forelock tugging had its place, but it took good looking perspicacious wives or daughters to properly pay homage. He would invite himself to the homes of his professional staff. He visited all homes once, but there was nothing random about his return visit.

Two years had passed since Bartholomew Cavendish's chance meeting with Norma Newman as she waited for her father at reception in his office building. Bartholomew Cavendish had all but forgotten about James Newman and his family; it had been nine years since he visited their home, once.

Norma knew the identity of the bull-of-a-man ponderously moving towards her as she sat flicking through a magazine. She had heard her father describe Cavendish as ugly. Her father had done his ugly boss an injustice, Cavendish was worse than ugly. Norma beheld the six foot plus amorphous mass, neck not visible. But having failed biology in the Leaving exam she guessed his neck had been sunk deep into his massive trunk by the weight of his huge bald bullet head. Gold fillings showed through a gash in the same head that had beady eyes and a flaring hooky nose that kept apart ears, the biggest she had ever seen outside the gates of Dublin zoo, ears capable of flapping on the energy generated by still weather.

The old bull had exuded lust and Norma signalled she was receiving his humping-bellow loud and clear. Lest his radar be on the blink, the crossing, uncrossing, and parting of her legs ensured Bartholomew the bull-bull received an eye full. Standing, she had extended her hand and smiling said by way of introduction, "Norma Newman! I have heard so much about you, Mr Cavendish, from my dear father."

Smothering Norma's hand in both of his, Cavendish had leaned forward intending to lessen their height difference but intending also to suggest a touch of intimacy.

"Yes! We do have a Newman on staff. Let me think…Please don't tell me. Yes, James!"

"I'm Norma, James's daughter. I'm waiting for him."

"You are truly beautiful, my dear. May I call you Norma?"

"But of course, Mr. Cavendish." replied Norma, coyly, leaving her fluttering eyelids to tickle his thinking and she hoped his few surviving hormones. If those same hormones needed oxygen or flippers, to swim about, she would willingly supply either or both, given the opportunity.

"Thank you, dear Norma. I distinctly recall visiting your lovely home, must be all of ten years ago now; your grandmother was living with you, correct?"

"Yes you are, Bartholomew. After all these years you remember, remarkable. Grandmother is still with us and I clearly recall your visit and the flowers. You have not changed one little bit, Mr. Cavendish."

"You flatter me, Norma. Norma, what a beautiful name and how appropriate."

"Now you have Norma blushing, Mr Cavendish, and in public."

Cavendish, conscious he was holding Norma's hand and sensing Norma had no intention of withdrawing hers until he indicated, suggested, "Perhaps we should continue our little tête-a-tête somewhere private, more comfortable. Observing males must envy me the company of such a beautiful young woman."

"Or observing females envy me!"

"Oh that I should be so lucky!"

"You have to have those London lovelies chasing after you in their thousands, Mr. Cavendish."

"Position does have its disadvantages, my dear."

"Disadvantages, Mr. Cavendish? Gorgeous women?"

"When one has mastered abstinence, then, and only then, is one truly in control of oneself."

"Norma has never had to exercise abstinence; Father spoiled me rotten. I have my own boutique in Dawson Street."

"What an amazing young lady. Business has its own appetites; success consumes the greedy. I suggest you leave a message for your father at reception. Better still, ring him from the comfort and privacy of my office."

"Your office, then! Actually father is not expecting me," blinked Norma in a way which was universal in its meaning. Bartholomew knew she was lying, but being a universal man he had a universal reputation to uphold. As they went in the lift to his office on the third floor, he bent and would have placed a feeler-kiss on Norma's cheek but Norma's quick thinking lips came in the way. Where others would experience revulsion Norma saw golden opportunity.

From that intercepted feeler-kiss grew a torrid relationship which happened to coincide with James Newman's career take-off.

When Norma's beguiling focussed, common-sense abandoned the brain of her quarry. The carcass did not matter: age, size, shape or creed made no difference. Power intoxicated. Without power, people meant nothing to her. She manipulated men without giving a granule of affection. She avoided the company of similarly equipped and motivated women. She allowed handmaids: weak, less confident females who saw her on a scale ranging from a woman with brass balls to a whore. Norma had no intention of playing life's game with a stripped deck.

With James's good fortune, Heather Dempsey could not have been more delighted. She was certain Constance would ensure David would be looked-after when he eventually qualified as an accountant. When Constance boasted, "Norma is truly a Newman, remarkable lady!" a knowing Heather remarked, "Indeed remarkable. God works in mysterious ways, dear Constance!'

Early Friday evening, before continuing on to her arranged appointment for that night, she would drop in on Constance Newman and apologise for her absence on the Wednesday. Heather's heavy schedule for that Friday would ensure David would be deprived of any opportunity of meeting his parents before they set out for West Cork the following morning, Saturday. To avoid the traffic, theirs would be an early start.

George asked to be excused from Friday's schedule. He confided in David: 'Surprise, surprise! Doctors do get old.'

Three cars were parked in front of Newman's when David and Heather arrived at six. One had English registration plates. Heather acknowledged her mistake, "I should have rung, Newmans have visitors. I will tender my apology to Constance for not calling and leave immediately"

"I'll wait, take your time, Gran," said David.

Heather's ring on the doorbell was answered by Trish who looked boyish in jeans, an oversized sloppy pullover and her jet black hair cut short. "Doctor Dempsey – how are you?" Trish exclaimed and continued, "Grandmother was so disappointed you could not visit the other night. She will be delighted to see you –please come in."

"Darling Trish, you have visitors. I do not wish to intrude."

"But you really must; Daddy has been promoted again and Mister Cavendish is here in person to congratulate him. Isn't that wonderful?"

"Marvellous, absolutely marvellous, I'm delighted for all of you. Please, a quick word with grandmother and I will be away."

"They're in the sitting room; Mr. Cavendish, Daddy, Grandmother and Norma. I'll get Gran."

Trish gently tapped on the sitting room door before opening it, and beckoned her Grandmother to come to the hallway.

A flushed Constance Newman came hurriedly to the front door, saying, "Delighted you called Heather on such a joyous occasion. James has received another promotion. I insist you come and meet Mr. Cavendish, he is in Dublin for a few days."

"At last your dreams are coming true, dear Constance. I am delighted for you and your family, but you will have to excuse me I'm on my way to the Jamesons. I called to apologise for the last evening."

"Heather, apology wasn't at all necessary I assure you!"

"Unpardonable, I had to call and apologise in person."

"Thank you. Is George with you?"

"Not tonight, David is driving."

"I so want to meet David."

When Heather had triumphantly informed Constance of David's prising from the clutches of Tim Pat and Emma and his moving into Fitzwilliam with them, Constance had been ecstatic at her dear friend's success. 'That will eat the very soul out of culchie Tim Pat. Culchies do have souls or is Constance presuming beyond reasonable expectation?"

To which Heather had replied, "Souls in some shape or form they would want to have. Dear Constance, hell would not be financially viable without an abundant supply of culchies."

"Forever has hell kept those peasant in line, the fear of!" laughed Constance.

Trish, listening to the exchange of pleasantries, volunteered, "Shall I fetch David?"

"Please, Trish".

"Just a few minutes then, Constance. Jamesons to be visited!" said Heather while allowing herself to be ushered by Constance into the sitting room.

The Norma Heather saw that evening presented an alluring severity in tailored pin-stripe suit. Everything concealed that needs no mention, and in Norma's case, that was a whole lot of woman. A woman beyond wooing, a challenge to be subdued.

Heather was introduced to a most polite Bartholomew Cavendish. 'Creepy,' she thought as shivers beyond medical definition domino-ed up and down her spine and trepidation had her rib cage chattering. Heather, as she viewed the two standing there side by side, placed Bartholomew and Norma in a mythical ring, and, not being particularly blessed in boxing parlance, decided the final bell would definitely come too soon for Bart and not soon enough for Norma. This was one contest Norma was guaranteed to win on a technical knockout. In her corner, Norma had the best in the business, Constance. The particular round when Bart would fall would be a matter for Norma's attorney and not for historians or turf-accountants.

Heather congratulated James on his promotion and said a sweet, "Hello, Norma."

Norma returned her greeting in a sweetly clipped, "Hi, Doctor Dempsey."

Norma, holding out a glass, said, "You must celebrate Daddy's promotion with a glass of bubbly, Doctor Dempsey."

Accepting the glass, Heather toasted, "Thank you, Norma, again congratulations James. And Bartholomew, pleased to have made your acquaintance."

"You are so kind, Doctor. Cavendish's are fortunate, not alone in having a gentleman the calibre of James with us, but shortly Leslie will be joining our ranks when he has done his finals. So, really it is a double celebration. Away at his golf this evening, I believe."

"Four handicapper," boasted James.

Unlike the Newmans, Cavendish hadn't the slightest interest in the comings and goings of golf balls, and when he did not comment on James's four handicap boast, the topic of swings and balls died a death.

The opportunity to mention David's name to Cavendish presented itself and Heather wasn't about letting the opportunity pass.

"Actually, Mister Cavendish, my grandson David, who is with me, has been advised by James to enter the accountancy profession rather than the medical, which is my own humble way of making a living," tittered Heather at her own self-effacement before finishing with, "Do you consider James's suggestion to be a wise one?"

"It is said medicine is in one's blood and accountancy is in one's pocket. I must confess to being an admirer of the persuasive powers of the latter, Doctor Heather."

The Newmans paid homage to their boss's wit with exaggerated laughter. Being forthright had never endeared Heather to persons who did not understand her. Constance would have preferred if Heather had been more circumspect when she questioned, "I do hope there is more to your life than money, Mr. Cavendish?"

Cavendish, on purpose dropping the doctor knowing it would rancour, responded to cheeky Heather Dempsey, "Most certainly there is more to my life, Mrs. Dempsey, but it has to be paid for. Because of money there can be so much more quality to one's life. More choice!"

Heather took grievous exception to the dropping of her doctor status at the first sign of honest discussion. Heather in turn dropped the formality of Mr. Cavendish. "Can moderation not be enough?" she challenged.

Constance knew Heather did not mean a word of what she was so earnestly suggesting. Constance was trapped. She could not give the impression of coming to Mr. Cavendish's rescue by intruding; he might resent that. Neither could she take the chance of offending Cavendish by siding with Heather, who she knew was being mischievous in the extreme. Wanting to put an end to the baiting, she was about to rush to the very bottom of the conversational barrel and drag from its bowels the subject of weather but Bartholomew beat her to the draw.

"Given people's differing circumstances, cultures, age, appetites, expectations, can there be a universally accepted boundary to 'moderation' or indeed 'enough' I should think not."

"I believe the ten commandments to be straight forward unequivocal boundaries." Replied Heather frostily.

Constance was developing a bout of flatulence brought on by Heather's propounding beliefs she spent more of her life breaking rather than observing. Constance wasn't to know, but Bartholomew was way ahead of the posse, he had already developed a bout from parrying bad quality horseshit from wounded Heather. It was to the relief of all when Norma ended the nonsense.

"Thank you, thank you. This is a celebration. More champagne, Bartholomew? Grandmother? Doctor Dempsey?"

Heather Dempsey gripped casual statements and pursued them. Not easy company. Norma considered her grandmother and her friend Dempsey well met. They were welcome to each other. She would ensure Bartholomew was not exposed to further hassle.

James, hoping a contribution from himself might help to calm matters, said, "I gave solid argument as to why Heather's grandson, David, should choose accountancy. Being the erudite lady that she is, she agreed".

Cavendish, casually, gave the plan his benediction. "Please keep James advised of David's progress, Doctor; Cavendish's would be pleased to accommodate David, his decision of course." Said Cavendish.

Heather had been reinstated to her doctor status, she would reciprocate by giving him back his name. He had remembered David's name; she was impressed.

"I will indeed, thank you, Mister Cavendish!"

Bartholomew Cavendish had taken a decision years previously to avoid ten commament women and was always willing to be rescued from salvation by beautiful young women; of late, one at the time.

Meanwhile Trish had introduced David to her mother Ann in the kitchen where she was busy making sandwiches.

"Where in God's name have you been?"

"Mother, it was I, handmaid Trish, who answered the front door, remember? Not abnormal Norma."

"Take no notice of me, David. I'm all fussed. Norma breezes in with Mister Cavendish. No warning. Those kind of surprises I can do without. Trish, butter those cuts of bread or we'll never be rid of them!"

Trish's polo neck, being one of her fathers, presented David with massive flashes of her glorious flesh.

"Norma, sister big bitch, brings into our home a gun-toting fossil and all mummy can think of doing is feeding him. We could all be blown to bits by bulbous Bertie and his side-kick abnormal Norm!"

"Respect, Trish, respect. And I wouldn't put too much credence in what that sister of yours says about a gun. You could get Mr Cavendish into trouble if you go around spreading that kind of malicious gossip."

"But it's the truth. Norma said it was a Derringer. A little silver one but it kills, the gun crooked gamblers have up their sleeves in Wild West films." David informed,

"Women carry them in their handbags in the same Wild West, Mrs Newman."

"Some mix we have in our house tonight, Mummy: a potential assassin and another an expert on the contents of ladies' handbags".

"Take no notice of Trish, David, – hurry with the sandwiches will you."

"I've had plenty practice at making sandwiches for the bog and the meadow. I'll help!"

David was about to pick up a knife when Trish subtly suggested, "I must wash my hands as well."

An embarrassed David did as corrected. Ann advised, "Don't you be getting that nice suit dirtied. Dark suits suit your complexion, David."

"When visiting with Gran, I have to wear a suit. She insists."

Having dried his hands, David took off his jacket and placed it on the back of a chair.

"And you change into something more presentable, Girl; wearing your father's polo neck. Look how well David is dressed." said Ann, not looking up from placing ham, cheese and onion on the bread's buttered faces.

"Indeed I will not change. One strutting hen in any house is more than enough."

"My father uses that expression 'strutting hen'. I wasn't expecting to hear it in Dalkey."

"Mummy, David hasn't heard of Dalkey hens!"

"What are you on about, now?"

"Dalkey hens are birds between brooding and boiling who successfully peck-empty the pockets of senior citizens …

Ann intervened, "Stop, stop that at once. What you are hinting at is outrageous. David, I can only apologise for my daughter's rude behaviour."

Without taking his eyes off the buttered bread in hand, David said nothing but did hazard a glance down Trish's father's polo-neck.

"I'd be a Dalkey chick myself but with no view to bedding a rooster for a long, long time!"

Again David said nothing but could not stop himself from hazarding another glance.

Ann threw her eyes to the heavens, "To think we sent Trish to a fee-paying convent school and we have to listen to this."

"Country nuns, country expressions. Father bought Norma a boutique in Dawson Street. the Strutting Hen Pen I call it. Now that really ruffles her feathers."

"Sibling rivalry, David, sibling rivalry. And David isn't here to listen to your immature squabbling. Norma is much more advanced than you."

"Some parts of the same hen are definitely much more advanced." Retorted Trish.

Trish's description heightened David's interest in viewing sister Norma. Being involved in the joint operation of sandwich making helped David to relax.

Wanting to support Trish in her declaration that she was not changing out of her casuals, he said, "I feel awkward in a suit. Makes me feel different. I feel I have to act differently. As if I'm a different person. My personality, such as it is, is forced to undergo a change. That kind of way."

"A suit can only hide so much, David. Truth will out eventually." said mother Ann.

"Polo necks? Does mine show too little or too much, David?" asked mischievous Trish.

"You'll burn in hell my girl!" said Ann.

"All I said was a suit makes you fell different." Said a blushing David.

"You are not the boy you were without the suit, right?" said a teasing Trish.

From the age of fifteen Trish had boyfriends. She liked David's type: no acne, tall, slim, athletic looking, talkative. On the debit side she thought him a touch cautious, too conscious of her presence, probably not used to the company of girls and therefore had no idea of how girls worked or expected to be treated. Given her own few years of experience she was not yet sure on which side of her sheets she would slot David O'Leary.

"Now you leave David alone young woman. At least until we get these sandwiches finished." Ordered Ann.

The mention of 'young woman' made David even more aware of Trish's breasts and he was satisfied these were exactly the ones that most pleased his dreams. As he glanced and glanced again and again he knew his father was one hundred percent correct in his declaration, 'You have to feel the flesh, son, you have to feel the flesh.' There and then was definitely neither the time nor place to begin, but his imagining was galloping out of control.

David went on full arousal; he felt huge inside his trousers, huge. Why had he taken off his coat, they were bound to notice. If there was a particular saint in the heavens or elsewhere who specialised in deflating horns he could badly do with his or her intercession. His bugle's cover had indeed been blown as Trish sweetly requested, "I have never been to a bog or I've never been to a meadow, David. Will David take Trish by her soft white hand through his heather and his hay and tell Trish the story of the birds and the bees and explain all all all that you know about the cute beaks of the birds and the soft bellies of the bees that you read about in those beautiful love poems and all all that. Please, David? Can Trish come away with you to the wild?" Struck by a flash of recollection, Trish added. "To the waters and the wild, child!"

Mother had previous experience of mischievous Trish, and knowing the effect her teasing had to be having on David she tried implanting a coolant into his fevered young blood,

"A swim in a cool stream or the cool sea is my heaven, oh the sea the sea the cool sea, I love the waves of the sea. Not that there's anything wrong with a shower!"

"Wouldn't you know mother also went to the nuns, David?"

"I'm afraid nuns aren't what they used to be, you hussy!" said Ann.

Given the cue by Ann and in the hope of encouraging a softening, David concentrated as hard as he possibly could on ice-caps, ice-bergs, polar bears, penguins, mackerel, tinned sardines. Why tinned he wasn't sure, but he suspected even the biggest and strongest sardine couldn't possibly survive in that hostile environment without a tin on. Unfortunately for David, penguin, polar bear, mackerel, tin-suited sardine et al were all rejected by red hot bugle. With the slightest of changes his father's annoying gift of wisdom came whispering to his ear, 'You have to feel the ice, son, you have to feel the ice!'

When distant ice had failed, David resorted to geography of a more local kind, "My bogs and meadows are far far away in West Cork, down in my father's home place."

"You mean you have a farm as well! I haven't heard of this farm."

As if Trish had told him, David knew his father and mother had been discussed in Newman's and she had overheard those conversations.

"It's not ours. It's been in our family for generations. My uncle Tom farms it now."

"But I haven't heard mention of this farm?"

"No reason why you should, Trish. I know virtually nothing about your family if your grandmother Constance is removed from the equation. And my knowledge of her is quite recent and very limited."

"More stupid equations on display in this house than you'd find on a chess board."

Ann smartly put an end to the conversation entering Newman politics. She asked David, "You could mistake Trish for a boy, couldn't you, David?"

Ann's cool sea and shower added to Trish's questions about his family had begun to work, but their effect shot into reverse at Ann's mention of mistaking Trish for a boy. David's brain whirled in a tizzy as his muddled brain tried formulating an acceptable form of words to answer Ann. The harder he tried concentrating on getting Trish's dual tits out of his brain, the harder he got. He figured if God had given women one tit instead of two he would now be smuggling around half a horn - his first lesson in accountancy. The desire for another glimpse tore at his eye muscles and – surprise, surprise- desire again won, eyes-down.

Trish eyed David and knew the question embarrassed him, but, interested in hearing his answer she had no intention of rescuing him.

"I suppose it is whatever one is comfortable in," said David,

again flashing a glance, but his glance was disappointed - wrong angle.

83

"But you would take me for a boy?"

"Certainly not, no!"

"Why?"

"I mean… the way you talk."

"So mummy is right"

"No, I'm not saying that."

"That is what I am hearing!"

"Well, you are obviously a woman."

"What can you see that mummy cannot see?"

"You have gone too far, Miss. Leave David alone. You are embarrassing him!" ordered Ann.

"Please, David, tell Trish, please! Trish could grow up with a major identity crisis. Could you live with little old me not knowing who I am, wandering around down in your heather, swimming in your streams, naked, no one around? Talk to wee Trish, David, talk to me. Do!"

"It's, it's everything… just everything about you." said David as his eyes looked everywhere except the area which confirmed his answers.

"So you wouldn't mistake me for a boy, but you really can't say why?"

"Not that I can't. You register with me as nothing other than a girl."

"Stop, Trish. God, you are terrible!" said Ann who was enjoying David's sparring, though Trish obviously had him under serious pressure. The boy was sweating. Trish intervened, "You point out to innocent Trish the difference between a girl and a woman."

"Television shouldn't be left into any Christian home," said Ann in resignation.

"I feel like a criminal in a witness box. Only I have no chance. What do you intend doing in college?"

"No boy's petty organs for me I assure you. Nothing so dull as medicine. Law for Trish."

"God help the opposition is all I say." Said Ann.

David was not as cautious in his looking as he had been. Trish again caught him looking and smiling, ensured he saw more rather than less.

"Nice suit, off the old peg is it?"

"Actually, handmade, bespoke."

Trish, bending in front of David, caught his trouser leg, providing his eyes with a gap so wide it accelerated his already thumping heart.

"First time fondling a real live bespoke. Pity about the trousers, appears on the tight side or perhaps things are much more than what they seem, O'Leary?"

"Trish, you're a demon!" said Ann too busy to concern herself further.

David began rubbing his eyes pretending they were smarting from the chopped onions.

"Open that kitchen door Trish; guests to be fed!"

On seeing David's exaggerated rubbing, Ann advised as she went from the kitchen with her tray, "Leave your eyes alone, David, rubbing makes them worse"

When Ann had left, Trish, ensuring privacy, closed the kitchen door behind her.

"It was the bold onions that hurt your eyes, wasn't it, David?" teased Trish bending low over the table tempting him to a view, though he continued rubbing his eyes. He feared he would explode. Even if Ann's holy water font was big enough, he wouldn't stick his problem in there; to do so would be a sin.

Trish, with schemes in her head, proposed a foreign body to be the eye's ememy, "David, onions get a bad press, could be a speck of dust you know!"

"Could be, I suppose."

Trish did not want David's problem to go away; she wanted to play. With handkerchief in hand she moved close up against David. David's Adam's apple shot to the terminus before returning to his dry gullet.

"My woman's eye wants to look deep deep into your onion eyes, Davey."

David regretted taking off his jacket; he wasn't thinking, he couldn't.

As Trish's body pressed him back against the table to conduct her examination, the kitchen door opened.

"Well, well, hanky panky in the pantry; what ever will my little sister get up to next?" said the most beautiful woman David had ever laid his onions on. A film star. An Oscar winning film star. His standing-to-attention-horn was left standing-to-attention as he straightened up.

"You would think of hanky panky. At least David is my own age. It's onions if you must know. Look after fossil Bertie, abnormal Norma!"

"Please continue with your panky. I'm getting some chocolate biscuits. Mr. Cavendish, your father's employer, has a sweet tooth."

"Can't be that sweet!"

"Now, now, Trish. Don't be bitchy, look after David's onions. You are David?"

A whole army of hormones were coming in the way of David's answering.

"He is!' said Trish in a higher pitch.

David's trousers made it obvious his problem couldn't possibly be an onion problem. Sister Trish needed smacking down, she should not have dropped the Bertie innuendo, even if David did not comprehend.

"Is onion still in there or has onion moved elsewhere?" asked Norma.

Before David could reply, Trish snapped,

"Elsewhere, onion jumped out when you jumped in, don't they always."

"And what does patient David think?" enquired Norma.

"I think 'tis gone." replied David, not sure what to say as he looked from one to the other.

"David, would you like Norma to take a look, I am especially good at eyes."

"Onions, if the truth be told!" snapped Trish.

As Norma moved towards David, he looked to Trish for guidance.

Trish hissed, "Bitch, bitch, bitch!" before exiting the kitchen slamming the door behind her.

"Sister Trish is one hot babe on positions, I'll give sister that," said Norma as she moved David into the same position as she had found him with Trish.

"Got to move right into you. Dave, your legs – open, open a little."

As she would a dummy in her shop, she moved him into position. Placing one leg between David's, she moved up against him. She could feel his awkwardness in attempting the impossible: to hide his muscle from her pressing and moving crotch. Placing an open hand either side of his face she whispered intimately, "Look at Norma, David. After all, it is your eye that is bothering you, isn't it?"

David barely choked his reply, "'Tis!"

Smiling, she kept moving and pressing until the starch left his face, and, with a wonderfully innocent sheepish grin he attempted to return her smile. He was smelling her - indeed he was. Relaxing her lower body against his, she moved gently, gently. She moved her shape, caressing his manhood, moving, pressing. To treble quick time, his heart pounded.

"Dear David your onions are in ship shape, believe me. Share them. Share them with Norma," she said tenderly looking deep into his treble-glazed eyes.

David imagined, imagined, imagined before exploding. Norma jumped back from David as his eyelids flipped flopped flapped in a multitude of different directions like a most unhappy Christmas turkey. Norma was once again satisfied she had executed her onion cure; this time with the minimum of fuss. Norma directed, "Go to the bathroom, take your time bathing your onions. First right, top of stairs, Sonny!"

David went as directed three steps at a time thanking his stars his suit was dark.

Trish on hearing David leave the bathroom met him in the hallway.
"Do you have the use of a car?" she asked.
"I have." replied David, more in hope than certainty.

"Would you like to take me to a disco?"

"Sure, sure I would!"

"Wednesdays and Saturdays are the best nights out here."

"Can I ring to confirm? Gran socializes a lot."

"You will find Newmans in the directory, Leslie."

"Leslie, Leslie, that will be great."

"It's best we put in an appearance; Norma and her oldies will think the worst – or the best."

"We will," agreed David, his manhood much relieved as they went to the sitting room. For a short time the conversation there revolved round the careers of Trish and David before Heather told of her commitment to visit a friend. Heather's exit was greeted with relief by all, except David.

Doctor Heather was in awe at the sacrifice Norma was making on behalf of her family and the willingness with which the family, in particular her great friend Constance, accepted Norma's obvious liaison with Cavendish. While the relationship disgusted Heather, she was forced to reflect on her own willingness to slide in under Norma's skirts when she had requested Cavendish to employ David.

Heather could only vaguely discuss the company with David as they went towards Jamesons.

"Those ladies have been spoiled by their father, too much freedom."

David knew who the ladies in question were but enquired innocently, "Trish and Norma, is it?"

"What are your impressions of Norma?"

Norma's electricity was still bubbling in David's veins causing magical static; he would never forget the greeting her body had given his.

"Well, I was only in Norma's company a few minutes, she seems… fine, fine, the finest!

David's idiom was the language of West Cork, and not with ease was it going to be replaced.

"And Cavendish?"

"A kind'ah beast ready to pounce but doesn't or or can't. A buzzard"

"Would Norma be a pouncing buzzard?"

"I wouldn't be the one to answer that now I wouldn't, but I suppose 'tis her duty to be extra polite to her father's boss. That's all I'll say. I helped their mother Ann with the sandwiches, she's a lovely woman."

"Ann is indeed good at that sort of thing. Norma has her own boutique in Dawson Street, you know that don't you?"

Visits to Dawson Street for David and his static would be a must.

"If the car is available Wednesday night I hope to go to a disco with Trish."

David's wanting to go to the disco had more to do with the hope of meeting Norma than dancing with Trish. Knowing his parents would be away, Constance said, "For the next two weeks we will give the visiting a rest, you go ahead and make whatever arrangement you want to make."

A vengeful Heather wasn't thinking of Trish as a daughter-in-law for Tim Pat and Emma; though there be an age gap, she smiled as she married Norma into that position.

David identified the handwriting on the envelope lying on the kitchen table when they returned to Fitzwilliam Square. He knew the way his grandmother looked at it and said 'A letter!' She would like to be made aware of its contents. Without making reference to the letter, David put it in his pocket. He would read it in bed. He dropped the car keys on the hall-stand. Not knowing David had promised his father he would keep his driving a secret from his mother until she had returned from West Cork, Heather took possession of the keys ensuring David did not visit his parents before they left for their Cork holiday.

Emma had called to Fitzwilliam, waited until eleven, and when they hadn't returned from visiting, she went home. David was to ring if he got in before twelve. Too late, it was twenty to one. Included was a cheque for two hundred plus one hundred in cash, with instructions to write for more if more was needed.

Tim Pat was attaching a roof rack to his car when a casually dressed David got out of a taxi at seven next morning.

Tim Pat's tossing and turning had kept Emma awake all night. It wasn't the first night his sleep had gone awry since David's move to Fitzwilliam. Tim Pat was a changed man. He had turned sullen, laughter had drained from him. It wasn't the leaving that was the cause of his maladies, it was Heather. Nothing would shake Tim Pat's belief his mother-in-law was out to poison David against his parents.

Tim Pat's heart swelled with joy when he saw David - casual dress noted. He put his arms round David's shoulders saying, "Me ould sagotia, a chip off the old block. Nice touch the taxi!"

Emma saw the two from the window and the taxi leave. A lump came to her throat; she could not have asked for anything more before setting out for West Cork.

"Packing early as usual, Dad?"

"Son, traffic is affright altogether; roads wider, straighter, and still it takes longer. They must be sticking in a few extra miles here and there."

"Is mammy up?"

"Up all hours packing. Nothing changes – we hope!"

David was receiving his father's concern loud and clear.

"I'll haul out the cases!"

"Breakfast first, cases after, nothing and nowhere is safe these days."

Tim Pat's whistling was sweet music to Emma's ears. She welcomed David as if he had been a prodigal of long absence.

Over breakfast David related, "Met a friend of your, Dad, well not exactly a friend, he knows our family."

The 'our family' rested as easy as a morning mist on Tim Pat's mind, he enquired, "Whoever would that be, Son?"

"Dinny Donovan, son of Bald Tyres Donovan from Clon. He said you would know his father."

"Summons after summons after summons from Bald Tyres. Small world. Where did you bump into Donovan?"

"You know him?"

"Not him, his ould fella."

"Dinny is our postman. Great West Cork accent, talk the leg off a pot," said David in his best West Cork brogue making a special effort to please his father and to heal his own bad memory of their last meeting.

"Donovan was a scourge, nothing bothered him only bald tyres on other people's cars. I swear a robin's dick would have more treads than the total of his own four tyres put together."

"He told me that as well!"

"What else had Dinny to say for himself?"

"He's a huge fan of grandmother."

Emma knew Tim Pat would enquire no further, and knowing David would not have brought up the subject except it was guaranteed to please his father, asked, "The story, David, the story?"

"He lacerated Gran, lacerated her. He went from no Christmas box, to her ignorance, to her slamming the door in his face and a whole range of other things. In language most colourful, he did not spare the language!"

David thought better of relating Dinny's story of her losing total control at mention of the O'Leary surname that had sent railings rattling round the postal district of Dublin two.

Tim Pat asked a question he knew David would be expecting, "How are they treating you beyond, son?"

"Fine, fine, Dad."

"Mother, let's hit the trail before them motorized lunatics come scorching from their wigwams".

"Leave the washing up, I'll look after it."

When Tim Pat was out of earshot Emma said a heartfelt, "Bless you, David, bless you for calling. Your visit is truly a life saver, thank you!"

A happier Tim Pat sketched alternatives open to David, "You have keys to your own home, son. And remember: there are plenty trains to Cork. Up the shaggen rebels, Dave, up the rebels."

"I'll tell Donovan you were asking for him."

"Do that, Dave. Never deny your own, boy!"

"Dad, Dave is an O'Leary. Dave won't!"

Early that summer's morning, there in the middle of the road David embraced his mother as they watched Tim Pat skip and jump like he hadn't skipped and jumped for weeks, shouting and punching the air, "Hup you boy you Dave, hup you boy you. Up the fuckin' Rebels, up the Rebels!"

Their neighbours went back to sleep; free range Tim Pat was back to normal.

CHAPTER 11

Tim Pat's conviction that city middle class youth were not streetwise would have received a jolt if he were privy to the appurtenance in David's trouser pocket when going on his twice-weekly date with Trish.

Trish had secreted two from Norma's supply and had produced them on their second date as they sweated tumbling and fumbling in the back of his grandmother's car. Knowing it was his first time, Trish assured him it was also her maiden voyage as together they attended to the sheathing of his dong. She had jumped as dong gushed at her touch. They had laughed and looked at it wondering what next it might think of doing as if it had a mind of its own, which dong had. David's mind was filled with Norma during those torrid engagements with Trish.

Leslie had always found Trish's boyfriends to be good listeners. That David knew nothing about the game of golf did not prevent Leslie from sitting in the lug of his ear and relating in hooks, slices, fades, chips, putts, his most recent round. Leslie, a member of his club's senior cup team, was not expected to suffer the company of scrubbers, but the bartering of twenty minutes of his time on the practice ground for a night's transport in David's car was affordable currency. Trish's approval on any given night had also to be paid for by Leslie. Where Leslie sourced the few quid was his problem, not Trish's.

One evening when David called, there was an air of excitement about the house. Leslie had won a competition and all, including grandmother Constance, were going to the presentation in the clubhouse. The Newmans were respected members. Grandfather Leslie had held every office, James had been honoured with the captaincy and Leslie junior was carrying on the family tradition.

On hearing the news, Trish put her own presentation in place for the evening. She met David at the door and excitedly informed, "They're going to the club, all of them!"

This news was greeted by David with a smile that had his lips running into his eardrums, and the tip of same ears point in dog-panting fashion in expectation of a lure being tossed.

Norma arrived from work by taxi having left her car in for service. On hearing of the exodus, Norma announced, "I'm going in David's car."

David couldn't take his eyes off Norma; she was more beautiful than even his wet-dreams recalled. Trish was furious; the cheek of Norma to walk in and assume control. They had used David's home a few times; they were cautious of over use, neighbours might talk. The one opportunity of abusing her mattress was being whipped out from under them.

Knowing what Norma would say if she said they were not going to the club, Trish declared magnanimously, "Senior citizens should not be abandoned. Room will be made for you!"

Norma left the insult pass.

When they arrived at the club, Leslie joined his cronies at the bar. The rest of the family sat together. James did the buying. Knowing their preference, he pointed to each person individually and enquired 'usual?' and was responded to by all in the affirmative. His finger hovered enquiringly towards David.

Trish ordered, "Pint of Guinness for David, please Dad!"

On their first date, on Trish's directive, they had gone to a pub. David, knowing the pub was part of her scene did not enlighten her to the fact that it was his first time entering a licensed premises without his father. She had asked for a glass of lager; pretending to be familiar he had ordered a glass of Guinness. He had often sampled his father's pint; the taste wasn't to his liking but he couldn't let on, it wouldn't be manly. David had felt tipsy after four glasses on that first date with Trish and while he had driven the car, he knew he should not have.

David was anything but comfortable as he sat among the Newmans with his pack of contraceptives in his pocket. His contribution to the conversation consisted of, 'Thank you, Mr. Newman,' when he was handed a pint by James.

'Thank you Mr. Newman,' he used four times, on being handed a fifth he staggered a 'ta-ta-thanks'.

He clapped the speeches when the others did. He was falling behind; a pint and a half stood looking up at him. He protested he had enough when next James Newman went to buy. He was left out of that round. When grandmother Constance said she wanted to go home, James, Ann and herself left but not before James again bought for those remaining. Two and a half pints stood looking up from the table at a shaky David.

Norma remarked, "I admire Guinness drinkers, something – something sexy about them!" David put the half-pint to his head and tossed it back in one gulp. He got the gulp down but a few seconds passed before his stomach managed to secure the gulp. Reaching out, he pulled the next pint towards him saying boastfully that which he had often heard his father boast:- "Mother's milk. Can't whack it!"

Trish raged at David's pandering to Norma's remark and the way he had stuffed himself with the half-pint.

"Solid and predictable easily managed like musty old men, isn't that right, Norm?" said Trish, voice laced with sarcasm and loud enough to be heard by others.

"I doubt David appreciates your stupid analogy. It wasn't at all what I meant, tricky Trish!"

David looked from one to the other. Old sores were being scratched back to life.

Trish replied, "David doesn't appreciate your presence no more than I do!"

"Sister mine, why are you so insecure - so afraid of Norma?"

"Why should I be insecure; you and I trawl in different centuries!"

"You will regret saying that!"

95

While the implications of the exchange ambled past David's muzzy thinking, others listening tittered.

Trish continued, "Go join brother Leslie. With his gift for carousing the intercession of your tits will be required to get him in and keep him in Cavendish's."

This time the collective intake of breath of those same listeners registered their shock at this public airing of Newman laundry.

Trish, who had not drunk too wisely, was in no state to appreciate just how shocking her public revelations were. She could not resist including the swipe at Leslie, who never invited her to the club or introduced her to his friends. But for her escorts' cars, he would have nothing to do with her.

Not losing her cool, Norma, in a measured voice, said,

"You insufferable moo-moo-cow. Grow up!"

Rising from her seat, Norma went with maximum movement to join Leslie and his company at the bar. Women's perjuring tongues swore they had not noticed the shimmying past of Norma's swivelling buttocks while their drooling partners indulged in mental ravishing.

"What was – was – what was all that about?" asked David in a voice much slurred.

"Miss supercilious, with all her so-called success, still chooses to live at home. I hate her!"

Encouraged by others, Leslie broke into a bar of a song and quickly a right session was in progress.

David's focussing was gone haywire; through a necklace of hiccups, he managed to mutter in verbal fragments, ' Go-go-going going to toi-toi-jacks!".

"Are you sure you're alright, David?" asked a concerned Trish.

"Co-co-course!" hiccupped David. A faltering indignation lacing his 'co-co-course'.

To hammer home his faltering indignation, David slugged from his fifth pint. Trish, familiar with drink associated hiccups, anticipated David's dinner arriving on a gusher. When David returned there was another full pint standing beside his still three- quarters filled fifth. Trish knew he needed that extra pint like he did a hole in the head.

"Compliments of a senior citizen, scared we will leave without her. You don't have to drink it, leave it after you!"

"Let it never-ever be said an O'O'O'O'Leary left a pi-pi-pint or the two chee-chee-cheeks of a wom-woman's arse after them."

David appeared to be masticating regurgitated porter before returning it, with the greatest difficulty, from whence it had come.

"O'Leary, your true self is surfacing. Can we expect fists to fly, jaws to break, furniture to smash?"

"Oh God, no-no-no, not-nothing like that I… I… I… assure you, Nor-Norma!"

"O'Leary, you dare insult me. You dare call me Norma!"

Trish's indignation nailed him to his seat and put on hold his regurgitating porter.

David's fogged brain scrambled in search of his mistake and having found it attempted a recovery. "I mean Orma. No, no, not Orma. Trish I mean!"

"Call me Orma or Norma once more and I swear I will kick your stupid head in!"

"Must, must be the heat, aw-awful wa-warm," muttered David reaching for the glass.

"That pint is flat, take the fresh one!" Trish's plot was hatched. Vital to its success was the keeping intact of David's cargo.

Norma sat in the front with Leslie doing the driving, David and Trish sat in the back, David sitting directly behind Norma. Trish, sticking her loving tongue down David's throat watched both his eyes bulging their alarm; and though his guts were heaving their turmoil she kept her tongue in position until that split second before the tsunami came ripping from his stomach. Trish, forcing David's head forward he gawked and gawked over Norma's head and back. Norma's hysterical shrieks filled the car as her arse sat transfixed in a pool of porter seasoned by carrots, cabbage, potatoes and masticated meat.

Grandmother Dempsey was a great believer in vegetables and plenty of them. Five a.m. found Trish rousing David from the couch in the Newman livingroom. On the newspaper covered floor sat a plastic basin.

"What happened?" David ventured to ask as the Artane Boys Band hammered a rousing march within the confines of his throbbing skull.

"Get up, cleaning operation to be done on the car before your grandmother sees it."

David was led with scoop, hand brush, detergents, cloths and boiling water to the car.

"I did all this?" he gasped, having looked and smelt the car's interior causing dry-retching to rack his frame, the ferocity of which had the ferrule in his arse attempt an escape through his mouth.

"Gra-Gran-mother, what am I going to tell gra-grandmother?"

"Volunteer nothing. If grandmother asks, tell her Leslie got sick. Leslie's suggestion not mine. If you are grounded, Leslie's travel plans will be seriously curtailed."

"What happened?"

"Apart from Norma requiring counselling to get your dinner out of her brain, nothing really."

"She'll never again look at me, never!"

"You fool, she has never looked at you in that way, sonny, never has, never will!"

The unorthodox manner in which he had shared his vegetables with Norma put an end to David's parading up and down Dawson Street.

Having scrubbed and scrubbed in shower and bath, every stitch of clothing Norma had worn went into the rubbish bin. She had enough of Trish. Norma ordered a meeting with father James and grandmother Constance. When asked by James if she wanted Trish, Leslie, and mother Ann present, Norma had told him it was a meeting for adult minds, only. Mother Ann's kitchen vocation was not to be disturbed.

Knowing it was her public remarks about Cavendish in the club that had caused Norma to call the meeting, Trish set about courting her grandmother's support.

"Once again Norma is making trouble for me, Gran. Never stops interfering in my affairs."

"In what way is she interfering with your affairs?"

"She never stops playing games with David, flirts to a point where she believes if she snapped her fingers he would come running to her like a puppy".

"And you believe that as well, don't you?"

"She only does it when I'm there, makes a fool out of him."

"Not like Norma calling a meeting for what appears to me to be nothing more than a bit of fun."

"It isn't fun to me. It isn't fair."

"Trish, there has to be more; grandmother knows you wouldn't be worried if there wasn't. It's best you tell me; I'm going to be told at this meeting, forewarned is forearmed."

"She is overreacting, I haven't had a serious argument with that one for weeks."

"Overreacting to what?"

"I said things about herself and Cavendish."

Constance did not like what she was hearing from her favourite granddaughter.

"In public?"

"Only once!"

"You know something that obviously I do not?"

"When she hurts me, I hurt her back".

"So you smack her with Mr. Cavendish, your father's boss? What kind of things did you say about Norma and Cavendish?"

"Not nice!"

"You suggest her friendship with Cavendish is more than platonic, would I be right?"

"Yes."

"A man of his age - ridiculous!"

"If it is ridiculous why has Father been given two promotions in

99

quick succession since Cavendish took a fancy to Norma?"

"Your father deserved those promotions; for too long he has been passed over."

When Trish did not comment, Grandmother continued, "Do you want Norma to stop escorting Mr. Cavendish, that she should make him aware sister Trish is spreading scandal about them? That her father was not to be promoted again, that Leslie should not join Cavendish's, that David O'Leary should not be employed there either, that by doing any of those three would confirm your disgusting suspicion?"

"I'm happy for father. I know those promotions mean everything to him," replied Trish in a more conciliatory tone.

"Would you have invested your time in your father's career to the extent Norma has?"

"I honestly don't know".

"Well, Norma has. She is a hard-nosed businesswoman. In one way, I despise her and in another way I admire … no, not admire, I'm in awe of her determination. That's what it is, determination! Do you really want your father to confront what you are suggesting?"

"It wasn't me who called this meeting. I'm not invited to the meeting."

"When you tell your father his promotions are because of Norma's so-called affair with Mr.Cavendish, as you have suggested, it is certain to destroy him…,and this household along with him. Could cause him to resign from Cavendish's"

"Didn't think of all that".

"Well you better think of that. Your suggestion, your public suggestion was despicable, could eventually reach your father's ears. Have you discussed this grievance of yours with David?" "No, I haven't".

"Was he present when yourself and Norma argued?"

"He had more than one too many. He didn't have a clue what was being said and Mister Cavendish's name was not mentioned, I'm sure of that, I think. I accept I have wronged Norma. I don't want Daddy upset. What do I do?"

"Norma could have challenged you over dinner but she didn't. She is giving you time to think, perhaps even to consult with me as to what you should do. Now you stop this meeting by apologising to Norma for your stupidity, because that is what it was and tell her there will be no repeat. Understood?"

"Yes, Grandmother."

CHAPTER 12

On Emma's and Tim Pat's annual sojourn to West Cork, Emma and Mary, the wife of Tom O'Leary, could be found binging socially. Their attendance could be found at fashion shows, theatres, gymkhanas, bowls, cross-roads dancing, and everything and anything once the location was within a reasonable driving distance from the farm. When Mary was otherwise occupied, Emma, in full riding outfit, was away riding through the countryside.

Porter followed by pillow-talk had Tom tell Mary of his jodhpur fantasies and she, with haste, confided in Emma while sharing two bottles of wine while the men were away at the pub.

" Tom told me your jodhpurs and crop turn him on big time. Mind you I have noticed a definite increase in activity when you are around". "Are you complaining?"

"Does a cat like milk? But when your jodhpurs go back to Dublin his appetite declines."

" Tom kinky!"

"I have to drive to Cork to get confession; contraceptives are the bane of my life".

"Do you really need them?"

"He likes to think so, keeps him young.

"Why not go local for condoms: petrol is expensive?"

"Being married to the local teacher makes a difference."

"What difference does that make?"

"Tom does not confess that we use them, says it's our own business and no one else's. 'In the conscience of every good Catholic there has to be wriggle room for condoms', says he. Teacher does have a way with words."

"I agree with Teacher."

"Teacher has me wriggling to Cork. You know when the priest asks at the end of confession, 'anything else?' That question catches me; if I say 'no', my silly conscience has me believing I've made a bad confession. Blast my conscience".

"I'd tell Reverend and leave Reverend do what he likes with condoms."

"There's the catch; I'd be making a liar of Tom if I told the truth."

"Because he doesn't tell?"

"Correct."

"Priest must be wondering to whose box do you take your custom."

"Living with God and sleeping with Tom isn't easy".

"And would the priest know everyone who goes into his box?"

"Priest could put a name to every shoe that falls half way down the church."

"In that case very little spice in what he hears."

"Summary jurisdiction stuff is all, even from those who haven't the transport to go elsewhere."

"Felonies, misdemeanour, rubbers and selected offences to Cork or interred with their sinning bones. Spicy stuff at all times exported."

"Exports don't affect priest's employment."

"We have no such problems."

"You mean . . ."

"No, no, no, heavens no. Anything but. We enjoy our sex. It isn't how I'm oversexed, but I do admit pussy to be a creature of habit".

"That's a relief. I couldn't have pussy galloping around the farm the way Tom feels about those jodhpurs if your husband's machinery wasn't in working order."

"I'd give up confession before the other, says you."

"I suppose David has plenty girls".

"Not that we are aware of and we would know. Nothing for David but study, study, study."

" Has to be every parent's worry, wondering if their children are -

what is rightly or wrongly called - 'normal'".

"When I discuss David's lack of social life with Tim Pat he says, 'Soon enough he'll have a fistful of arse in his paw'.

"Crudity and O'Leary's are two sides of the same butter box. You must have been one right ticket in your day?"

"My sisters and I grew up in a house of silence, dreadful silence. Even now I shudder when I think of my childhood. No freedom. David has all the freedom in the world and he doesn't make use of it".

"Those jodhpurs – you must loan me those some night and the crop. I promise to report how I get on … maybe!"

"Be warned: no Cork box for crop and jodhpur. Sin would definitely have Vatican status. Rome for absolution."

"'Twould be worth it. We could have a second honeymoon: our first was a wee bit rushed".

Tim Pat had a month's holidays but Emma had to return to work after a fortnight. He drove her back after what they agreed had been a glorious holiday. At Newland's Cross, on the outskirts of Dublin, Tim Pat informed Emma of David's driving. The silence that greeted this information confirmed the wisdom of not telling Emma before the holiday. Fury raged in Emma.

"Your permission wasn't sought?" she snapped.

"No!"

"Would you have given it?"

"You know damn well where I stand on that driving business".

"Did David tell you?"

"We met".

"The idiot, the idiot, the idiot".

"I had a word with him".

"It's not him, it's that woman".

"Don't I know".

"She will do anything, anything to drive him from us".

"I'll kill her, I swear I'll kill the bitch if anything happens to David. As God's my judge I will. There's a graveyard of difference between dodging cows and dodging traffic in O'Connell Street."

"Thanks for not telling me before the holiday. I wouldn't have gone. What's to be done?"

There was a long pause before Tim Pat replied, "Has me addled. Might be better to say nothing, advise him to be careful, and for your health's sake, tear strips off that mother of yours."

"We leave him drive?"

"No alternative if you don't want him abandoning us".

Tim Pat returned to West Cork next morning.

Emma, anticipating the confrontation with her mother, found concentration at work impossible. She went direct from work to Fitzwilliam Square.

There was no concealing father's delight on seeing her. Getting up from his chair he kissed her. In his low sincere voice he welcomed her only to be drowned by Heather's haughty voice coming into the room and flopping down on the chair George had vacated.

"Ho, ho. Jungle Emma has survived another trip to the outback."

"My son David, is he here?" asked Emma tersely, dismissing her mother's insult.

"Not at all, not at all; away golfing with his new found friends."

Father George would have liked to impart that bit of, what he considered, good news but left the stage to his wife as was his custom.

"How does David come and go to these new found friends, may I ask?" questioned Emma.

"Car, of course. Zooms off every evening full of the joys of life" declared mother glorying in her victory.

"He drives himself?"

"Come, come now. This is the latter part of the twentieth century; it may not have arrived in some quarters but it certainly has arrived in Fitzwilliam Square.

"David drives?"

Mother, still sitting, declared: "Of course David drives!"

Happiness abandoned George's face.

"You know we had forbidden David to drive."

"I decided your decision could not be sustained given David's maturity, ability to drive and my generosity in allowing him use my car." "It wasn't your decision to make, and you should have consulted with me before you even considered offering him the car."

"Well, then, you should have stayed in Dublin and not gone off on safari to bush country."

"It was my concern for you and father that I asked David to stay in Dublin. You had no right, absolutely no right to go against our wishes."

"It was your concern for father not your mother. At least be honest about that."

"David is too young to drive," said George, more an observer than participant in the argument.

"Of course David is too young. Thank you, Father!".

Heather, feeling at a disadvantage sitting, stood up and eye-balled her daughter.

"What kind of grandmother would I be if I did not listen to the pain of my grandson and act accordingly in his best interest. And if you had been listening to David instead of wasting your life with that most uncivil of civil servants, David would not have had to confide his anxieties in me. I have every right to listen to my grandson's disenchantment."

"What exactly are you saying David said?"

"He said nothing to me." remarked George.

The words registered with Emma; she was pleased to hear them. She repeated, "What are you saying David told you that he could not tell his parents?"

"Stupid, that is the point. How could a son confide in a father he is embarrassed having."

"David did not say that; you dare say David said that about his father."

Emma considered looking to father for denial of the statement and was pleased when he volunteered, "Nothing he said to me would suggest other than he loved his father."

This time Emma acknowledged father's comment.

"Thank you, Father."

Heather glared at George.

"Are you accusing me of lying?"

"Father said he never heard David say what you are suggesting he said. Father is stating a fact, not calling you a liar?"

"I stand over what I said," snapped Heather.

"Did David actually say he was embarrassed having Tim Pat as his father?" queried Emma

"Not perhaps in so many words."

"Use as many words as you like – what perhaps did he say?"

"I have no intention of breaking a confidence."

"You are a liar, a liar!"

"From the moment you were born, you were trouble, a brat. You were the cause of your sisters being expelled from that excellent school in England. You brought shame on this house when you married that, that rustic."

"From the moment I was born!…well, well. At last you've said it after all these years. What a bitter disappointment it was for you to be presented with a third baby girl."

"What has my disappointment got to do with your obduracy?"

"It has everything to do with your attitude towards Florence, Stephanie and myself. You considered yourself cursed with three daughters and me being the youngest incurred the focus of most of your disappointment.'

"How dare you try hurting me like this."

"I cannot hurt you. Florence or Stephanie cannot hurt you, because you have never loved us."

"Your needs were met. Is it not reasonable that I would want a son along with daughters?"

"Pity you weren't satisfied with the will of God."

"You are quick to invoke God. You, who have not been to the sacraments since the day you married."

"Better than being a hypocrite."

"You dare insult me in my home."

"This house was never a home," said Emma bitterly.

"And I suppose yours is when your only child is happier here than living with you".

"I'm sorry this day ever happened," pleaded George.

"It had to happen. She married that O'Leary to spite me".

"It was never my husband you hated. I was stupid thinking it was. Tim Pat was a convenient peg to hang your bitterness on. It was me you hated. You said it yourself and to think I still call you 'Mother'."

"I'm listening to no more of your rubbish. Leave my house, now."

A fretting George anguished, "No, no. This arguing has to stop. Emma do not leave. This is home to all our children. A cup of tea perhaps? All this anger coming out into the open now. Have I been blind."

Heather blazed from the room. Emma put her arms around her father saying, "Oh Dad, I didn't mean for you to get involved."

"What have I not said, what have I not done that made you say you had an unhappy time in this house, my dear darling Emma".

"I didn't mean you when I referred to this house."

"But surely being the father, I must take most if not all of the blame for your unhappiness."

"I assure you none of your daughters see it that way. Mummy is domineering. You are the kindest, most gentle father in the whole world".

"I'm beginning to think that is the worst thing that can be said to a man married to a woman like – well when one is married to mother, shall we say."

"We all love you, Dad."

"I don't suppose I would be any different no matter who married me."

"I wouldn't want you to be any different, Dad. None of your daughters would," lied Emma.

CHAPTER 13

After the altercation with her mother on the Monday, Emma received a phone call from David saying he would call the following night.

"It's easier for you to visit now that you are driving," said Emma caustically when David arrived. There was a long pause before David enquired, "Daddy told you?"

"Not before I was back in Dublin."

"You don't mind then?"

"David, that is not what I'm saying. I was terrified on being told."

"I'm very careful. You don't have to worry, honestly."

"I will worry!"

"I drive to Dalkey most evenings, I play golf with Leslie Newman. Well, actually, he gives me lessons"

"It pleases me you are playing golf, but your driving is against my better judgement and your father's. I'm saying no more, but for God's sake be careful".

"Mother, you can be sure I will."

"Did grandmother tell you I called to Fitzwilliam?"

"No, granddad did. He said you were fine and you enjoyed your holiday"

"Did grandmother mention anything – say anything?"

"No! Should she have?"

Emma avoided David's question by asking," I expect Leslie Newman is Constance Newman's grandson?"

"That's right; you must know them?"

"Not since I married your father have I met Constance Newman."

"Unusual. Her being Gran's best friend. Leslie's father James, mother Ann, and his two sisters live with her."

"Seems you are enjoying yourself."

"Oh, I am, I also go to discos with them. Really good fun."

"Discos?"

"Anything wrong with my going to discos?"

"Mixing with your own age group has to be good."

"I was afraid you might object."

"Why ever would you think that?"

"The driving. I drive as Leslie doesn't have a car but he does have a licence."

"No speeding mind. If I hear of you speeding, grandmother or no grandmother, your driving will come to an end!"

"Grandmother knows how careful I am. I've been driving her all over the place, not as much as a scratch."

"One mistake on the road can be one mistake too many, David."

"No fear this David will make a mistake."

"Surely the Newman's have a car?"

"Course they have. So has Norma but Leslie doesn't get to drive either car, and he's three years older than me. That's how good I am."

"David, me thinks the Newmans know their Leslie. He's a drinker, isn't he?"

"When he's with his father in the golf club, he does."

"David, believe me, he drinks to excess and his parents know he does."

"He has just passed his second, or did Trish say third year accountancy exams. Norma is the eldest she owns a boutique in Dawson Street and then there is Trish, she is my own age."

"What's the name of Norma's shop in Dawson Street ?"

"Norma's,… I think."

"Original!"

"Trish travels with myself and Leslie to the discos.
We get on really well."

"That's good. How is grandfather today?"

"Himself and Gran must have had some kind of argument, they weren't talking. Don't say I told you, I don't want to be labelled a carrier of gossip."

"Of course I won't."

"How is Uncle Tom, Mary and all the work?"

"You were missed, but all are agreed you didn't have a choice."

"Grandmother never stops thanking me for coming to live with them, gives me plenty money along with the car."

"Your parents will give you all the money you want. What one might consider generosity is oft-times intended to compromise the recipient when making decisions."

"Some mouthful, Mother. I can't very well not take the money when she practically throws it at me."

"We expect you to consult with us before making decisions, serious decisions. We wouldn't want to think you were not happy with us as parents."

"Dad mentioned this decision business to me before. It can't be because I didn't go to West Cork. You told me to stay and look after them - that was your decision."

"It has nothing got to do with West Cork. We want to ensure you don't grow away from us."

"Where would I be growing to?"

"It could be suggested that you look at us in a different light."

"It's Daddy you are talking about, isn't it?"

"Grandmother has not been saying nice things about your father, never has. I hope you are strong enough not to be influenced."

"She does go on a bit about Dad, how his West Cork accent and wardrobe do not transfer to Fitzwilliam Square."

"And how does David respond to those statements?"

"I take them as a joke."

"You don't stand up for your father?"

"Of course I stand up! You can be sure I stand up, but she always says these things jokingly. Says I'm too sensitive, and that I would not

111

be that way if I didn't believe there was a little truth in what she was saying. She says that jokingly as well."

"Be respectful but in no way subservient. Remember this is your home not Fitzwilliam Square."

"This has something got to do with them not talking today, hasn't it?"

"There was an argument between your grandmother and myself, Granddad was caught in the middle."

"Can I ask what the argument was about?"

"Old sores were lanced and now that they have been lanced, it will take goodwill on everyone's part to cure them. Forgetting is not an option."

"Bet Father was one of those sores?"

"Surprisingly, father wasn't half the sore I thought he was."

"If it wasn't daddy, who or what was the argument about?"

"The argument was between grandmother and myself. She wanted me to be a boy. Stephanie and Florence also, but me, for definite."

"That's all this great big argument was about?"

"Her third pregnancy was a third unwanted baby girl. The value of a male child in a house of women is inestimable".

"Where would dad be without you, where would I be? Granddad seems happy. To me he does anyway."

"Full time masochist, full time pacifist, full time whipping boy. Every relationship meets needs. Sometimes those needs can be unhealthy."

"You've lost me. They don't seem to exist for each other. That's all I'll say."

"Tell me what you mean by 'they don't exist for each other'?"

"Well, they … they're like two units moving in the one area without common purpose. Do you know what I'm trying to say?"

"Are you saying it isn't like our home? Not like myself and your father, warm to each other even in thunder?"

"That's it! That's exactly it. Warm in thunder. Raw West Cork lingo, the crème-de la-crème of languages."

"Of that particular crème, Heather does have her own strong views. Enough has been said on the matter."

"Taking money from Gran and her remarks about dad, you think she is trying to turn me against you, don't you?"

"Of your grandmother's intentions, your mother cautions circumspection."

"Worry not, I will. No point in telling Dad about all this."

"Definitely not. Perhaps everything will have blown over before he returns."

David had no sooner left the house than Mary rang from West Cork.

"I have the house to myself, Emma. The two are still at the hay. Forecast isn't great."

"David has just left, driving grandmother's car. Honestly I'm the proverbial bag of nerves. That mother of mine is a right bitch. It's all her doing."

"You were complaining about David not socialising. Cars have the gift of making their drivers very popular. You mightn't be seeing much of him from now on. Tim Pat told you about David driving?"

"On the way back he did, and when we talked about the car and under the car and around the car, I'm not as upset about the whole business as I was. But when the phone will ring at night, the first thought that will come flashing to my mind will be David."

"Only natural, Emma. We can all worry ourselves to an early grave about one thing or another. Listen, I have to tell you about our whip and jodhpur saga. Just between ourselves now, between ourselves do you hear?"

"Mary, Emma's jodhpurs are sealed and a knot is in her whip".

"Well, the night Tim Pat drove you back, my boyoh gets me to put on the jodhpurs. Raring to go was our Tom, stretched out starkers on the bed smiling like a Cheshire cat. In true military style, I ordered him over onto his belly, raised my crop, lash after lash I flaked down on his backside, and did he yowl? Yowl? He terrified the weather-cock into crowing hours before the dawn itself thought of breaking. His language was blue, blue, blue. I thought a seizure was on the way with his leaping and jumping. 'Blow on my bum! Blow my bum!' he begged. But Mary no blow, Mary, no blow. 'Newspaper, newspaper, fan, fan, fan!' Mary no fan. Without a thought for the cost, he begged, 'Rub, rub butter on, butter rub on.' Naturally I refused, when I offered margarine instead he cried, 'Great, great, great, great'. I looked in the fridge and was pleased to tell him we didn't have margarine. When I told him his arse warranted a tetanus injection, he wouldn't hear of calling-out the G.P.. So kind hearted Mary suggested the old reliable 'iodine' as a last resort. He agreed. Well the weather-cock's cock-a-doodle-doodles went into overdrive in keeping with his agony. Naked, he shot from the house to the haggard where he ripped off outer cabbage leaves and rammed them you know where, yelping. Shep all the time running rings around him. Jodhpur fantasy had died a death in that haggard. When all parts cooled he bent over the kitchen table, posy of cabbage leaves still in situ, declaring jodhpurs should not be worn in bedrooms by ignorant countrywomen especially when fridges had no margarine. How's about that for a fantasy cure, Doctor Emma?"

"No doubt you've saved his soul and left extraneous matters to cabbage leaves and iodine. "

"Cabbage leaves and iodine! Pleasure administered with purgatory."

"Not in equal measure. Anticipation of pleasure died at first lash, purgatory does go on a little longer. A sin for the Cork box."

"Wrong! Not for parish box, Cork box, Vatican box, letter box, snuff box, no box! It's hardly the stuff of eternal damnation. Anyway, a wife is guaranteed indulgences for doing her husband's bidding"

"Sounds as if there won't be a next time. Did you draw blood?"

"A few ridges of red. They didn't really bleed. I'll whip you if you say a word."

"I won't if you promise to tell me how you get on in Cork."

"How could you tell that in a confession box? Where would you begin?"

"You should have thought of that beforehand. Peeping-Tom-God is always watching."

"I assure you tractor seat is extracting maximum atonement. He is blessed to have Tim Pat: he does most of the tractor work."

"Makes up for the penance he is ducking for not telling about the condoms. What cannot be framed should be photographed for posterity."

"Not late yet. You know something, it must have been the hand of God that struck those blows. I only meant to tap tap tap but welcome be the squeals and weals of God. When I said it was a pity you weren't here, he said doctors are like policemen, the bums were never around when you wanted them."

"Bet you enjoyed the sense of power the crop gave you?"

"Not saying!"

"I want my crop back. Without the blood, thank you, lest I be accused of cruelty to animals."

"I'll kill you if you breathe a word."

" Tim Pat has to be full of curios questions."

"You never heard anything like the questions. He goes on and on. Tom told him he sat on a plank with a rusty nail. Tim Pat wanted to know the plank and why he didn't take his backside for an anti-tetanus injection? After inspection he declared, 'Christ there must have been a dozen nails on that plank seeing as both cheeks are infected'. He asked if I had inspected the plank, wanted right-or-wrong to ring you. Honestly, I couldn't stop laughing, and, as true as God, if he didn't say, 'If I didn't know better I'd say you two were up to something kinky'. Well you should have seen poor Tom's face. Fair play to him, he replied, 'Don't you know well we were!'"

"Do you think Tom will tell Tim Pat?"

"You never know with Tom. After a few drinks he yaps and yaps. But one thing is for sure he'll not tell until his backside is on speaking terms with the tractor seat."

"Will I send you down ointment?"

"That would be great. I'm smearing baby cream from jars and times well passed onto cheeks at the minute. It gives him as much relief as heaven allows."

"If Tim Pat returns complaining of sitting on that plank or any other plank, I'll scratch your eyes out!"

"Now, there's a thought."

CHAPTER 14

At seven a.m. the frying pan was crackling as Tim Pat sat at the kitchen table watching Mary cooking breakfast. When the phone rang, Tim Pat sprang to his feet but fear stopped him from picking up the phone. "David! I know 'tis David. That fucking motor car!"

Mary on answering the phone gave a thumb's up sign to Tim Pat, signalling the news wasn't at all bad. "Your dad died in his sleep. Oh Emma, this is terrible news, terrible".

Tim Pat gave a skip, and, punching the air, murmured "Terrible news my arse: miracle misfortunate-George lived as long as he did married to that bitch of a hoor." Before handing the phone to Tim Pat, Mary told Emma, "He's right beside me….in the kitchen, the kitchen mind. Handing you over".

Tim Pat was feeling no pain when he spoke to Emma. "Sorry about George, Emma. Gentleman, a gentleman if ever there was one. A gentleman. Were you with him when he passed away?"

Regret was all too obvious in Emma's voice when she answered, "No, I wasn't. It was David who rang me just this minute".

Tim Pat was only taken slightly aback with Emma's answer when he asked, "Have you spoken to Heather?"

"No, I haven't spoken to Heather. We had a blazing row in front of Daddy. She ordered me from the house. Sorry to disappoint your ego, but the row wasn't about Tim Pat O'Leary this time".

"Without her venom, my ego would have died years ago. You are going to be blamed for your dad's death, you know that?"

With resignation, Emma acknowledged what Tim Pat had said to be true.

"Yes I suppose I will. How Daddy hated unpleasantness. Why did he have to witness the row? It was my last time seeing him alive."

"Was David there at the time?"

"Thank God, no. He called here last night. I told him Mother and I had an argument in front of Daddy".

Tom walks into the kitchen and asks Mary, "Who's on the blower?"

Mary whispers, "Emma's father George died in his sleep last night".

Tom made his feelings known in a guttural. "Bollocks to George. Tim Pat might have to go back."

Mary taken aback by Tom's coldness, "Of course Tim Pat will have to go back."

"George will be planted without us that's for sure. Hay down, turf in the bog and the state of my arse, what a time he decided to pull out."

"Raw time to be sure, but welcome be the will of God."

"Don't you try telling me God had anything to do with your crop turning savage on my backside."

"Far be it for me to tell a national teacher God had turned savage."

Tom gingerly feeling his backside said mournfully, "My backside can't sit down."

"What ever will backside do when you take backside to Sunday Mass?"

"I'll take backside to Saturday confession instead".

"I'll drive to the funeral in Dublin. You kneel on the passenger seat and pretend you are a rear view mirror".

"Funny, funny, funny. You don't expect a doctor to cut-out without giving some kind of notice. Anyone that lives long enough to put a bulge in eighty can't complain".

Putting his finger to his lips Tom ordered "Whist!" Himself and Mary did not hide the fact that they were listening to Tim Pat's conversation with Emma.

Tim Pat, on the phone, listened to Emma before replying, "Because your mother wouldn't come to my parents funerals, George could not come. It's as simple as that. That doesn't stop Tom and Mary going to your dads."

Having listened to Emma, Tim Pat replied, "I'll tell Tom and Mary they're not expected to travel, but, knowing them, they will want to go no matter the amount of work they have on hand. Innocent country folk and their corporal works of mercy. I'm hearing you Emma, the decision is theirs. They'll make up their own minds".

Tim Pat had heard enough and wanting to end the conversation said, "I'm sitting into the car this very minute and driving back. After the breakfast of course. Can't have sheepdog Shep putting his health at risk eating Mary's greasy fry. Bye, bye! See you later Emma".

Tim Pat dropped the handset on the receiver saying "Mouse George to die and that rip of a bitch left standing. No one's to blame but God for that miscarriage of justice."

Tom's work-load got in the way of his being charitable when he asked Tim Pat, "She'll be expecting you back, will she?"

Mary warned, "If Tim Pat wants to be castrated, he'll stay here."

Tim Pat was going to tell them he was his own man.

"There'll be no castration whether I do or I don't".

"Why, is Emma superstitious?" smirked a disappointed Tom.

"Emma won't be expecting you to travel to Dublin. Time of year, work, and all that," said Tim Pat, to which Tom replied falsely but firmly "There are certain fundamental decencies to be fulfilled in this life, and one of those fundamentals is burying the dead. Us country folk might be simple folk but we get our fundamentals right, don't we Mary?"

Mary agreed, "Tom, I want you to know your wife is right behind your sentimentals".

Tom corrected, "Fundamentals, Mary, fundamentals." To which Mary replied "Yes Tom, sentimentals".

"Wife, there'll be work there when we're dead and gone".

"Tom is the boss Tim Pat; if Tom says we're funeral bound, then funeral bound are we."

Tim Pat, in disbelief, looks at Mary askance.

"I won't forget this, and neither will Emma. I knew you'd turn-up trumps. She'd be delighted to see you there supporting her in her hour of need."

"That's us. That's us. Trump turn-ups. That's what you said we were, Tim Pat, wasn't it? Trump turn-ups?"

"Mary, it's 'turn-up trumps." Explained Tom.

"Trumps or no trumps, we'll turn up."

"Thanks Mary."

"I'll be tossing a few bits and pieces into a case for the both of us, Tom."

"We'll travel in convoy, me leading, you behind driving with Tom's ass winking at me in my rear view mirror".

"Tom's arse isn't squinting anywhere. And neither is Mary's".

"That has to be the fastest turn around since the hairpin was invented".

"Morning and night, cows tits to pull, hay to haul, turf to draw, sheds to paint, gutters to fix. Will I go on?"

"You've gone far enough. You're on the outskirts of being overrun by work."

"Fundamentals aren't what they used to be, Mary."

"Fundamentals take a back seat to the weather, and right good weather is what we have right now and here you are shagging off to a funeral, and you should know better too Mary, then you're a townie and weather doesn't affect townies bank accounts".

Tim Pat, remembering, said, "George was a nice man, which his wife isn't".

"In fairness very few wives are nice men." Said Mary.

In the full knowledge that Tim Pat was definitely returning to Dublin for the funeral, Tom changed his tune.

"We're only joking, Tim Pat, Emma would have us certified if we left the farm at this time of year".

Mary teased, "Tom, you shouldn't be telling lies about your fundamentals. Boys have had their bottoms whacked with a riding crop for less. Right, Tim Pat?".

"I knew it, I knew it, I knew it. Plank, my arse. Rusty nails, my arse. Emma's riding crop whacks teacher, bloody hell bloody arse!"

CHAPTER 15

Emma hurried to Fitzwilliam Square having rung Tim Pat in West Cork with the news of her father's death, When Emma entered the master bedroom, she found her mother sitting at the dressing table dabbing the final touches to her public face. Father George seemed to be asleep beneath tossed bedclothes. With venom, her mother hissed at Emma's reflected image in the mirror, "My husband is dead because of you. You'll remember that because your sisters will and so will I!"

Rising from the dressing table, she quickly left the room, not affording Emma an opportunity to respond. Emma had no intention of so doing. Emma left her lips on her father's cold brow before sitting on the side of the bed holding his hand where David found her in quiet reverie.

Doctor Heather had first rung Constance Newman, then her daughters Florence and Stephanie, and in martyred proportions identified their sister Emma as the cause of their father's demise.

David was handed a list of his grandmother's acolytes who needed to be contacted as a matter of urgency. David's mother Emma did not appear on that list. Within the hour, Constance Newman had arrived and was ever present at her friend's side during those most public of days. Doctor Heather gave a sublime performance as a newly arrived widow whose anguish was multiplied by the infliction of her three daughters, two of whom had at least married within their own class, but Emma had church-buckled herself to a rustic. Her friends had no doubt that God had not been kind to Heather in regard to her offspring, but George's passing at this time would be seen to be a blessing when the mud had settled on his grave. George had been sickly of late, mildly cranky and had the temerity to repeatedly ask Constance to make him tea and toast at the most inconsiderate of times. Yes, things were looking up for their dear friend Heather if not for George, who never could drive and God in his wisdom had planted grandson David in Fitzwilliam Square, knowing, as was his wont in such matters, George's demise to be on the horizon.

Doctor George Dempsey's funeral would be family and close friends only- so ordained his wife Heather and so read his obituary both in the death column and also a notice on the back page of the Irish Times. It did not matter to Tim Pat that his mother-in-law's hand stayed by her side when he proffered his in sympathy. As they tend to do, the practical aspects of the funeral went without a hitch: George Dempsey was buried.

By Norma's attendance at the funeral with her family, David believed he would know if the odium attached to his belly's indiscretion had been forgiven. James, Ann and Trish arrived. Norma did not show - more than David's belly was disappointed.

Somewhere in the midst of the obsequies, Tim Pat, Emma and David came face to face with Constance Newman, her son James, his wife Ann, and their daughter Trish. Like a stoat sensing danger, Constance's osteoporosis-inflicted spine straightened and stiffened, adding inches to her height, her eyes pinched to mere slits and the clamping of her thin lips hid from view the pencil line of purple lipstick as Trish and David casually dispensed the introductions. Constance gave full expression of her loyalty to Heather when her hands, in broad sweep, swept behind her back where her fingers entwined in knuckle-white obstinacy when the customary handshake of condolence should have been accepted by Emma and possibly Tim Pat. Disbelief rendered her own family speechless, even the irrepressible Trish was silenced. Fumbled pleasantries died a death given their grandmother's naked hostility. Knowing Tim Pat's rage because of Constance Newman's rude and insulting behaviour towards his wife had Emma on tender-hooks less he should explode in the only fashion Tim Pat ever exploded, which was akin to a duck in thunder. Emma smartly earthed

Tim Pat's fury by leaning heavily on his forearm thereby beseeching his quick fire fists and in this case quicker tongue to keep his rage on-hold. Once again, Emma's earth-ing worked.

Constance Newman turned on her heel and literally shot from them causing Tim Pat to remark, "That turn would leave room on a sixpence for a four hand reel."

Trish, attempting to mitigate her grandmother's discourtesy, joked, "Gran never misses an opportunity to practice her pirouette."

Ann explained, "Gran has to be in need of a sleep. The dear dear woman has to be exhausted, she has been with Mrs. Dempsey since since she got the phone call."

Accompanied by a wry smile from Tim Pat, Emma offered without conviction, "Exhaustion has never been a considerate companion."

James corrected, "Exhaustion is no excuse for bad manners, Doctor Emma."

James had been brought up on a diet of 'Doctor this' and 'Doctor that' by his mother Constance, who was complying with Doctor Dempsey's insistence on same.

Tim Pat considered what Ann had said to be a load of naive bollox, while wife Emma was so impressed she humbly confessed, "Your charity puts me to shame, Ann. So kind, so merciful, and please do call me Emma, James. Within the curtilage of hospitals or in my surgery I am Doctor, but outside I appreciate informality, none of that middle-class snobbery."

Tim Pat was being Tim Pat when he poked fun at his wife and lied through his teeth in support of Emma.

"Like Doctor Emma, you put me to shame too, Ann."

Emma and David threw sceptical eyes at Tim Pat while Ann, uncomfortable with the sainthood status, shrugged and denied, "Indeed I'm anything but kind and merciful."

Trish quipped, "I'm living proof of that."

Tim Pat admiring the sexuality and spirit of Trish said casually, "Trish, you're a joker, I'm thinking."

James saw fit to mildly correct Trish, "Missy, you remember those kind words Doctor Emma has said about your mother."

Thinking-tumblers in Trish's brain were meshing at the rate of knots. James had provided his daughter with a glorious opportunity to twist the conversation so that she might innocently douse her sister-bitch with vinegar for the collective palates of the O'Learys to savour - in particular David - before Father James would inevitably get round to boasting about his hugely accomplished eldest daughter Norma. Trish, knowing her father would not have the balls to dismiss her lure with a peremptory, rubbish, as her mother assuredly would, feigned psychological damage as a result of the low esteem in which she was held by parents who gave all their love to Norma. Her thinking had cautioned her to toss Leslie into the mix to show Norma was not totally to blame. She cast her lure.

"Missy Trish takes after her dear mother, Ann. That is why missy Trish is the black sheep of the Newmans."

Sure enough father came clear out of the water to bite the lure as Trish expected. Too late, James realized Trish had hooked him into requesting an explanation of her 'black sheep' reference.

Trish's and Norma's scheming had in common that foxy colouring of 'don't throw me into the bushes' factored in. In sham disbelief but in the certainty Trish would not hunt her 'black sheep' down Cavendish way. James queried "Black sheep, my Trish?" In a voice suitably pitched to match her doleful countenance, Trish said, "Your Trish is too kind, too merciful, too forgiving. I'd be better respected if I was as cold and calculating as Norma. Not that Leslie is much better. Neither of them are here to pay their respects, are they? But Trish is here. I wouldn't thank that one to drag herself away from her rags for a few minutes to be here. After all Dawson Street is but a step away. You put up the money, all the money, just because she refused to go to school. Didn't have the intelligence I know, but she could have tried. She was handed everything, everything."

The memory of Norma's moving in on David's onion-eye had her rant continue longer than she had intended.

David considered Norma's non-attendance as sufficient justification to enquire as to her whereabouts but exercising a modicum of savvy, which was about as much as he had when it came to thinking about Norma, he resisted.

In the many arguments between Trish and Norma, mother Ann was blessed with the wisdom of Solomon; she left them at it, while their well-meaning father invariably succeeded in fanning what would have started out as little more than a contentious ember to a full blown conflagration.

Emma, while pleased to have someone to talk to, thought it time to move among the mourners. She said, "Not that there is anyone here wanting to meet me but it is proper that I should mingle."

David looked at Trish who said, "Mingle with your Mum, David!"

When the funeral party split in two after the post-internment meal in the Shelbourne, Tim Pat, in the popularity stakes, won by far the bigger half. Grieving Heather, grieving Constance, and all their grieving supplicants plus the three Dempsey daughters and two grieving sons-in-law retired to Fitzwilliam Square. It did not escape Heather's withering eye that David and Trish went skipping away with Tim Pat's eclectic crew. Tim Pat was chuffed and reckoned the maid Trish was having a good influence on his beloved son David.

The reputation of Tim Pat and Emma for holding impromptu ding-dongs was legendary and these shindigs were welcomed by neighbours, all of whom, like himself, were settlers or sons or daughters of settlers. After those ding-dongs David and others of his generation hauled their bleary eyes into classrooms as a consequence of tormented music turfed-out by an assortment of instruments at the mercy of mostly uncultured hands, aided and abetted by knuckled saucepans, Emma's spoons, and a Tim Pat O'Leary original West Cork washboard. David's 'refinement' having been brought up in that loving but erratic environment was a source of disappointment to his parents and wonderment to his neighbours.

125

There was nothing impromptu about this particular ding-dong. Faster than a benevolent tsunami news of George Dempsey's death swept through their cul-de-sac. Tim Pat would do the right thing by Fitzwilliam George - of that neighbours were certain. No sooner had his car touched-down than willing hands helped haul the cargo of booze, minerals, cooked ham, mustard, Chef sauce, pan loaves, kitchen towels and yellowish toilet rolls into his house. It didn't cross the mind of any of his Christian neighbours to offer condolence or enquire about deceased George without whose cooperation the ding-dong would not be taking place. Neither had it crossed Tim Pat's mind that any of them would.

The musicians had rasped their way into the 'Rakes of Mallow' for the second time before Emma squeezed her way into the thronged hallway. She was immediately spotted by Tim Pat who had been certain she wouldn't go the distance in Fitzwilliam. Emma's nervous smile could not hide her distress at her early return. Tim Pat ushered Emma out onto the front lawn where they could chat in private.

"It's official, Emma's the cause of Father's death. Bad, bad day at Fitzwilliam, Tim Pat".

What surprised Tim Pat was Emma's surprise at being blamed. "Didn't you know you'd be blamed? No parent was ever loved as your Dad was loved by you. You can look yourself in the mirror and ..."

Emma finished his oft repeated phrase, " shave with a clear conscience."

"Dad was a softie, a real old softie. I loved him, always will." Tim Pat, believing Emma should have had natural allies in Fitzwilliam, enquired, "Stephanie and Florence, did they not side with you?"

"Incredibly, after all their years of being rejected they believed mother. Unbelievable!"

"Worry not. I give good odds a blazing row is in progress as we speak. The two will be given their walking papers. Mark my words, they'll be back, they'll be back to you, Emma".

Emma, shaking her head, said, "I wouldn't want them falling-out with mother on my behalf."

"Heather will manage that falling-out all on her own. Sorry to disappoint you."

Emma having unburdened her grief onto Tim Pat was now more relaxed. Again, she chose to confirm what Tim Pat and all the Shelbourne-returnees to their house were certain of, "No booze in Fitzwilliam and Heather's tea was on the wild side."

"That's Fitzwilliam for you - wild on the tea side. Seriously, Emma, if you think this ding-dong isn't a suitable celebration of your good father's long life, we can always hold another up ahead".

"O'Leary, 'up-ahead' is reserved for impromptus. This ding-dong is our first ever planned. I know you've been working on this since you received my phone call".

"Caused me a lot of hassle has George's ding-dong. Important we get everything right for him. He'd appreciate the effort I've put into this. That man would've loved me if he was let. I know he would."

Emma smacked her lips.

"Could do with a shot or two of brandy if all the wild tea is gone".

A concerned Tim Pat enquired "You've a touch of a headache, haven't you?"

"Just a touch Tim Pat, just a touch".

"Later, my love, later".

Emma smiled.

"But for the carburettor of a Morris Minor and mechanical-Finbar I could have had a wonderfully boring life."

Tim Pat holding Emma at arms length said, "Now for the good news, son David has leapt clean out of his shell…inside with Trish. Remember how you used gaze into Tim Pat's eyes..."

"No, I don't!"

" I knew you'd remember. Well, they're glued, glued. She's looking over her bottle, he's looking over his bottle, I'd be thinking those bottles are jigging their way into sweet music." Emma kissed Tim Pat saying, "Oh, for the Rakes of Mallow'.

Tim Pat corrected, 'The Rakes of West Cork, Emma, the Rakes of West Cork."

Emma threw her arms around his neck crying, "My raker and saviour, my raker and saviour, O'Leary Tim Pat!"

Tim Pat and Emma shuffled their way to a flushed David and gamey-eyed Trish. Doctor Emma and West Cork's Tim Pat knew for certain the energy between the two hadn't had its origins in the waking of Doctor George.

Knowing David would want Trish to be properly welcomed, Emma requested Trish to visit again soon. And Trish wanting David's parents to believe this was her maiden voyage was pleased to lie.

" Now that I know where you live, of course I will; that is if David would like me to visit". "Of course he does, Trish!" answered Emma on behalf of her blushing son.

Curious about his mother's quick return, David asked, "You didn't stay long in Fitzwilliam, Mam?"

Tim Pat had the gift of what he considered appropriate lies which invariably necessitated a thicker lie being overlaid by Emma. Tim Pat told the father-and-mother of all lies even by his own high standards.

"Son, your father is hurting, hurting badly. George and myself were very close, very close when he was let, which he wasn't. That's the reason Mother has came home. Your father is hurting, hurting badly."

So outrageous was the lie, David's jaw almost hopped off his knees on its way to the ground; the dig at grandmother Heather was one of his father's usuals.

"It's not good for one's health to keep emotions bottled up. Emotions are best released. Your father finds unburdening very, very difficult. That's why mother has come home to be with him, David."

This time round, David did bite the bottle he had put between his lips. Their lying, even by West Cork standards, was outrageous. David had boasted to Trish his home had everything except moderation. This was not the father David had painted so vividly for Trish. No such confusion reigned when Tim Pat corrected the coughing David in a tongue she had been told to expect.

"And all the times your uncle Tom warned 'clean bottles before sticking them in the gob', you didn't clean the jowl, did you? Rats and what have you jumping and pissing and shitting and farting all over them."

David had to go along with Tim Pat's lie, which again confused Trish, who had been led to believe, by David himself, that he had no experience of drinking. David kept the lying-ship at full speed ahead when he added, "This ding-dong is a grieving ding-dong, Trish. Our Christian neighbours can be relied on to come and help us grieve. Ancient Irish custom: drinking and grieving and drinking."

Trish, scanning the merry Christians passed the unguarded remark, " The definition of grieving is badly served by the Oxford dictionary."

"Trish, Oxford is an English dictionary; we wouldn't be expecting any favours from that crowd."

Tim Pat's remark put Trish thinking: stories David had told her about the Black and Tans and West Cork. West Cork, another planet away as far as she was concerned.

David, wanting to be as outrageous as his father, added, "Without the music there wouldn't be that many serious grievers here."

Trish, looking and listening to the merriment, said, "I've this Christian brother, Leslie, who doesn't know the meaning of grieving, but he certainly has what it takes to be one of your serious grievers."

For his parent's enlightenment, David said, "Leslie, Trish's brother, serious golfer!"

No more than Cavendish was interested in golf, neither was Tim Pat or Emma interested.

When Emma confided, "I play the spoons, Tim Pat the washboard!"

Trish, all excited, requested, "You must play, please!"

Tim Pat explained, "Wouldn't go down too well if we played given the day that's in it, Trish".

When Emma complained -"And I do have a headache" - Trish

smartly handed her bottle to David, and even more smartly went up the stairs, saying, "I know where there's Panadol."

How many times Trish had been up those steps Tim Pat and Emma did not know, but up those steps she sure had been. Tim Pat put his arm around David saying, "Great you're home, Son, Great!" David's response was everything Tim Pat and Emma could have wished for, "Home dad, home!" he repeated, clattering his bottle off his father's in celebration.

Trish returned with a glass of water and two tablets. "Take those and you'll be right as rain, Doctor."

Courteous Emma said "You'd make a wonderful Doctor, Trish, wonderful".

"It's law for me, my brother Leslie, accountancy, and when he's finished he's going into Cavendishes and David has also been offered a position in the company when he qualifies."

Too late she remembered David had told her his parent's wanted him to do medicine.

Tim Pat, not liking what he was hearing, said, "I thought we had settled on medicine?"

David, fearing his father's wrath, had not mentioned changing from medicine to accountancy. Mother Emma might be displeased at the switch but there it would end.

"Accountancy is by far the more lucrative profession and one can plan ahead, make arrangements, no working week-ends, like Mum."

Tim Pat lashed, "Heather's hand is in that decision, I know 'tis! If we wanted you to be an astronaut that rip would send you down a mine shaft."

Emma calmed the waters, "Your life, David. If you want to do accountancy by all means do accountancy. If you decide to switch faculties at any time, you will have your parent's backing."

"Thanks, Mam."

Trish, in recovery mode, highlighted positives, "We will practically own Cavendish's. Daddy high up, Leslie as good as in and David later."

As far as Tim Pat was concerned the arse had fallen out of George's ding-dong. In temper, he left the skin from his knuckles stuck to his washboard as into the early hours songs were brayed, tunes were chewed, their grace notes savaged.

CHAPTER 16

Tongues that had become accustomed to wagging since the touching down of Ms. Norma Newman onto the lap of their supremo went awag-wag-wagging when her father James, now second from the top, parachuted his pass degree son Leslie into the firm. Staff, not aware of David O'Leary's connections, caused no such tongue- wagging when he joined replete with his honours degree three years after Leslie. Promotions, always unpredictable, now took on a definite inevitability. To the chagrin of all, nepotism was alive and well and flourishing in Cavendish's. A silent frustrated workforce watched the manoeuvrings as Leslie was promoted and, hoping to deflect some attention from Leslie, David too was promoted by James.

Bartholomew Cavendish was eternally grateful for the life of debauchery which money had bought him. His promiscuous dick had him roam over acres of flesh. Without his wallet the bunnies that had scrambled by the wagon-load to burrow under his tonnage would have scampered screaming far away o'er the mountains given the absence of even one redeeming physical feature in the length and considerable breadth of his carcass. His mother had pity for him - she had told him so. Knowing his mother to be an honest woman, he did not kill her. His mother had bullied him as indeed Norma was now bullying him. He got a sexual charge from being dominated by Norma; it fed into his need for a buzz. Norma quickly rumbled to Bartholomew's sexual proclivities and satisfied his every whim withholding just the one. The withholding made it the one he craved for. Not that she had any problem pissing nor scruples about pissing down on him but it had to be withheld - a carrot or a drenching just beyond his reach. Her ace in the proverbial hole to be played when that ace was absolutely necessary. After all she was boss; her role demanded that his desire be smacked down; to feed his buzz he needed to be smack-smack-smacked.

Bartholomew was not about facing the few short years left to him on this earth without his nymphet Norma. He was smitten and nothing his nymphet demanded was denied. At her suggestion, a house in Rathgar was rented - nothing pretentious but luxuriously appointed.

Having had her father promoted to second in command, Leslie and David O'Leary on the staff, Norma considered what further reward she might screw out of Bartholomew before Gabriel's bugle horned the old buzzard to the bone-yard.

A devil for nursery rhymes Bartholomew's insistence on playing 'Humpty-Dumpty' had more than Norma's heart in her mouth when he would tumble from a bean bag knowing the same tumble played havoc with his vertigo. While his head, with effort, recovered its equilibrium from its Humpty tumble she purred as she fumbled with his layered dewlaps, "Norma exists only for her Bartholomew, her very own Bartholomew". Now sitting astride Dumpty, her hair brushing his bald pate, tits teasing across the puce lipped chasm furnished with gold filled teeth, never once had she considered what had gone in or out of that mouth no more than his dentist would have; only the stench of garlic was a problem. Bartholomew was in ecstasy at the appropriation inherent in Norma's expressed, 'exists only for her very own Bartholomew'.

Being ever so slightly comatosed, his dodgy heart having once again survived the mild excitements of another Humpty-Dumpty tumble, vanity had him entertain the ridiculous as he dreamily asked, "What is it Bartholomew can give his Norma as a gesture of his love and affection?"

His heart did not miss a beat when Norma requested a wedding ring. Norma was a businesswoman her humping was business. She had her family fixed-up to her satisfaction; she now wanted to know what was in their continuing relationship for herself. Norma would marry him to get her claws on the company. He knew this is what she wanted and had foreseen its coming. He had nephews and nieces in his London office but they didn't have the slightest interest in moving to Dublin.

"A most sincere thank you for asking, my love, you flatter me. Marriage at my age would be absurd, ridiculous, not necessary. Perhaps we can make my Dublin office a joint venture. It would please me greatly to share it with you. Tomorrow I will instruct my solicitor. Forty-nine percent to my beautiful Norma".

For Norma the resolution was two points short of perfect. As she teased his expectant mouth with her nipple before placing it within, she whispered, "Fifty one my dearest Bartholomew, then no one can bully or compromise your Norma ...ever!"

As he slurped his eyes smiled knowing Norma was well aware of the concept of 'no such thing as a free lunch'. He took time-out from his slurping to ask, "Will Bartholomew get his shower, if he's a good Bartholomew and makes yours fifty one, Mama?"

"Bartholomew will get his shower, but not today Bartholomew, not today."

Before reverting to his slurping, he asked their percentage arrangement be kept secret until after his release from this world and her thighs of pleasure. Norma chastised him for his doleful outlook and earnestly prayed his signature would be on his solicitor's parchment before that release.

The reputation of his company was no trifling matter for Bartholomew. The least he expected from Leslie Newman was that he would turn-up for work and be on time when he did. Norma would deal with his anxiety. "A staff member you promoted is not working even to his own ability; Norma, I would thank you to see that he does!"

Norma was taken aback at Bartholomew's mentioning of brother Leslie. Knowing Leslie to be a wreck beyond patchwork she attempted deflection, "Is it Leslie you've been thinking about and Norma all excited about our being together like this."

Bartholomew was not about to be deflected. Keeping the tip of his index finger on the button of Norma's nose, he gently persisted, "My dear, your a success because Norma is a hard nosed businesswoman."

Cute Norma wasn't about teasing out the ramifications of that particular statement. Knowing bad news put on weight travelling, and Leslie's load was mountainous to begin with, she supported his 'hard nosed businesswoman' definition by telling him, "Remedial rather than disciplinary action is already in train, Bartholomew."

"Bartholomew can rely on Norma to do whatever is necessary?"

"Be assured your Norma will do whatever is necessary, Bartholomew."

Though David's promotions sickened his colleagues, his ability merited their reluctant admiration. The list of business calls handed to David at reception each morning and his tray stacked with files vouched for his standing among Cavendish clients. Company business more and more moved effortlessly round his energy.

David's presence magnified Leslie's limitations much to the embarrassment of father James. Leslie, knowing intellectual improvement was beyond him and his employment to be in the gift of his father, conducted himself at work in the full nature of a company squireeen.

The one commodity in complete absence among the Cavendish workforce was loyalty. A-sprinting that gallant band did go to Bartholomew's eardrums and of late a trickle to James Newman's with every snippet of scandal or gossip that the informer hoped would wound, mortally or otherwise, a true friend and colleague. Censored from James Newman's trickle was his own son's lack of performance.

Cavendish did not have to ask those informers how Leslie Newman was performing, at every opportunity, he was assured by them Leslie's graph showed no signs of bottoming-out. The fact that these same callers did not mention David O'Leary, he interpreted as proof positive of O'Leary's ability.

When Norma met father James at a prearranged family meeting to discuss what was to be done with Leslie, she asked, "Where is he, where is grandmother? I wanted them both here?"

"Leslie's at the club; he'll be back shortly. Constance is about. Your mother will stay in the kitchen, or attend to her flowers, or whatever, she will not involve herself in our meeting. No harm to have Trish out of the way. Workaholic O'Leary couldn't take time off to go with her to Greece. Busy- busy-busy."

"Father, ultimatum time has arrived for Leslie. Our plan for him to take your place when you retire is in tatters if he does not change, and change drastically. O'Leary's name is never mentioned to Cavendish, which in itself is a tribute to O'Leary's ability. Our problem is getting Leslie to change his lifestyle?"

James saw this as the lesser of two problems, "How is one made intelligent?"

A car door was heard slamming.

"That's him!"

"Call him in!" ordered Norma.

James was not fashioned for confrontation; he would prefer if Norma handled the situation on her own. There were times he envied Ann who earnestly believed the world would be a better place if matters were left in the hands of God.

"He will have a few on board. Perhaps we should wait for another time?"

"In here, now!" snapped Norma.

Leslie's bounding up the stairs came to a sudden stop when James ordered in the frostiest voice he could muster,

"Leslie, a minute!"

Norma's car had been parked in the forecourt. The tenor of his father's voice told Leslie it was Norma who was demanding his presence in the drawing room. On the stairs his steps were measured knowing trouble awaited. Constance had heard Leslie being peremptorily summoned and went to the drawing room. Constance stepped into the room behind Leslie.

The dogs in the street knew of Leslie's alcohol abuse, but

grandmother was also aware of his substance abuse. In a drunken stupor he had boasted to her his lines of coke did not affect his performance at work. Her retort had been lost on him, 'How could it, you don't have a performance!'

Bright and early that following morning, Constance was waiting to tackle Leslie on the drugs issue. She could have stayed in bed, he could not surface till mid-day. He denied having told her he used cocaine, swore he had never used drugs of any kind, and could not recall being told he had no credible performance at work for drugs or booze or anything else to affect.

Nervous Leslie glanced from ice-cold Norma to stern-faced father and grandmother. The drinks he had at the club had given him the sort of courage one gets from drink. Leslie touched his jaw, his nose, his ear, before tapping his eyebrow, "Does Leslie spy with his insightful eye a structure beginning with G... Gallows? Definitely isn't a promotion. Leslie's nose would have sniffed promo... on his nostril radar."

"Sniff again brother Leslie." Snapped Norma, "Radar on high has you charted as a drunken waster and take that stupid, innocent, injured look off your face. You are a disgrace to this family, a disgrace, you have let father down, family down. Fool! Your father grooming... grooming cannot be the right word, brazenly promoting you. Mr. Cavendish is concerned about the image of his company and who could blame him? He demands corrective action be taken, and if that doesn't work, you are to go, sacked!"

Leslie, feet apart, left hand extended, splayed fingers on parade, ready to enumerate with his right index the many reasons that had fashioned the Leslie he now was, had the ground whipped from under him by father James. Normally a mild-mannered man, James needed more than wished to speak given the dam-burst of emotions that were sledging to exit from his chest. "In late, out early, golf club's swinging, practice putting on your office carpet, spurious business lunches that booze and booze until breakfast time and beyond. An expense account that exceeds all others, including my own by a multiple of five, you don't even have the common sense to keep a low profile ..."

When irate James paused to catch breath, Leslie, with index still poised over his now wiggling splayed-on-parade fingers, attempts an entry, "Am I entitled ...?

He was flattened by James's juggernaut of emotions as James rattled on, "Unshaven, no tie, blasted runners, hours on the phone, ignorant guffaws ringing round the building, even the cleaners treat the boss's son as a joke, and you're incapable of seeing it. The humiliation!"

When again Leslie attempted an entry, "Am I entitled to defend myself?"

Norma cut him dead, "You don't have a defence, coward!"

When Leslie blurted-out, "Coward, coward, now I'm a coward?"

Norma shouted, "What else are you but a coward? In spite of your pathetic CV father had the guts to promote you and you thank him with this loutish behaviour!"

Leslie's splayed on parade fingers and right index dropped to his side in surrender. Grandmother Constance, believing enough had been said, advised in a more conciliatory tone,

"Take it on the chin, Leslie. You must realise all Cavendish employees are watching, wondering what promotional opportunities, if any, Cavendish's hold for them."

"And I'll be sacked with you" Said James in resignation.

Leslie retaliated, "I find that very interesting. My conduct at work; tell me when did you last send me an account of any consequence to work on?"

Father James was silent at the accusation. "You can't remember because there is no remembering!"

James resisted highlighting Leslie's incompetence any further. Instead he reproached his own inaction, "This conversation should have taken place ages ago. Now that it has we can all go forward, together, as a family. That's what is important, family."

Grandmother queried, "Do you agree or disagree with these accusations, Leslie?"

"It's not as simple as it is portrayed!" retorted Leslie.

"So there is a reason or explanation for your behaviour?" asked Grandmother.

"God damn right there is! How would any of you like facing into a workplace where you know you are perceived as a second-class citizen – with their honours degrees – bunch of intellectual snobs, and not one of them playing golf off single figures, scrubbers the lot of them! And don't forget a lot of business is generated on the golf course. It's called networking."

James, considering he had said enough about Lesie's expense account remained silent. Norma had no such qualms', "I know what you lot generate in and around golf clubs. Show me an expense account and I'll tell you what you are?"

Norma's comment was greeted with silence. Grandmother and James worried lest Leslie, in anger, would give expression to the bartering benefits of Norma's friendship with Cavendish. It did enter Leslie's head but there it died knowing to do so would have him banished from home and family.

Grandmother's advice occupied that awkward silence, " New chapter, family Newman moves on!"

There was a smugness about Norma as she observed, "Always remember most accountant's business is generated by successful business people like myself – without any university degrees! Brother, if you believe there is an ability gap, I assure you it's nothing hard work cannot overcome."

Grandmother in false indignation, said "Leslie is much more intelligent than any of that Cavendish lot. Leslie has not applied himself, that is all."

Without visiting his own limitations Leslie said, "Let's not kid ourselves, Dave O'Leary is in a class of his own. And that includes everyone in there."

Grandmother gave Leslie something to cling to, "But they have chosen O'Leary to compare you with!"

Doleful Leslie nodded agreement. "Unfortunately that is the case, Grandmother."

"David O'Leary has to be let go, sacked, from Cavendish's!"

Like a scalpel the content of grandmother's words sliced through the discourse.

As could be expected the first to react was a delighted Leslie, "Brilliant!"

James expressed incredulity, "Jesus Christ, am I being asked to sack my brightest and best?"

Resignation loaded Leslie's voice as he whinged, "There you have it – his brightest and best. That's what I'm up against every hour every day, his brightest and best."

"Mother, you are serious?" asked James.

"Think about it, James, Newmans before all else!"

Norma would have liked to be the one who had thought of the firing solution. Trish and her relationship with O'Leary had not been mentioned; which would not be unusual in their household where only-son, Leslie, was God.

Merits of O'Leary's sacking would be in vain without action on Leslie's part.

"It is drastic and will have to be backed by your absolute commitment, Leslie."

Said grandmother while James was panicking at the boldness of the suggestion.

"Hold, hold everything. This, this is monstrous!" said James.

"Do you have a better solution, James?" asked Grandmother in the certainty that he had not. James, feeling the pressure, opened the top button in his shirt,

"Sacking O'Leary is not a solution. Sacking O' Leary is bad business!"

Businesswoman Norma, said in a knowing voice, "O'Leary doesn't have to be fired, ask him to leave."

"Thank you, Norma. That makes it easier. Explain yourself?"

Norma did explain to James, "I expect it is well known O'Leary is setting up on his own? Anyone as bright as he is would be stupid not to." Leslie supported Norma's logic with common-sense facts.

"He has made all the right contacts, he has been in the right position to do so."

"No one from Cavendish's has ever left to set up their own company."

The manner in which James made the observation indicated Grandmother's suggested remedy had at least grabbed his attention. Leslie confirmed his resolve.

"I will do my part!"

When an uncertain James enquired, "Will Cavendish buy into his sacking or leaving or whatever you call it?"

The three swivelling heads in her direction confirmed for Norma her liaison with Cavendish had her family's full support.

"If what precipitated this drastic action is packaged properly, then I cannot foresee a problem."

Grandmother expressed her admiration. "Spoken like a true Newman, darling Norma."

Chapter 17

On arriving back at Fitzwilliam after work, David's ritual of calling 'Grandmother' while standing his briefcase and hanging his mackintosh by the loop on the hallstand, did not happen on this late Friday evening causing a concerned grandmother to enquire when she heard the door opening, "Is that you David?" She wasn't at all sure what David meant when he replied, "Cometh the sack, cometh David!"

While giving grandmother her customary peck on the cheek she was taken aback by the aberrant smell of alcohol. David had never socialised after work, had always returned home first, changed, and then gone out. Putting aside National Geographic she viewed his carelessness as across the back of a chair he tossed his mackintosh.

"Would grandmother greatly mind if an unemployed – I beg your pardon – sacked accountant accompanies you on your daily botanical stroll?"

David's sense of humour, she knew, did not stretch to cracking jokes about being sacked. In a most serious vein, she enquired, "Sacked, sacked – you are joking, David? Tell grandmother you are joking."

"Grandmother, I lie not – given the old boot. Be-gone, O'Leary, be-gone!"

A lot of venom had leaked from Heather Dempsey since George's death. The ferocity of Emma's declaration that she, Emma, had been 'hated' because of her gender Heather would not agree with. Heather accepted she had felt no warmth towards her, had purposely deprived Emma of her mother's love but believed that Emma's response to what was considered a cruel act of fate justified under the circumstances. Since the funeral she had not allowed a night to pass without giving

Emma a ring, more often than not for no other reason than extending the olive branch. Even Tim Pat made it easy for her, she would hear him call, "For you, Emma, your mother!"

All their lives, George and herself had walked the same shallow crescent through Stephen's Green to mass in University Church. They never strayed to the enchanted core where a granite fountain effortlessly cascaded its pearls amid the splendid ostentation of preening flowers alive in their manicured beds vying for the eye's attention. Never dwelled, dawdled or admired shrubs, flowers, trees, or noticed the serenely paddling ducks, drakes, water-hens on the man-made lake no more than they did the busy pigeons pecking what had been tossed by visitors of all ages and in particular children, or see the poets, patriots, scholars, perched on their eye-high plinths.

Now that Heather was on her own, she wandered round flower beds and lakes, and was at a loss in understanding why herself and George had avoided the wonder and splendour that flourished a mere step-inside their rigid mass-path crescent. She accepted that decision had been hers, as all, even the most innocuous, had been hers – never George's.

Heather's shunning of discourse with the working classes while not exactly ending on her first encounter with an attendant in Stephen's Green, but end it did shortly after having first verified information casually imparted by the attendant on the species of flowers she had been admiring.

When next they met she ventured a tentative, 'Hallo?'

At their first meeting Heather had been so filled with the exquisiteness not just of those particular flowers but the park's totality, that she had not noticed the attendant's approach. Neither was she sure which flower he was referring to when he said without pointing, "Nemophila, my favourite, and won't you look at little Nesembryanthemum behind. The darlings, the darlings. Ahhh! Such beauty, such beauty!"

She would prove this cap-back-on-pole blue-coated attendant of low-station a chancer. No commoner was going to pull the wool over Doctor Heather's eyes. Old habits die hard and prejudices even slower. Midst all the beauty, it was the blue uniform she heard talking not the wearer. Her swivelling head assured that no one she knew saw this operative speak to her. She would have had to explain the discourse was not of her choosing, it was imposed. She did not make comment on the uniform's soliloquy, but purposely moved to another flowerbed and from there onto another. She could not reconcile the man's station in life with his knowledge. His high colouring she attributed to a blood pressure problem common among his class, because of their dietary habits and propensity to over indulgence in alcohol.

As a shadow would, he again appeared at her shoulder saying as he looked past her at the flowers.

"It's you that has the eye for beauty, ma'am. Limnantes. So, so delicate. Them are all my little children, my children. Limnantes…limnantes."

Then the slouched shadow went from her with hands clasped behind its blue back. Heather committed to memory the names he had given the flowers. If her memory failed, then pictures would unlock the flowers' identity.

Carnations, chrysanthemums, tulips, roses and many other varieties bought in the florists and placed in expensive vases at the expected places in homes of the quality was statement of the dwellers, love of flowers. Queries as to their source had very rarely elicited the pride-filled answer, 'Grew them myself, thank you." Neither had Tim Pat's green fingers been credited when visitors enquired about the fresh-from-the-garden bunches brought by Emma to Fitzwilliam Square.

Grandmother rang Emma the evening of that first encounter and asked her to bring some of her husband's illustrated gardening books. Emma did not query her mother's sudden interest, but drove straight to Fitzwilliam with a stack of Tim Pat's best.

Heather searched for her flowers, first in pictures and then by name; those books disappointingly confirmed the attendant to be correct. With book in handbag she returned to Stephen's Green next day. Opening the relevant pages beside the different beds, she examined and read their profile; no doubting, he had been correct. She sensed being watched. Sure enough the knowledgeable attendant waved and smiling came towards her. Embarrassed at being caught, she said her first 'Hallo'. Knowing full-well there was no disrespect implied or intended in his not acknowledging her, 'Hallo', Heather's social posturing scaled from her and she was open to being educated by a definite blue-collar worker. He just rambled-on-and-on about his flowers, saying, "Blue Blue Eyes, easy to grow. It's heartening for us to see people coming with their books checking, learning about our many different varieties."

But thanks to Tim Pat's pictures, Heather knew the common name for Nemophila was Baby Blue Eyes. She boasted, "I admit to being a complete novice but Nemophilia I do know."

"There you are now, missus, sure don't we all arrive late at appreciating something or someone and them there under our noses all the time. All the time there and not seeing – not seeing!" he mused.

The import of his words stung. She heard him saying he had regrets – also. His uniform was changing into a person. A full life existed within those blues.

"You know something, missus, the wife never once came to see where I worked – never once. All those years and never came. Not even the once to see my gardens. That hurts now. An awful, awful lot it hurts. Gone now – God rest her, gone. Never ever saw my flowers. Can you imagine that? I told her she'd love them, didn't make no difference. Should have made her come. She would have thought the world of me if she knew my flowers. No! Wouldn't come. Made sandwiches though, good ones, the best. Might as well be working down a mine as far as my good woman was concerned. But, ahh, she was great… great. God rest the good woman's soul."

"Regrets, regrets! Sorry your lady wife has passed on."

To which he casually replied, "Thank you."

While tipping his flowers, he said, "Little slips of regret to be sure. Haven't we all got them in plenty. Slips, little slips of regret. No guilt though; if you know what I mean missus, no guilt."

Heather attempted an entry inside the apparent tranquil mind of this stooped man in blue who never ceased tipping flowers, pinching earth with caring fingers against fragile stems, who seemed to be talking to the flowers as much as he was speaking his life's story to the person standing beside him. Beyond his humility and humanity, she could not see; and though knowing the Good Book declared 'envy' a sin 'envy' she could not resist committing.

"Truly it must be marvellous to watch something grow from seed to full bloom".

Heather paused before adding, 'Though their dying you must also witness."

"Isn't it nature is all, missus, nature. We comes we goes. Just like children: we love them, rear them, sends them to school to give them wings and then they fly fly. But with the will of God and a little luck, we will be well gone ahead of them, well gone. Ahh, life is great, great! A few pints the weekend, a bob each way on the ould nags, and back to me darlin' flowers on the Monday. Could anyone or anything in this world whack a garden ? No, can't be whacked. Can't whack a garden. Flowers on Monday. The sandwiches aren't great no more though. Makes them myself now, I do. But what the heck! Don't smoke though, never did!"

Heather was forced to consider her bullying of George and her treatment of her daughters: guilty was her silent plea on both counts. She had avoided being available for her children when love was needed, had abrogated her responsibilities to nannies and a boarding school. Her daughters Stephanie and Florence, had rarely brought their children to visit their grandparents, and when they did bring them, she knew it was to please grandfather George, not her.

This prompted Heather to ask the gardner, " Do you have grandchildren?"

"Don't they come all the ways in here to see their granddad's farm? ha-ha-aah…. His ducks, and his drakes, and his flowers, and his fountain of pearls. Granddad's huge farm at the top of Grafton Street.

Aren't children the life us? I hope you've plenty around you, missus. Children keeps the life in the bones of the world!"

"I'm afraid I don't see much of mine – never have, my own fault really".

"Can't be easy with them overseas. Thank God mine are all within a whistle of me. Honest to God, don't they swarms all over me wanting to hear stories from my farm? and of course, the couple of coppers. Ah yes, the couple of coppers: they know they're guaranteed from granddad."

"My daughters aren't overseas in this city actually. I didn't make time for them when they were young. Grew apart. My fault. I should be ashamed to admit it. In my defence, I would say I have many many loyal friends whom I have helped down the years and still do."

She wasn't interested in reasoning why she was admitting guilt to this uniformed park attendant she was meeting for the second time, but she felt better for having done so, in a way cleansed. Here in the soul of this park where flora are cultivated and fauna near domesticated; in their presence, one's worldly importance is reduced to insignificance and confession to little more than an honest chat. Heather pondered the value of her friends knowing she had never confided in any of them, not even fully to Constance Newman; or were they too, like George, dominated by her and of no value when it was she herself needed help.

The gardener continued, "Spread anything too thin and nothing prospers, not even friendships. Bet now your friends were thankful for your strength, but you had no one to draw from. The strong are their own worst enemies. The tree that doesn't bend. We know what happens that tree, don't we? And aren't you here smelling the roses. Never easy to make amends, admitting to being wrong is not easy, but what the heck, what the heck. Walk a little with me and I'll show you my Hibiscus, Hollyhock tree. Call me George."

Not once did he look at Heather's face while he spoke. Always stooping down, squinting, tipping, peaked cap tilted back. If he had looked at Heather, he would have seen her startled at his mentioning of the name George.

Four consecutive days, Heather visited the park. George made no secret of his enjoying her company. He would hasten to her, informing, answering, suggesting what she should begin with in planning her garden, considering the aspect to her side of Fitzwilliam Square. They allowed niches in conversation's flow to slot in personal experiences. George accepted her invitation to visit and she insisted on him staying for lunch. Saturday was fixed: he would be on a half day.

Before parting George asked, "By the way Missus, I don't know your name."

"Mrs Dempsey… Heather. George…Heather."

"By jingo! First Heather I ever met. Right-e-oh, I'll be there Heather. Looking forward I am to lunch. Heather …Calluna, one species; many, many varieties."

The door bell did not ring on the Saturday. Heather fumed and reproached herself for not knowing better. The likes of a park attendant keeping an appointment, how naive could she be? A week passed before she marched angrilyto the park. She searched, George was nowhere to be found. A young attendant mooched around the fountain at the centre of the park. She had not seen him before. The other attendants had seen herself and George together but they did not approach. George would have told them about her and about his not turning up for their date. Blast them in their blues; they would definitely be sniggering at her; blast them. She would enquire from this new attendant and avoid being made a laughing stock.

"Is George on holidays?"

Cheekily her question was answered, "Yeah, you could say that."

All her old arrogance was back as haughtily she demanded, "Young man, what is it you are trying to tell me?"

"Dropped dead, didn't he. Wearing his Sunday best last Saturday. Just about where you are standing I'm told. In his best clobber he was, with a bunch of flowers gripped in his hand. Creepy when you think of it. Must have had a notion he was on his way to the other side the way he was decked out. It's an ill wind. Got his job I did. Ha-ha. Got George's old blue bonnet ha ha ha."

"My God! Oh my God!" gasped Heather, placing her hand on the granite fountain for support.

"Are you all right?" anxiously asked the attendant of the ashen-faced Heather.

"I will rest a little, I'll be fine, thank you."

Heather stayed sitting alone with her thoughts for a long long time before slowly making her way to University Church. There she knelt as shadows lengthened not capable of gathering her senses. Unable to talk to her God, she stiffly got to her feet and made her tired way home.

The running of the house had eased onto David. For the first time in her life, Heather allowed herself to experience the concept of pampering and liked it. David had become her star. She got confused digesting David's news of his being sacked.

"The end of the world is not at hand I assure you, Gran. David O'Leary has been considered surplus to requirements in Cavendish's. So described by my erstwhile friend James of the Newman dynasty."

"Surplus to requirements. My God! Shocked, I'm shocked!"

"Roll over O'Leary, Leslie is a coming … Leslie is a coming! Get off his tracks. O'Leary make way! You are not to be fretting yourself. Trials and tribulations and all that. Rent money, what will I use for rent money, that is the question."

"Now is not the time for joking David. Is Leslie behind this?"

"Definitely not! He doesn't have or never will have the intelligence?"

"Cunning?"

"Nope!"

"You believe there is an ulterior motive, don't you?"

"Common sense – not modesty – forbids me from ever seeing myself near poll position in the Cavendish-stroke-Newman empire."

"Go on?"

"Leslie is – no, not nasty baggage – incompetent baggage. He actually makes me brighter than I am; the corollary of which is I make him look duller than he is. Therefore to brighten the dark they remove the light. A contradiction? Yes! But it does work."

"For the life of me, I cannot see Constance agreeing with your sacking. Our life long friendship jettisoned because of misplaced ambition. Still, the sacking wouldn't have taken place without her knowledge if not her sanction. She hasn't been on the phone - she knows about your sacking. To my shame I've actually been in awe of Norma's sacrifice on behalf of her family I really have. Not once has Constance mentioned Norma's relationship with Cavendish, not once. And she has never withheld any secrets from me. I'm late in saying this but hers is a guilt drenched in shame. Not that Norma and Cavendish's relationship is any of my business, but I assure you now it is."

"Everything has been well considered by them. Trish conveniently in Greece for a month. It stinks. The whole God damn thing stinks."

"It would be foolhardy to rush to judgment on Trish. Trish takes after her mother, Ann. Trish is not a Newman."

"Bet my replacement in Cavendish's will be of a lesser candle-wick than Leslie. 'Candle-wick' one of Dad's analogies."

"Would you consider taking legal action over your dismissal?"

"Definitely not!"

"For unfair dismissal you could be awarded thousands."

"My life is about job fulfilment not thousands, or for that matter high-station."

"Another Tim Pat analogy?"

"Correct!"

It was David's first time hearing grandmother mention his father's name in a tone approximating to friendly. A change had taken place in his grandmother, a change that had her engrossed in gardening matters.

"Constance will be expecting a reaction from me, I will not disappoint her. How dare she! When is Trish due to return?"

"This day week. She was gone a fortnight before I was shunted, and returns a fortnight after the foul deed was done."

"You haven't had time to inform your parents, have you?"

Previously 'mother' had been substituted for 'parents'- a significant development thought David.

150

"I will give them a ring."

"You will not, you will visit. You will be the better for visiting."

"May I ask how you intend spending your evening?"

"Trot along, David, trot along, away with you."

Tim Pat on hearing the news belched, "Them shower of fuckin' hoors! Not a minute's luck will they have!"

An ash-faced Emma was speechless.

"Whips shit altogether! What in the name of Jesus is the world coming to?" Tim Pat's discharge towards the Newmans had begun and would never abate.

"And to think my wife goes out friggen riding with one of them and my son walking –her-out! Fuck me pink!"

"It isn't the end of the world, Dad." was the hollow response from David.

"One is used to arse-holes promoted in the civil service, the guards, the army, but not in a private company. Companies can't afford that carry on. Or so we are told."

Tim Pat marched up and down the kitchen, his shoe lashing out in all directions at his Newman quarry while Emma's immersing in decades of Tim Pat lingo said in desperation, "Well, honest to God. Honestly! The whole thing is… is ridiculous. What do we do? I know what I'm going to do, I'm going for a pint before I blow a half-dozen gaskets."

David, in agreement, asked, "Dad you heard patient Emma, sick bay for gaskets urgently required, where to?"

Tim Pat, making it unanimous, ruled, "Not to that fuckin' golf club, that's for sure. By Jesus, murder is festering in the marrow of O'Leary's bones."

"Tim Pat, easy on the language!" said Emma, knowing she was wasting her breath.

"My arse, I will!"

Emma set out their itinerary giving the words a colouring of most gracious living. "Martin B's! And the O'Leary clan will feast on fish and chips on the way home to our castle."

CHAPTER 18

Heather Dempsey requested the taxi driver to wait before going to Newmans' front door. Constance Newman had been expecting Heather Dempsey from the day of David's dismissal. Heather would grasp the nettle immediately as was her wont and Constance had no intention of handing the advantage to Heather by affording her the opportunity of refusing an invitation to the house. The altercation that was certain to take place would take place on her doorstep where un-welcomed visitors could, with ease, be dispatched. The fact that the visitor in question was a life-long friend made this strategy even more attractive.

On opening the door and without a semblance of salutation, Constance shot, "Sorry it had to be David."

"It was your idea, then?" levied Heather.

"No particular one's idea. It was our only option."

"Newman's only option for what?"

"Is it not logical a boss would protect his company?"

"From David?"

"He was contemplating starting out on his own, you must have known he was."

"Is this the lie you sold to Cavendish?"

"The truth can be unpalatable."

"Never as disgusting as lies!"

"You dare call me a liar!"

"Your reprehensible action will one day be seen for what it is, Constance Newman. I wish to speak to the boss. Be that Norma or James or boss designate Leslie, or all four of you Newmans, together!"

"You dare insult my family, get away from my door, get away." fumed Constance, before slamming the door in Heather's face.

Heather, livid with rage, kept her finger on the bell. No response. She banged and banged loud and hard on the knocker. No response. Returning to Fitzwilliam Square, she acknowledged she could have expected no other outcome.

A courting couple were cooing in Martin B's snug when Tim Pat, Emma and David entered. Neither party took any notice of the other. Tim Pat and David were into their second pint, Emma half through her first, before the matter that had them there was mentioned.

"I needed that. Bastards!" uttered Tim Pat as he appraised what was left of his second pint.

"They knew recourse to courts would not be an option I would consider."

Emma, wanting to be optimistic.

"Every cloud has a silver lining!"

Tim Pat, looking askance at Emma, said "Is that the best you can do? Every cloud has a silver lining? This isn't a cloud or even a cloud formation, this is a whole God damn tornado, woman!"

"Not much point crying into our drinks now is there?" retorted Emma, more than capable of holding her own in the cut and thrust of debate with O'Leary.

"You're right, you're right. Sure enough there isn't," apologised Tim Pat.

In anticipation of discord breaking out as much as wanting to be on their own, the lovers thought it safer to vacate the snug.

"For what its worth, my integrity is intact. I'm enjoying these pints, and we know what the begrudgers can do."

"Here, here, David. That's the Dempsey spirit," proudly declared Emma, knowing Tim Pat would have something to say about that.

"My arse 'tis Dempsey spirit. How's the 'quare-one' taking the news?"

Recent happenings, including the borrowing of his books, which she had not returned, indicated a metamorphosis taking place in Tim Pat's favourite human being. David, looking at his watch, mused,

"Right about now I expect 'quare-one' is washing down the main course of grilled Newman with a bottle of Nuits St. George."

"She actually rang and reprimanded Constance?" asked Emma, willing David to confirm that mother Heather placed the injustice perpetrated on David before her friendship with Constance Newman.

"The mood grandmother was in when she ordered me home, quite honestly I cannot see her protest beginning or ending with a simple phone call."

Emma, overjoyed at her mother's as yet unconfirmed action asserted, "This is marvellous, marvellous news, isn't it Tim Pat?"

Tim Pat hesitated before replying, "I'll grant it's a significant development if it turns out to be fact. Some change, some change."

Praying her son's answer would be in the affirmative, Emma asked, "Was it mummy told you to visit?"

"Practically hunted me from Fitzwilliam."

"Your silver lining Emma, apologies!" said Tim Pat.

"I'm dying to find out about mother and the Newmans."

"Ring and find out. Curiosity will have you twisting and turning for the night if you don't. And keep me awake, which is worse."

No sooner had Emma gone to the phone than she was back, saying, "There would be coins stuck in the slot, wouldn't there! "

"Kiosks across the road. Go with your mother, David."

"David, stay where you are; mother is capable of managing on her own."

Ten minutes elapsed before Emma, robustly, entered the snug singing the revelation, "Newman connection severed, yupee!"

"Well, Holy Lord! Not even life-long friendships are sacred when it comes to nepotism!" declared a happy Tim Pat.

"And Heather wants me to move into their consulting rooms in Fitzwilliam."

David said, "Why not, they're idle."

Tim Pat half-turning his head giving the impression he was looking at the sky through the window. "Two full moons up there, better than any silver lining."

" Fitzwilliam is about consultants, is it not" said David.

"So what? It's GP's bring buildings to life."

"Pity GP's can't do the same for human beings," said Tim Pat.

"Those beings are best left to God." Said Emma.

"Between GP's and God, no one is safe!"

Smiling, Emma said, "David, it takes a Tim Pat O'Leary to change the natural order."

"And not before time an O'Leary did!" bragged Tim Pat. David asked, "You've accepted?"

"Of course I've accepted! Why not? Fitzwilliam is my home after all."

"Possession is nine points of the law. The ould bitch can't live for ever!"

"You bastard, your greedy eyes are on Fitzwilliam!" said a shocked Emma.

"Course they are! When it comes to inheritance, nepotism has to be ensured."

CHAPTER 19

David rang Cavendish's mid-week leaving a curt message for James or Leslie to meet Trish at the airport on her return from Greece that Saturday. Though certain arrangements would have been made by the Newmans, he considered his phone call a statement of decency.

David and grandmother Heather were listening to the radio while having breakfast on Sunday when the newsreader announced, 'one male dead, one woman seriously injured, and a second male slightly injured in a traffic accident in Howth in the early hours of the morning. No names have yet been released.'

"Youth, speed, drink: once again reaping its grim harvest," David added in support of his grandmother's prediction, "Once you hear the a.m. the probability of drink being involved increases one hundred fold."

"You would be an authority on a.m. drinking, David. You returned from one of your Newman visits with our car stinking of vomit."

"But I wasn't driving, Leslie was. I was a nervous wreck expecting you to enquire about that smell, why didn't you?"

"The whole Newman household was involved in the post-mortem into the destroying of madam Norma's outfit. Constance kept me appraised of the conflict that raged between the girls. The humiliation you must have suffered I considered sufficient punishment; was grandmother right?"

"That you would bar me from driving was my greatest fear."

"Leslie Newman does have a serious drink problem."

"His new responsibilities in Cavendishes' might straighten him out," remarked David, sarcastically.

"Not at all. Worse he will get. His lack of confidence will ensure that he does."

"Never saw mammy happier than when you told her about your altercation with Constance Newman. Gran's sacrifice was much appreciated, Dad and Mam were delighted."

At every opportunity, David attempted bridge-building between his parents and his grandmother, in particular with his father. Grandmother cogitated on the gelling effect a common foe had on former enemies. She registered the implication in David's statement.

"David, grandmother is also family. Your father has mellowed and myself perhaps a little." To which David replied, "I would have to agree."

The ambiguity of his reply had grandmother observe, "Tim Pat-speak I am hearing from you, David!"

David, answering, repeated her own words, "O'Leary's are family too you know."

No sooner had David left to visit his parents after breakfast than Heather received a plethora of phone calls giving details of the Howth traffic accident.

With a sense of excitement rather than grief she rang David with the news. When Tim Pat answered the phone, she asked, "A word with David if I may, Tim Pat."

Tim Pat's heart stopped before stumbling at pace on hearing Heather lilt 'Tim Pat'.

Nothing less than the miracle of a live George being pulled from the ground, against his will, must have taken place, Tim Pat reckoned. He told her, "David and Emma are gone to the newsagents. They'll be back shortly. Everything ok Mrs Dempsey?"

"There's been an accident, James Newman has been killed. Trish is in intensive care in the Mater and I am reliably informed inebriated Leslie lying on the back seat escaped uninjured."

"All due respects to the damaged car, Mrs. Dempsey, but my faith in natural justice has been restored. Sorry to hear about Trish. As regards Leslie being rescued by booze; pity, I say to that. Pity! "

The wry smile that spread across Heather's face was lost to Tim Pat on the phone as regrettably his words had assured her Tim Pat O'Leary hadn't changed one iota.

"Please ask David to ring me when he gets in, Tim Pat. And thank you for all those books."

Tim Pat knew Heather Dempsey never asked but to command.

"Plenty more where they came from. I'll tell David to ring you straight away, Mrs Dempsey."

Tim Pat heard the phone clicking off at her end.

Staring at the receiver in his hand he said, "Fuck me pink, O'Leary!"

Tim Pat's thoughts were not with the dead or injured, but with the phone call from a most polite mother-in-law when Emma and David returned with Sunday's bundle of newspapers.

Emma and David, when told about the accident, invoked the mercy of God in his judgment of James and prayed he would be given a bed in heaven. To which Tim Pat replied, "Norma will pull a few of what she is good at pulling to ensure dead James climbs into some corner of a scratcher in God's bunk-house."

The implication in his father's sketching of Norma's character displeased David, while Emma was not at all surprised by Tim Pat's callous reaction.

Clashing with the hurt Newman's collective abuse was having on him was David's craving for Norma's approval. What his father had suggested hurt him more than he dared admit, even to himself. He remained silent. Emma's feeble, "We must try to be charitable." did nothing for David no more than Tim Pat's bitter reply, "Not in me to try that hard!"

Not wanting to hear any further criticism of Norma, David rushed his intentions.

"Hope Trish is ok, must make contact, got to think things through."

"What's to think about? Newman's hammered a job on you, thinking business not required. Don't you be a sucker for them shower."

Emma ushered David toward the phone, "Ring your grandmother, David."

While David was on the phone, Emma asked Tim Pat that which she had been dying to ask, "How did yourself and mummy really get on?"

"Why wouldn't we really get on? Hasn't Tim Pat and mummy been palsy-walsie since that very first day she directed me to the basement in Fitzwilliam."

"I know, I know. Did she say anything, discuss anything other than the accident?"

"Nothing more than a polite request for David to ring and thanked me for my books which she has conveniently forgotten to return. Slipped my mind to tell you she called me Tim Pat"

In disbelief Emma exclaimed, "Never!"

"Tim Pat, you heard, her words not mine."

"Terrific! Calling you Tim Pat cannot have been easy for her."

"Only bloody name I have. Her difficulty was of her own making. Haven't I given her my precious books, haven't I? Your Tim Pat is a gentleman most fair, forgiving, but mad thirsty for blood."

"How is David going to contend with the Trish situation. I hope when all this is sorted, they will get back together."

"Now woman, you stop living in cloud-cuckoo-land. All the Newmans are involved, including Trish. Make no mistake, I liked the girl but failed assassins don't expect a second chance and failed assassins don't get a second chance from O'Leary."

"Just can't see Trish a party to David's sacking. I suggest you keep your thoughts on Trish to yourself. David loves that girl, and if you make problems between them you will be the loser. Warning you, Tim Pat."

"Your mother's objecting didn't affect our courtship?"

"Actually it accelerated my resolve to capture you. She has a lot to answer for."

"'Twas your Morris Minor drove my downfall into the fast lane."

David's return ended their banter. Tim Pat's curiosity had no sooner asked "Well?" than their door bell rang.

"I'll get that!" said Tim Pat rising from his chair.

David and Emma strained to identify the caller's voice. Straining wasn't needed; the high pitched voice of Larry Doherty, an accountant with Cavendish's assailed their ears. Doctor Emma diagnosed, "He's got a hearing problem!"

David's insider information disagreed, "Wrong. It's those that have to listen to him wish they had."

David was already on his way when his Father informed, "Larry Doherty – sitting room!"

"From the firm, shleeveen bollix, partial to Jameson!"

David was mean with those adjectives; it meant something when he did use them. Tim Pat gloried in hearing David use the West Cork vernacular where one word could give full colouring to a canvas, or, in Larry's case, carcass.

"Have fun, Son, have fun. Water on the way for Paddy," said Tim Pat, slamming shut his all-knowing right eye, a gesture well known to David in it's meaning. Touch not his favourite whiskey brands.

Larry Doherty came from that mentality where honest application was a recourse of last resort when arse licking and stroking had failed to deliver. Ambitious subordinates took their lives in their hands when pre-ceding him down a stairway.

Faster than a sputnik, Larry's hand shot from his tweed sleeve in greeting when David entered the room.

"My great great friend, called to Fitzwilliam. Your grannie said I'd find you here. Grand woman for her age. Grand woman, aye, a grand woman. Sad, sad, sad about James and the way he went and all that, but sure the Man-Above has the road mapped out for all of us. He has, he has. James today, or was it last night, whichever; me tomorrow; and your good self, David, away, way down the road away, with the help of God, always with the help of God, have to say that."

His father's advice came hurtling to David's mind, 'Have fun in all situations, especially when impossible.'

"A hoor for the same road maps was James and as you say, God is a dab-hand at charting the same road maps."

"In the style he was accustomed to and all, company car, top of the range. I asked I did, I did. For no reason at all I asked was it the company car, I did."

Bending, David made sure Larry saw the assortment of whiskeys and whiskys in his father's well stocked cabinet before taking out a full bottle of Paddy Whiskey, leaving behind in particular the Jameson so beloved by Larry. This manoeuvre was greeted by the barely audible but distinctive smacking-nibbling which is solely associated with hot soup-tasting-lips.

"We know not the day nor the hour." said David as he poured a glass of Paddy for Larry, none for himself. Larry had no intention of interfering with freedom of choice no more than he had a problem with a bottle not shared.

"Your firing was as much a surprise to us as 'twas to your good self, my friend."

"Actually, friend, when I said 'we know not the day nor the hour', it is James's death I'm referring to, not my Cavendish expulsion."

Not remotely interested in being introduced to someone so basely described as a 'sleeveen', Tim Pat opened the sitting room door and set down on the coffee table a porcelain brown jug that had two blue parallel bands circling, "Too early for the Waterford glass," said Tim Pat, before exiting with haste.

Larry chuckled, "Telepathy of a high degree. Can't beat country. Your father I take it?" to which David replied without a semblance of a smile, "On my father's side, yes."

Larry tossed back his Paddy, but not before adding a tear drop from the jug. Before putting down the bottle David refilled chuckling-Larry's glass.

"Ho, ho, hoo, I can see the rest you're having is doing you good.

Can't beat resting the bones. That's what they say down-my-country. Us that are left in Cavendish's can thank our lucky stars that baldy fucker's axe didn't fall more widely. Four or five good years left in Larry Doherty, after that for me twill be …

David completed Larry's farming idiom, "Out to grass!"

Larry had all the tried and tested buttering-up phrases and he was about to spread more of the same when he rhetorically asked, "Your father, West Cork? Would Larry be right? Only an honest country man like myself would know them phrases."

David again heard his father's advice come whispering to his mind, 'Give their tongues whiskey. Be patient, load and listen!'

"You have to be in the running for high office, Larry, now that James is gone to his accountant in the sky."

"Between ourselves now, Larry knows he can trust his friend Dave. Must be all of thirty four years ago, myself and Gloria weren't long married, didn't Cavendish visit our new home. My whore, didn't he drop the paw! Gloria lit him, lit him, lit him. I must have been in the jacks myself or somewhere for I never heard a tittle, not as much as the littlest tittle"

"They don't make balls that tit-tit-tittle no more; sorry, walls that thick no more: Freudian slip."

"Gloria didn't tell me about that paw-job until recently. Never came back after that first visit did Cavendish, in spite of me asking him again and again. Never came back. I'd have split the whore from ear hole to arse hole if I'd known. I would, I would."

"You would, you would. Seems Cavendish always had a reputation as a drop-paw-job. You must have known that, Lars?"

David regretted saying it, it gave Larry the opportunity of mentioning Cavendish's relationship with Norma; he needn't have worried, wily Larry knew better than to mention Norma … at this stage.

"Taking a man's character is a serious business and show me the man that hasn't attempted something stupid in drink and I'll show you a bullock squared."

Knowing Gloria's present dimensions, but no more than that about the good woman, David mused, "He must have been drunk!"

Larry chose the acceptable interpretation. "'Tis common knowledge yourself and James's daughter Trish were friendly. I'd have to say 'were' after all that's happened, but there can't be anything between you and the Newmans now they've sacked you. James would never have got to where he got but for that Norma-one. And remember, that's a good thirty years after my Gloria shooting his ..." "Paw down!" interjected David.

Larry continued, "Something deadly slippery about that Cavendish, deadly."

David was tiring and the Paddy was going down.

"Larry, what brings you here?"

"Larry is organising a bit of a send-off for yourself, myself and a few of the lads. A bit of a presentation, don't you know."

"A reject being feted by his erstwhile colleagues? Doesn't sound appropriate."

"That's a load of cobblers, David. A load of bloody cobblers."

"This presentation, you had it organised before James's demise?"

"When myself and Gloria recovered from the shock of your leaving, I floated the idea. The lads are all for it."

"Now that James is gone, a few might turn-up. Don't suppose Leslie is part of your organising committee?"

"That shit! Definitely not. I want to discuss that fellow's promotions with you."

"Me, why me? I'm finished with Cavendish's. That's why you're organising this presentation, remember?"

"David, friend, here's the scenario: I was resigned to settle for what I have after James's jumping the queue. But now James is gone if Cavendish was to give that top job to pass-Leslie he'd have a mutiny on his hands. More than a half would leave and form their own company."

By now Larry was doing his own Paddy pouring and had

abandoned the tear drop.

David enquired, "Where does David O'Leary figure in your scheme of things?"

"Cavendish will listen to you, I know he will. Drop the hint about the threatened split if Leslie is promoted. Now, he cannot very well offer you your job back, but if your friend Larry is given one of the top jobs as God's my judge you'll be at Larry's right hand the very next day. You will, you will. You have Larry's word and Gloria's word on that you have."

What disgusted David more than the ramifications of the carrot of Larry's right-hand-man was Larry's opinion of him being of his ilk. He had a good idea where Larry and Gloria's plan was heading; he wanted his suspicions confirmed.

"Shrewd Cavendish will make no hasty decisions. Promoting people downstream is one thing, but the top job for Leslie? No way."

"The big white banana is in love, my man. The steam from baldy's balls is clouding his vision. That's where you come in."

"What do I do? Take a fan to baldy's banana?"

Tim Pat had got it right, 'Give their tongues whiskey, be patient, load and listen'. David was wallowing in the power of Paddy.

"Never once has he mentioned your name on the phone, not once. Whenever I mentioned how excellent you were, …he never made a comment. He holds you in the highest regard; he will value your opinion on this important issue."

"Recent happenings would bear that out."

"You are assuming he knows the truth about your leaving."

"Obviously you are on the phone to banana on a regular basis?"

"In relation to work related matters, yes. Banana rings me."

David knew he was lying through his teeth. "It's a wonder one of my presentation colleagues didn't inform him as to the true story behind my leaving?"

Larry knew David was being smart but pressed ahead.

"Cavendish will listen to you. Go to that funeral and make it your business to talk to him. Tell him Larry Doherty is the man for James's job and on my mother's grave, you will be Larry's number one. That will give it up the arse to them Newmans."

"What do the others think?"

"Naturally I didn't tell the others about your coming back as my deputy, but we are at one in not accepting Leslie. No Siree. No Leslie! This world is for them that grab it, shake it and gather up the apples. A golden opportunity this is. Grab it, man, grab it."

"The rest will be up in arms when you bring me back!"

"Fuck the rest! They couldn't organise a snowball in Lapland. You leave Larry Doherty to deal with them shower."

"So I forget my sacking, go to the funeral, and have a grave-side pow-wow with Banana, right?"

"Precisely! Business David, business. No room for virtues, stupid pride, all that horseshit."

Given the near demise of the whiskey David believed it safe to play an arrogant card.

"In your planning, Gloria and yourself must have considered the prospect of Cavendish inviting me back. Putting yourself in my position, you know the price I would demand?"

The puckering of Doherty's eyebrows told David that Gloria and himself had not contemplated that prospect.

Larry had been glad to see the back of whiz-kid O'Leary, as were most of the seniors who had good reason to feel threatened by his presence. If flattery or any other potion or poison was required for Larry to gain the prize, he would cock it up, lay it on, lick it on, or take it on.

"Every man must have ambition, where would one be without ambition. But you have time on your side, David, you are young, not that long in the company either. Patience, David. I swear I'll look after you. I'm not going to go over all that again, but you can trust your friend, Larry. You will have happy memories of this day and thank God for the visit of Larry Doherty."

The thickness of the patronizing had David's belly churning.

"Now, the way I read the situation is, yourself and Gloria have a lot of homework to do, a lot of homework."

Puzzlement furrowed Larry's brow as he ruminated. "How's that now? How's that?"

"Well, from what you've told me, I cannot see any progress, no matter what I say to Cavendish".

"Go on, Larry's listening."

"This incident between Gloria and Cavendish - you don't mind if I call Gloria, Gloria?"

"Carry on."

"Well, if Gloria remembers Cavendish's paw-drop all those years ago, you can be certain Banana's recall of Gloria will be all the more vivid."

"Keep going."

"Banana isn't going to put himself into the position of having to deal on a daily basis with a man whose wife spurned his paw. Consider the embarrassment?".

"Should have thought of that, should have thought of that. Keep going, keep going." worried Doherty.

"All is not lost, Lars. All is not lost," counselled David.

"Stupid bitch! All is not lost. How the hell is all not lost?"

Larry's 'stupid bitch' reference confirmed for David that Larry, knowing the kind Cavendish was, had given Cavendish a free run at his new bride in their spanking new house but Gloria had properly smacked his paw down all those years ago. A smacking-down that had pegged Larry to a middle-ranking rung in the firm, and both Larry and Gloria knew that. For all Larry's most public guff and bravado, it was common knowledge that Gloria was boss in their house, and, while Gloria was full of ambition for her husband she stopped short of trading sexual juices to attain his goal.

David knew he had Larry hooked.

"Lars, you get Gloria to go to that funeral – both days – Banana could very well welcome her company. Definitely worth a try. Business! Silly virtue should never get in the way of business. Grab the tree, shake the tree, the apples, Lars, the apples! I'll leave it at that."

For having suggested such a dastardly plan, David knew he had lowered himself to Doherty's standards. He regretted having done so. Doherty was made of sterner stuff.

"A second bite of the apple, fuck that Gloria anyhow." To which David replied,

"Forget what I said about Gloria going to the funeral. Your ambition requires low-life like yourself to succeed. No more than Gloria had, neither do I have that strain of sleeveenism required to execute your brand of connivance."

"What! What, fuck! Are you calling me a sleeveen?"

Indignation had raised the volume of Doherty's voice.

"I'm not sure whether I've been more insulted by my sacking or by your considering me of the ilk that could be propositioned in the manner you have just done."

Doherty's chemistry did not allow conflict, he ensured doors were kept ajar. Seldom he barked but for definite he had never bitten. In a huff he stood up saying, "This is the thanks I get for for... for having your interest at heart. More fool Larry."

"I think it's best your considerate offer of a presentation to me be forgotten. Don't you lick arse, Lars?"

David knew he was pushing the insults but his father had told him people like Larry learned at an early age not to be offended by either truth or lie.

Before setting out Larry knew the selling of his package would be difficult. Gloria had cautioned it might. He hoped now, when all else seemed to have failed, to extract a guarantee of silence from whiz-shit O'Leary.

"Can I take it what has been discussed here will not go beyond the two of us?"

"But Larry, I've got to ensure your coming here does not link me to any overt or covert action done in the future by you or any of my ex-colleagues."

"God, David, but you are warping my honourable intentions. What I am trying to do is… is stave off the prospect of a split in the firm. Nothing more."

"Whatever you are doing, Doherty, will be done without David O'Leary."

"Will you have that word with Cavendish for, for Gloria's sake if not mine?"

Larry mentioning Gloria disgusted David but it did not surprise him.

"I won't be meeting Cavendish, tell that to Gloria."

"But you are going to the funeral?"

"Haven't made my mind up but I doubt I will."

"Have forgiveness in your heart, David. Don't blacken the poor man's memory," ministered Larry in his most priestly plead.

David opened the door intimating it was time his visitor left.

"What will you do for a job?" Larry posed, hoping the collision of David's mind with the stark reality of being unemployed might cause him to re-think his attitude.

"I can assure you the end of my professional life is not nigh or anywhere near nigh'ing, Lars Doherty!"

On the doorstep Larry's sputnik hand again shot from his tweed sleeve, saying, "Between ourselves now!"

"Larry Doherty, good night. And Trish Newman will be fine, thank you for enquiring."

The importance his father placed on pressing-the-flesh absolved David from considering it a discourtesy when he ignored Larry's proffered hand before dismissively closing the door. A door that could do with a lick of paint as could the windows.

"Hearing confessions?" enquired Tim Pat when David joined himself and Emma in the kitchen.

"That scoundrel was in our house over an hour and not once did he mention James' death in the context of a tragedy and neither did he enquire about the severity of Trish's injuries."

Emma said, "I've just been speaking to the Mater, while Trish has multiple injuries, fractured pelvis, fractured right femur, fractured tibia and fibula of the left, fractured ribs, she'll be fine."

The listed injuries shocked David.

"She's in bits, bits, God!"

"It will take time but she'll be fine. No brain damage, that is what is important."

"How long will it take before she is up and about?"

"You never know with these injuries. Rough guess, nine months."

Emma, reading David's mind, continued "She will not be seeing any visitors for a few days, time enough for you to decide about visiting."

"About this funeral business?" Tim Pat lazily broached the subject, knowing hard decisions had to be made.

"I've no difficulty with that funeral. O'Leary ain't going!"

David's decision did not surprise his parents but the emphatic way he said it did. "You have every good reason not to, David," affirmed Emma.

"Bloody sure David has, and so have we," supported Tim Pat gruffly.

"Doherty asked me to go to the funeral, crawl to Cavendish and convince him that he, Doherty, is the man who should replace James. Did you ever hear the likes of that. All this importuning to take place at the side of an open grave. Christ Almighty that man has some neck."

"You told him where to stick his importuning?"

"Father, I surely did."

"Good. His likes will have a plan B primed for activation."

With a critical eye, Emma looked around the kitchen.

"Perhaps Doherty has a paint brush primed for activation you could borrow!"

Tim Pat loved working in his garden but would endure endless goading before finally tackling any tasty job round the house. Painting and papering he detested, there was very little else to be done when those two were ruled out but still he bitched at the 'very little else'. No way would he allow a tradesman inside the door, his pocket was hypersensitive that way.

"Your mother never stops badgering about painting this or painting that. To keep her tongue quiet, one of the days, I'll give this place a lick." Said Tim Pat.

"Martin B. might loan you his retired paint brushes!" Said Emma.

"I'd best be going. Gran will be expecting me." Said David.

"Doherty polished off the Paddy, would my supposing be correct?"

"The price suited his pocket."

"Your grandmother spoke civilly to me today, called me Tim Pat – it's an ill wind!"

"She did?"

"As God's my judge she did!"

"She did, David!" said Emma, confirming the miracle.

CHAPTER 20

"You're awake are you?" asked Larry Doherty in a failed drunken whisper having pounded up the stairs and noisily entered the dark master bedroom.

"You stink! Turn on that light, damn you!" snapped a long-suffering Gloria. Larry always asked that stupid 'You're awake are you?' and would keep asking until he got a reply.

Fumbling, Larry did as directed. He had previous convictions for sticking his head through the wardrobe when he had stumbled drunk in darkness. The light had to be left on all night when Larry was in this state, otherwise the possibility of him pissing into the wardrobe in the dark was a real possibility. Cute Gloria, not wanting to leave the light on, had locked the wardrobe, tidy Larry pissed into a drawer. The light was left on. As a consequence, Gloria would not sleep and this caused her on occasions to move herself and her chattels to another room. Tonight was different, she knew the mission her Lars had been on.

"Did you convince O'Leary?

She expected Larry home round twelve; when he hadn't arrived, she had gone to bed at one.

"That O'Leary bol-bollox will go – will go – nowhere in this life or to the fun-fun-funeral either, he won't."

Gloria knew he had drawn a negative.

Larry, full to the gills with Paddy and porter, sat on the side of the bed breathing heavily. Cajoling had earned him the facility of a late drink in his local while the barmen cleaned-up after official closing. He had lashed back five pints on top of his disappointment and O'Leary's bottle of Paddy. This particular after-hours facility did nothing for Gloria's nuptial bliss.

As Larry bent to untie his laces he left off a screamer of a fart. In a flash Gloria was out of bed and marched from the room clutching her hot water bottle. Open-mouthed and bleary-eyed, Larry gawked after her muttering, "What…what in the name of Jesus have I done now?"

Standing, his braces slipped from his slouched shoulders. A shake saw his trousers down round his ankles. With palms flat against the wall, level with his head, he looked down at the slow shuffling of his feet as they accomplished the difficult task of extricating themselves from the harness of shoes and trousers all at the one time. Standing on the shoes and trouser-mound, he straightened and eyeballed the wallpaper full on. Giving himself a few minutes to gain composure, he moved in shirt, socks and long-johns towards the room where Gloria lay in a single bed facing the wall.

"As I…. as I was saying, there was no re…reasoning with the the the Whiz. Everything, everything we had disk…disk…talked about I… I… I… told Whi…Whi…Whiz. But no good. No good. Nah! No good."

He watched for some reaction from Gloria, but there was none that he could detect in the full length of her. He would plough on: Larry Doherty with Paddy and porter on board had guts, pucks of guts; he'd give plan B a shot, play his last card, though that card was no longer the trump that it once was. He had thought long and hard in the pub about what Whiz had suggested; after all, Gloria had as much to gain as he had.

"Refused to talk to Dish…Dish…Cavendish. No …no …no …he won't even go to the fuck…fuckin' funeral."

No reaction from Gloria. Larry didn't feel great, and standing didn't help. But he was afraid to sit on the bed: his arse might fart again; it definitely wasn't in any condition to be trusted.

A chair had a mound of clothes on top. Mortal sin to sit on clothes that Gloria had ironed. He wasn't sure that they were ironed but that was another chance he wasn't going to take. What he had to say was important. His loaded belly has his mind screaming that his life depended on what he was about to propose.

"I would def...defini' get the the od... the nod... if you play... played. I mean talk... talk to Ban-Ban-Banana sor-orry-sorry Cav-Cavendish."

Gloria heard him alright, by God she did. She said nothing but her ears were really pricked for what her Lars had planned for her.

"Mean to say... I mean...we, we're people of the world now we are...and business is buss...buss...business ...my chance... our chance will never ever...ever never again come ...ever. Only... only die the once can JaJa-James."

Larry saw Cavendish's golden throne beckoning as he slurred his way through his alcohol-prepared script.

"All you you've to do is be kind...kinda nice to Ban...Banana Cav-Cavendish like, I mean not ... not like... like the other time like... you know like."

Gloria knew exactly what her husband was suggesting. She had married a hail-well meet nod-and-wink man – a non-violent man he held flaccid convictions but high ambition. Superstition and a side bet on Heaven's existence had him wedge his snout inside God's door on Sundays between his purchase of newspapers and their browsing while quaffing pre-prandial pints. He tailored repartee to please the assumed whims of listeners. Gloria had witnessed him laughing while a dog nonchalantly pissed against his trouser-leg because the mutt's master had gifted him with a complimentary ticket to a rugby international in Lansdowne Road. He had no need to scrounge or take backhands, they had full and plenty. He had never questioned the management of their joint bank account. Gloria's misfortune, was, Larry believed the world's eyes were watching the hierarchical structures in Cavendish's and the worth of an employee was judged by the rung he or she occupied. Unintentionally, Gloria was carried along on the current of his ambition, but she had never given her Lars the impression of promotion at any price.

Larry had never previously been as forthright in blaming her for his lack of position as he was now doing. She was devastated at his suggested remedial action. Her husband of thirty three years and seven months to the day, now that it was after midnight, was telling her she should have allowed Cavendish have his way with her all those years ago, and here he was asking her to prostitute her honour. She prayed to God he was parroting, in his drunken state, advice given by O'Leary.

"Is that O'Leary's strategy or your own, Larry?"

He was in no condition to register the desolation in Gloria's voice.

"My own, my own, of course my own…. You didn't marry a total idiot you know. I thinks …Lar…Larry Doc…Doherty winks, thinks, for himself," he boasted.

"But you did discuss it with him?"

"I didn't, woman. I didn't!"

"Why was it necessary to visit O'Leary if you had this great idea before you went to him?"

"Shrewd mover …. A little shit. Yeah, a little shit, but-but shrewd."

"You value his shrewdness?"

"Cute, cute hoor that fellow. Sees… sees the bloody angles. Can I sit down?"

"This bed is too small. What did he think of your plan?"

"Great, bloody great!"

"So you did mention it to him!"

"He said, well actually, I said…. I did mention about that happening …' he belched'… scuse…scuse me, … that paw…paw thing years …years ago, the paw."

"And he said to give the paw-paw another opportunity, isn't that right, Larry?"

"To be honest, honest, I think he did say …I'd have no chance, that's if Cav… Cavendish and you was wasn't weren't talking."

'That is Cavendish and me weren't talking?"

"Zac… zactly - what he said!"

"And he said I should not be so stupidly prudish this time round?"

"Ah now now Gloria… you… you're confusing me. Where am I? Right…'it was business'… that's right… that's what he said, 'business'."

"That I should be more… accommodating?"

"Well no… actually yeah."

"Of course, you did not disagree?"

"Right, Gloo…Gloria… the opp…opportunity… James gone… I need, I need for us to win… last chance… just play him, play him along. He couldn't rise. You know what I mean Gloria, could… couldn't rise anyway."

"You want me to go to bed with Cavendish?"

"Ah Gloria you are… you are…at his age. Larry don't want to know…. You know, business, Gloria,… business!"

"But no matter what happens you will turn a blind eye. I would be correct in saying that?"

"By God, Gloria, a blind eye I swear… we will shay…shay… shake on the blind eye."

In one movement, Gloria was on her feet facing a wretched vertical Buda supported on two spindly varicosed pegs which were not as off-putting as his porter stained puss. His outstretched hand to clinch his suggested infidelity deal with Gloria was short only a condom. In revulsion she demanded, "Where is the silver, Doherty, where's the silver?"

"Sil…silver, …ha ha… Lars lo…loves his Gloria's sense of… of… of hue…hue…humour, Gloria."

Larry's arms moved to encircle Gloria. With little difficulty she banged him sideways knocking him against the wall. Tall and lissom in her youth, Gloria was now in possession of more poundage that should accompany advancing years.

"What… what…easy… easy… easy!" stammered Larry, barely surviving with the aid of the wall.

"Maybe Lars has a few more in mind for his Gloria to copulate with: free tickets to Croke Park, the Curragh racecourse, Lansdowne, free pints, free fish and chips! Damn you! When I've put up with you all these years, I should be able to lie down with any tramp. Get out! Tramp! Tramp! Tramp!"

Larry made a physical and verbally inarticulate attempt at begging forgiveness but was clattered across the head by Gloria's hot water bottle before being violently shoved from the room. As he supported himself along the corridor a vase hit the back of his head. Blood flowing down his back gave Gloria immense pleasure. She locked her door.

Through the night Gloria searched for stepping stones of her design that might have led Larry to believe she would stoop to his suggested level. She had soothed his discontent, believing it to be a wife's duty to support a husband's ambition, nothing more.

In the early hours she heard him on the phone. The door bell rang – she heard a car drive away. The Mater Hospital rang at 10a.m.

"Mrs Larry Doherty?"

"Gloria Doherty, yes."

"Your husband is being kept in for observation; he has a nasty wound to the head."

"Good, very good, excellent, keep him. Be warned he has a fetish for flower vases. Thank you for ringing."

A perplexed staff nurse looked inside the mouthpiece of her Mater phone as the line went dead.

From his third floor window Larry had an excellent vantage point as he surveyed the funeral cortege of James Newman leave the hospital. The dressing of turban proportions round his head bore testament to Gloria's unerring strike; neither did Gloria attend the funeral.

A contrite Larry returned home next morning having shredded from his vocabulary, 'Cavendish', 'promotion', 'O'Leary', his 'mother's grave'. 'business' and 'banana' he most definitely obliterated.

His Sunday sojourn to the House of God had him at such a distance to Gloria's rear, to a casual observer he was more stalker than trailing husband. Gloria's imposed eleven pm curfew was an even greater embarrassment, but a blessing to bar staff who had long tired of his brand of bullshit. But for the intersession of a major miracle Larry believed his brownie points would forever be in deepest red and they would lie with him in the single bed.

CHAPTER 21

Constance believed God had wreaked vengeance on the Newmans for embracing mammon. She missed her confidant Heather Dempsey, and her incessant searching for Heather's face among the mourners did not cease.

Norma, certain of the reason for grandmother's all too apparent distraction, gently squeezed her arm and whispered, "Your friendship with Heather Dempsey is dead and gone, but it is my father and your son James we are burying here this morning.'

It had taken James's death to bring home to a tired Constance the odium of her actions, which now so nauseated her as to prohibit her from seeking forgiveness from Heather.

A distraught Ann mourned the loss of her dear husband James; Trish, in her hospital bed, was inconsolable at the loss of her loving father; Leslie felt vulnerable at the loss of his security, while Norma was planning ahead.

Norma, in the certainty Cavendish would not approve of David's sacking had instructed her father not to seek Cavendish's prior permission. Norma was especially confidant of her ability to caress any tantrum he might throw when he did find out.

Cavendish would never cut-short the whisperings of informants; he would leave them crawl to their own closure, and so it was with the stream of phone calls he received telling him of David's sacking. Larry Doherty confided to Cavendish that O'Leary would be a tremendous loss to Cavendish's and hoped there was no truth in the rumour that he was starting out on his own. The time was not yet right for Larry to assassinate his principal opposition for James's position but shortly he would confide the lie to Cavendish that these pretenders too were planning to join O'Leary. Cavendish thanked all informants and never failed to encourage their loyalty. Bartholomew censured James and chided Norma, not for sacking David but for not telling him of their intentions. When James tried persuading Cavendish that the haste employed in David's sacking was for the good of the company, Cavendish had replied, "The stench of nepotism is all too pervasive, James Newman!"

However, Cavendish did not give expression to his disbelief when Norma's beguiling failed to convince him that his perceived stench was not justified considering David O'Leary's involvement with her sister Trish and their grandmother's friendship with Heather Dempsey.

Norma's attitude confirmed to Cavendish that which he knew: the Newmans were unprincipled. Just how unprincipled he anticipated would be borne out in the aftermath of the funeral.

Leslie and his mother Ann preceded Norma and Cavendish from the graveyard. Norma, severe in black, said firmly, "Brother Leslie has much changed since Father's passing!"

Every member of staff had attended the funeral and sympathised, especially with Cavendish, with one noticeable exception.

Cavendish observed, "Larry Doherty and his wife did not attend - either day".

Norma vaguely knew Doherty to see but had never met his wife. She knew Doherty to be Bartholomew's principal tout.

"Do you consider Doherty's absence in some way sinister, Bartholomew?"

"Not without good reason would Doherty miss this funeral. Only contender absent."

Norma knew the filling of her father's post was in Bartholomew's mind.

"Perhaps he is joining O'Leary in his new venture. It lends credence to the rumour after all?"

"Your family breathed life into that rumour."

Norma knew better than to deny the accusation. Norma needed

time to appraise the situation with her grandmother.

"Replacing father so soon after his tragic death would really be most insensitive, Bartholomew, most insensitive?"

No one knew better than Bartholomew that Norma did not have a sensitive bone in her body, and, be his eyes open or closed, he had intimate knowledge of each and every one of Norma's insincere bones. Cavendish continued. "Uncertainty is never helpful. Respect my judgment, Norma. Do not consider Leslie for James's position; concern yourself with having Leslie looked after by whoever it is you do appoint."

Bartholomew was telling her not to force him into rejecting Leslie. She would ask that he afford her the opportunity of proposing an acceptable nomination or solution.

"Darling Bartholomew, do trust your Norma to make the proper appointment."

Cavendish did not doubt her resourcefulness.

"Before I catch my London flight, I will visit Trish."

"Kind of you to offer, Bartholomew, but Trish is not allowed visitors, family only. You should have said yes when I asked you to marry me."

Cavendish smiled his admiration; this was his Norma, proposing marriage among the headstones.

Norma, among the same headstones was doing her own processing of their conversation, and with a rather devious inquisitiveness asked, "Is there any one else you do not want considered for father's position, Bartholomew?"

"Doherty!"

That night Norma consulted with her grandmother; she had no one else to consult with. An exhausted Constance was beyond analysing their predicament, but then again, grandmother was not in possession of all the facts, Norma's fifty one per cent stake in the company. Bemoaning her actions, in a tired voice, Constance said, "Why did I slam the door in her face?"

"Who's face, Grandmother?" enquired Norma, knowing it was Heather Dempsey's but hoped by speaking about the slamming her grandmother's pain might be eased.

"Heather would have humiliated me if I had allowed a discussion on O'Leary's sacking. That is why I could not allow her into the house. I slammed the door."

"Grandmother, you did what you had to do, correct decision. But for father's death, you would have lived comfortably with your slamming. You are tired, vulnerable. I assure you you will soon forget Dempsey. But a problem we do have is that Cavendish will not accept Leslie's appointment, so, for the time being, I have to find someone temporary, a caretaker."

"A caretaker, I see, or do I?"

"Norma is privy to information; trust me. Newman's have a firm grip on Cavendish's, but I do have to nominate someone acceptable to Cavendish, someone preferably who can be removed in a few short years, someone who can be trusted to look after Leslie."

"There has to be an employee coming up to retirement age who would be delighted to accept the post under those conditions."

"There is, but Cavendish has ruled him out."

"Why?"

"Grandmother, believe me, you don't need to know."

"Problems have been solved by reversing previous decisions and indeed relationships. Your sister Trish is going to be incapacitated for quite some time."

Grandmother was telling her to keep faith with her tried and tested tits-and-bum business formula.

"Message received Grandmother, love you!"

CHAPTER 22

When Norma, hands hanging, entered the private ward Trish's greeting was everything she had expected.

"Get out!"

Trish too got the response she expected.

"You're on the mend, Sister mine."

"What have I got that you could possibly want to steal?"

"You got that right, Trish. There is no advantage in knowing you. I don't mean to be waggish, but you are comfortable, albeit reasonably so?"

Trish's hands embraced her helpless situation as Norma surveyed the traction harness and mound created by a bed-spread covering the crib beneath.

"You are waggish. Mummy has taken me through every last detail of Daddy's funeral, several times, so do spare me your business version and pray God spares me a visit from that drunken fool, Leslie. That night in the club, how father and himself laughed and boasted about their stupid Newman dynasty. It was then I heard about David's sacking and don't you insult my intelligence by telling me you had nothing to do with it. Perhaps I'm wronging you. It was you who suggested his sacking to Cavendish so as to afford Leslie a less embarrassing run to the top when father … but alas, Norma, you are now faced with a problem: Cavendish will insist on father's position being filled. Decision time, Norma. Choose Leslie, choose revolt! But you can do it, Norma. You've got the balls for revolt, Norma. Go for revolt, or you could lose your Newman dynasty."

Norma, in the certainty grandmother Constance would with ease parry Trish's attack when that attack would inevitably take place, told her, "I was present when grandmother suggested David's removal, but if you think we waited for you to be out of the country before removing him, you are wrong. It was a family decision with Newman's interests foremost in our minds."

"Am I not a Newman? Was my interest not considered?" exclaimed Trish.

"Why not view you're absence as fortuitous, because you were not here the damage to your relationship has to be limited."

"Fortuitous!" cried Trish, "For whom fortuitous? Mummy told me none of the O'Leary's attended Daddy's funeral. Can there be a more definite statement of… of hostility than their not attending?"

"All the more reason why you should tell David and his family the truth. You two have been together for too long to throw what you have away on a misunderstanding. You might tell him I had nothing to do with his sacking, either."

Norma didn't need a medical stock-take to conclude Trish had nothing physical to offer David other than an uncomfortable tubular chair to baby-sit her broken bones for at least six months. Wonderful grandmother was so right when she hinted, 'Problems have been solved by reversing previous decisions or relationships.' Where a family member should properly bleed for Trish's predicament, sister Norma had possibilities taking root.

Trish was all too willing to clutch that wisp of hope that had been pointed out by Norma. She would write to Emma.

"If you want to tell David you had nothing to do with his sacking you go ahead and tell David yourself for I won't. I have my own entreating to do with David thanks to you lot."

"You're the boss, Trish. Really, really can't blame you."

The visit was going nicely for Norma. She liked to afford her subjects the feeling of their being in charge, and for that reason had asked that the message of her not being involved in his sacking be delivered to David in the full knowledge Trish would refuse. Norma had invited the firm rebuff she expected, but knew she had sown the seed of reconciliation with Trish. Grandmother Constance would be in admiration of her deviousness.

"Trish, contact David when you feel up to it; his pride has to be in tatters." Said Norma, and was quite pleased with her progress when Trish replied. "His family will be against his having anything to do with a Newman."

"His mother wouldn't"

"Emma is different, Emma will know I had nothing to do with this ghastly business."

"There you are, the ideal intermediary!"

"Why are you so interested in my affairs?"

"We have lost our father. Whatever you may think of me personally, us Newmans must face the future together as a family and family includes you, Trish."

Norma considered it appropriate to excavate her handbag, her fingers reappeared holding a tissue with which she dabbed a dry nose but conjured a sniffle, twice, to prove her sincerity.

"And family Newman must not make the same mistake again?" wryly remarked Trish.

"What is past is past, Trish"

"But family must look after Leslie!"

Sarcasm laced Trish's words but Norma unapologetically responded,

"But Sister mine of course we must look after brother Leslie."

"No Fuehrer to protect bruder in zee job now, mein sister!"

"Agreed mein sister Trish. I do have to go. Pluck up that Newman courage and ring David. Anything I can get you?"

"Newman treachery I do not have to pluck, and no, there is nothing you can get me!" .

"Hospitals are about pain management. No need to suffer, Trish."

"As indeed are some relationships."

Norma kissed the crib. An act so ridiculous in Trish's estimation that pain attended her every joint when a hearty belly-laugh escaped.

"Darling Norma, kissing a bed is unhygienic. Could induce a bed-pan or two for the unfortunate occupier."

At the sclera-corneal junction of Norma's right eye, one teardrop appeared but required a definite blink to send it coursing over her painted cheek. Norma's tear duct failed to muster a second.

Norma considered her mission successful – a wrong word could undo all her good work. She left.

Telephone enquirers about her condition who did not leave a name sustained Trish's hope that David or Emma might have been one of those callers. Because of this hoped-for call, she had delayed writing to Emma.

Norma again called the following afternoon and casually enquired if Trish had made contact with David or Emma. When the response was in the negative she suggested silence on Trish's part could be interpreted as her being guilty. She dwelt no further on the subject and left if for Trish's consideration.

The double chance of David or Emma answering the phone in Fitzwilliam during surgery hours clinched Trish's decision to request the hospital phone. If Heather Dempsey answered she would replace the receiver. Tension had her knuckles white as she gripped the phone and firmed it to her ear. She could hear the ringing search every corner in Dempsey's inviting someone to answer. It felt like ages before she closed her eyes in relief on hearing Emma's voice say 'O'Leary surgery'.

"Trish, Emma!" was all she could manage.

Emma heard and heard Trish crying. Doctor Emma's tears flowed in shared grief.

"Thank God you are fine Trish. Oh, thank God!"

The release of sorrow and tension that had swollen Trish's heart and mind gushed unbridled. Her waved arm signalled the nurse to retreat when she arrived into the ward concerned at the crying.

The astute nurse placed a 'No Visitors' sign on the door.

"Keep crying, keep crying, I'm crying with you Trish," came the tranquil tones of Emma's mothering over the phone. Minutes passed before Trish gained sufficient composure to gasp a broken sentence.

"You have… have not… rejected me?"

"Trish, we all love you."

Emma's cuddling words wrung the last vestige of abandonment from Trish.

"I had nothing… nothing to do with David's… David's leaving and neither had mummy…I knew nothing about what had happened until that last night in the golf club… nothing!"

"I know, I know Trish…. . You leave everything to Emma. David is tormented, his mind dragged this way and that. I don't have to tell you he has good reason to be tormented, but you are his only real concern. That I can assure you."

Trish, in her own grief, could sense the heavy substance of Emma's worry over the phone.

"I don't know what to believe from my family. Poor mummy is lost, lost in all their scheming. She came to me directly from the graveyard; none of the others did. All the time repeating, 'Daddy is gone, Daddy is gone!' Nothing about Cavendish's … or their rubbish promotions, Daddy is gone!"

"I expect the morning is the best time for me to visit?"

Trish was certain Emma's timing was to avoid meeting her family.

"I'm sure they won't mind a doctor being present no matter what they are doing with me in the morning and they have plenty."

"Professionals don't like other professionals observing, but Doctor Emma promises to be discreet."

"To see you would be such a relief, please come."

"Sorry about your father. Please understand why we could not attend his funeral."

"How could you attend after what my family did to David. I am so pleased I rang. My heart is so so heavy."

"Well, you can 'un-heavy' your heart now, Trish."

"I will miss the horse riding."

"Days are short and murky this time of year, concentrate on getting better. Doctor Emma's orders."

"Do you have patients waiting?"

"Not at this hour I haven't. Like your legal profession, by appointment only in Fitzwilliam."

"Please ask David to be at the phone this time tomorrow, if possible."

"He will be in shortly. He will call you back."

"Tomorrow will be perfect. I'm much too happy now to receive David's phone call."

"As you wish, Trish."

The calmness emanating from the room had the nurse listen, then enter and lift the phone from beneath the hand of the sleeping Trish. Experience had taught the nurse to identify the different categories of sleep and Trish's was the desired deep drag and slow exhaling that comes with contentment.

Constance Newman stood examining the 'No Visitors' sign on the ward door. When the nurse, writing-up charts in her office, did not come to Constance, Constance in a huff went to the nurse.

"I'm Mrs. Newman."

"Yes?"

"My granddaughter Trish is a patient, I wish to see her."

"Are you a doctor?"

"I employ doctors when I need doctors."

The nurse seemed dismissive of this visitor's presence as she continued writing while answering, "In Trish's case visiting hours only for relations; persons specifically asked for by Trish at any reasonable hour. Right now you will be pleased to hear your granddaughter is sound asleep."

Constance had deliberated long and hard before making this visit; Norma had told her she would have to accept responsibility for the decision to sack David. There was no room for argument on that score: it was business. How Constance explained matters to Trish was her problem, but Norma's name was not to be mentioned. Constance looked suspiciously at the slip of a nurse and concluded she, Constance, was the victim of a conspiracy between Trish and the nursing staff to frustrate her visiting.

"Am I not being allowed visit my granddaughter?" she challenged.

"A patient's welfare is primary and we ask all – including grandmothers - to co-operate," lectured the nurse.

"Perhaps she is awake?"

"I said Trish is asleep, I have just visited," replied the nurse irritably, who was catching up on her office duties. .

"Did Trish have visitors this evening?" questioned Constance.

The nurse, expressing surprise at being asked to divulge what would be considered by staff as privileged information, exclaimed, "I beg your pardon?" She had stopped writing and stared at this impudent visitor.

"Trish is a private patient. I am entitled to visit," pointed out Constance as she chanced invoking a hospital rule, not at all sure of the rule's existence.

"I suggest you talk to matron. She is in her office on the ground floor. I am not leaving you in. Now, please. I am extremely busy!"

The nurse, bending her head perused the documents open before her. No way was Constance accepting dismissal by a state registered nurse. Smartly, she stepped down the corridor and coming abreast of the ward door reached for the handle and pushed hard. Not unlocking the door properly, there was a loud clatter as the door burst open causing her to stumble inside, but Trish did not wake. Embarrassment enveloped Constance as she was marched unceremoniously out into the corridor.

"Matron will be expecting you. Get out!" chastised the furious nurse while picking up a phone. Constance slithered out of the building without a whimper.

Fortified by her grandmother's experience, Norma never visited without leaving a gift for the nursing staff. Norma's patronising soon had her on first name terms with all, and they in turn volunteered at her slightest prompting any information sought. They informed her that they could set their watches by the visits of a Doctor Dempsey and the handsome David. Doctor Dempsey called each morning at eleven and was gone by ten past. David did not visit as regularly but always at twelve thirty and left at twelve forty five. Trish, on purpose, had not mentioned any of these visits to her mother Ann, because mother Ann could not keep a secret.

It was Norma's third morning in a row keeping watch on the Mater Private. Twelve forty five exactly, Greenwich Mean Time, as reported by her nursing informants. David came through the door of the Mater Private having visited Trish. David was indeed a handsome man, Norma opined as she smartly crossed the road in the certainty her guile would succeed, "David, how are you?" she charmed, offering her hand. David was stunned by the warmth of her greeting. Apart altogether from the monstrous happenings of the recent past Norma had been hostile ever since he showered her in the Morris Minor. Now was not the time to puzzle her attitude change. David took the proffered hand of a woman whose body he had desired from his eyes' first feasting, he said, "Hello, Norma," adding as an after-afterthought, "Sorry about your father."

"Thank you, David. And how are you?" she tittered before continuing, "after what my horrible grandmother did to you, my question must sound frightfully insensitive."

The way Norma delivered her grandmother as sacrifice on the hospital steps as author of his sacking made the foul deed sound farcical. David laughed, their hands still together, warm Norma doing the holding. She released, having given their touching an importance.

"Trish was so so lucky," said David while his loins breathed in the beautifully groomed Norma. Norma, feigning surprise at David's visiting, said, "Oh, you have been with Trish . That is good. Really really good."

"Every day there's an improvement. She's coming on great."

"Trish didn't mention you visited."

"Obviously I'm not that important."

Norma asked in the certainty of not being refused, "Important enough for Norma to ask David to lunch."

."Difficult as it is for us unemployed to make time, I'm pleased to make an exception in your case, Norma."

"The Shelbourne, then. Shelbourne okay for you?"

"Why not?"

"I came by taxi," lied Norma knowing David had a car. She wanted his hormones at her body's mercy in the car's intimacy. Her own car could be picked up later.

"Are you driving, David?"

"Parked up the road, will you wait here?"

"I'd much prefer to walk, with you"

As they walked, she snuggled close as she linked David towards where his car was parked. Though David was perplexed by Norma's warmth, he had no intention of obstructing.

"It really is chilly, David."

"It's the time of year, Norma."

Ladylike, Norma waited for David to open the passenger door. As David walked round the back of the car having seated Norma, he practically bumped into a cap- wearing Larry Doherty . Doherty wasn't a cap-wearing man, and it's comical perching on the back of his pole, peak tilted near vertical, had David comment, "You are either taking that cap to casualty for straightening or returning from a botched hair cut. Which, Lars?"

Larry, as long as he lived did not want reminding of anything even remotely connected to that near fatal plan of action devised by David in the presence of the late Paddy bottle.

"Nothing could be further from the truth mister fucking know-all Leary. If you must know, Christian Larry's performing one of the corporal works of mercy, visiting a patient from home. That shower down the country think every bloody hospital in Dublin is plastered up against Larry's gable-end. Yourself now, you were in visiting the Newman lady, weren't you?" probed Larry as his cap dipped a few degrees attempting to identify the woman inside the car. Whether or not she was identified David could not be sure.

Larry's phoney ebullience concealed the monster ache in his head having had several stitches removed from his pole in casualty.

David askcd the question that he knew would guarantee Larry's departure.

"Before I leave you, any developments on the you-know-what paw plan, Lars?"

Bending from the waist, Larry, tipping the cocked peak of his cap saluted the woman in the passenger seat before making haste away, saying, "Good luck to you both now, good luck, ha-haah-ha!"

Both for their own reasons hoped Larry had failed to identify David's passenger but Larry's ha-haah-ha had them both worried.

"Doherty relates the smallest tittle-tattle to Cavendish. He wasn't at father's funeral. Neither was his wife!"

"What?" David asked in surprise.

"I said he was not at father's funeral! More than you were surprised he wasn't there," said Norma, recalling Cavendish had expressed surprise at his absence.

"Well, well!" A flummoxed David could say no more.

"What is the meaning of your 'well well'?" enquired Norma, knowing there had to be another dimension to Larry's non-attendance given David's reaction.

"He was the one man I was certain would ensure a high funeral profile."

"Me thinks there is more to your 'well, well', David. Do tell Norma, pleaseee?"

David laughed and observed, "He knew you were a woman!"

"Does that surprise you?"

"He gets right under my skin. His type I cannot stand."

"Does Norma qualify for 'under your skin'?"

"David would require a degree of qualification to put some structure to Norma's use of the metaphor."

"Structure, structure. Let's see now, Norma would hope her femininity hasn't escaped the eye of handsome O'Leary. Pleased with that structure, David?"

"Norma well knows she is the possessor of those attributes associated with the female form and none other."

"You rascal! You have noticed!"

"Indeed rascal has!"

Norma's fidgeting legs ensured her dress rode higher and higher as they drove towards the Shelbourne. Though David tried his damnedest to conceal his admiration, Norma numbered his caught-glances at twenty seven, not accounting for the few he could have missed at traffic lights.

Over lunch they spoke about everything and anything, but skirted Cavendish's until Norma said, "Your association with Cavendish's must not end, David. You have been wronged and grievously wronged and a way of correcting that wrong has to be found. Norma would like to play her part in making it up to you."

"The humiliation of being sacked has to be experienced to be believed, and to know that you have been unjustly sacked compounds that humiliation. Quite honestly, Norma, if Cavendish and all his crew fell into a deep-fat-fryer, David O'Leary would not toss any one of them a deep-fat life belt."

"Not even a deep-fat 999 call?"

"Is David getting the scent of a distress call?"

"David, please consider my suggestion as the righting of a wrong, and please remember there is a grandmother pining for the lost friendship of a dear friend she so scandalously insulted."

"All that you have said is indeed true."

"There is you, there is me."

"Let's not worry ourselves today, dear Norma."

"Will there be other days, David?"

"Being a gentleman, I insist on returning the lunch."

"Why not make it dinner some night?"

"Why not indeed!"

"There is one thing!"

"Norma's one thing is?"

With an alluring look that tempered David's muscle into steel, Norma suggested, "Norma thinks it is best our meetings should be kept between ourselves. It could distress patient Trish if she knew we were … well … having meals together."

Tim Pat would have been proud of him when, with a calculating look that sent a chill down Norma's spine, David replied, "I agree. Bartholomew might also become distressed – not in his power to fire a man twice, but there could be consequences for Norma."

"David, I would like to explain my relationship with Mr. Cavendish. My kid sister and others believe there is a sexual connotation to our relationship: well, nothing could be further from the truth. The adorable old man fawns on me. Definitely, he is very, very possessive, but I assure you he is not one of those dirty old men one hears about. He is one of the nicest, kindest, persons I have ever met, a gentleman. Whatever he may have been in his past life, he certainly isn't now. It is absurd to think anyone his age could get up to any shenanigans. Well, honestly!"

Meaning to copper fasten her statement, Norma laughed while David smiled as he contemplated grandmother Heather asphyxiating on Norma's woeful ditty. Prompting Norma to ask, "Whence the smiles, David, do you not believe me?"

"You really did look cute delivering your homily."

"Homilies with lies can be interesting. Unfortunately the truth is invariably boring. When are you taking me out to dinner?"

"Can Norma keep her appetite on hold until tomorrow night?"

"With effort!"

"I'll be in Rathgar at nine. Your idea of not telling anyone – and I mean anyone – appeals to me."

The prospect of an affair with the damsel Norma blinded David's true feelings for Trish, and also diffused his declared hatred of the whole Newman clan. Norma, on the other hand, was satisfied she could get David to rejoin Cavendish's once she had him negotiating on his back.

CHAPTER 23

"My dearest Bartholomew, your Norma has an excellent candidate for Daddy's position, one I'm sure you will approve of."

"Norma's pretty head never ever sleeps."

"The solution was so obvious I should have thought of it immediately."

"But you did think of it and I approve."

Norma, taken aback at the inference in Bartholomew's words, threw back the covers exposing their nakedness. Propping herself up on an elbow she asked, "You actually think you know the identity of this person I have in mind?"

"Bartholomew has given his approval."

"But you don't know. You can't know. I haven't discussed this person with anyone. I haven't even asked the person in question would they consider my proposition!"

"You correctly wanted my benediction before so doing."

"But of course! I do hope we have the same person in mind."

"We all know what great minds think, don't we?"

"Tell me then?" Norma challenged

"Would it be a young man recently jettisoned by – we won't go into that particular insanity?" said Bartholomew as his hand gently moulded the shape of Norma's breast.

Norma was hurt by his insensitive use of the word 'insanity'. She would have thought a word like 'blunder' to be quite sufficient, but quickly realised businessman Bartholomew was correct in calling an insanity an insanity. Every day was a school day for businesswoman Norma, she would learn from 'insanity.'

She dismissed the notion that Bartholomew was having her

followed by a private detective. Hot on the heels of her detective theory came the memory of Larry 'The Cap' Doherty. Larry 'The Cap' was a real live possibility that she would have to deal with if indeed such a calamity had befallen her. She had to think positive, she would think positive, Norma firmly believed in Guardian Angels.

"I don't – I don't believe this, you actually know it is David O'Leary?"

When Bartholomew was wrapped in ecstasy, all those upper and lower gold fillings went on display. Norma's laughter stirred the cockles of his dicky heart as she flopped back in disbelief.

"Incredible!" she exclaimed.

"Guesswork wasn't required Norma; it was my belief in your business acumen. A Newman will marry O'Leary. Can't have an outsider at the helm of our company can we? Brother Leslie has to be looked after."

On occasions like this Bartholomew's words were carefully measured; they looked after his sentences. Norma knew that by his stressing 'Newman' rather than specifically naming Trish, he was not ruling out a liaison between herself and David, but not before chimney sweeps had recycled his mouth-full of gold fillings. Bonuses for crematorium workers did not exist but perks did. Even in death, perks made for a happier work force.

"You have taught your Norma well, Bartholomew."

Bartholomew thrived on Norma's patronizing.

"That which business ordains does not have to interfere with our happiness, my pet. When one has mastered abstinence then, and only then, is one in control of one's self. Do you recall when first Bartholomew said that?"

Remembering, Norma chuckled, "In the lift when my lips first intercepted yours."

Bartholomew smiled and said, "Correct, you did not exercise much control."

"Nor you much abstinence, Sir."

"And you, young lady, introduced me to the concept of love being

195

a malady when love cannot be satisfied in a one night's stand."

"You bold, bold, boy you. I believe you to be the author of that truism," said Norma as she playfully plucked his flabby cheek. Triggered by the memory, Norma caressed and delicately played her body on his before turning him over onto his belly and sitting astride his hulk. Norma's carefully choreographed session had spent Bartholomew. His eyes now closed in his half-turned head that rested on his interlocking forearms; the epitome of luxurious satisfaction. Barely audible, he murmured, "Beauty's tenure tumbles with ageing, nothing is left. Nothing without the presence of a mind. You have both. You are the possessor of both, my sweet one."

"Your Norma's next move should be?" she asked slowly, not wanting to fracture their intimacy.

"How far has your relationship advanced?'

Again the spectre of the bending Larry 'The Cap' had her hesitate in her kneading and knew this hesitancy would be interpreted as progress having been already made. When Bartholomew probed, as he was doing now, she experienced a sensation she believed akin to the taking of a lie detector test. Prudence told her to tell no lies but sketch in some truths in the knowledge Bartholomew rarely asked questions he didn't know the answers of.

"We had dinner together, we met at the hospital."

"Has he been here?"

"He has." she replied, as casually as he had asked.

Trepidation had stopped her kneading as she sat akimbo on her exhausted bronco.

"That is good!" he said, ratifying her strategy.

"Have I upset you, Bartholomew?" she enquired, loading her every syllable with vulnerability.

"Be careful of O'Leary. Being brilliant does not necessarily mean being broad- minded."

"No matter what happens between me and O'Leary, my relationship with you stays exactly the same, Bartholomew. I love you"

"Careful Norma, careful. Business before all else. There will always be business that will need your attention."

"Bartholomew, you don't mean that. Please say you don't. Business will not come between the two of us, never!"

There wasn't a woman in the world who could deliver bunkum like Norma, nor had the good fortune to deliver their bunkum from that throne of all thrones while slowly brushing her comb up and down the length of his back. Before they had ever needed gold, Bartholomew had cut his teeth on such bunkum but Norma's bunkum was as good as any bunkum he had ever been hosed by.

Norma worried that David's affection for Trish could fade if the accident left her with permanent injuries. She knew Trish's support would be needed to get David's legs back under a desk in Cavendish's. Her constant harping on about their grandmother's distress at losing Heather Dempsey's friendship and Leslie's vulnerability had the desired effect. Trish was foxed into suggesting David should be enticed back into Cavendish's with the carrot of filling James's position. Norma had congratulated Trish on her brilliant suggestion. Having achieved that objective, Norma now considered it in Newmans' best interests if her butt rather than Trish's heart married David and to that end she fed David a meagre diet of mattress. The mattress's pleasure bent his reasoning to her desires so much so David believed his father and mother erred badly in judgement when they made scathing attacks on his decision to accept the offer. So ferocious in intensity did these attacks become, David moved overnight from Fitzwilliam into an apartment, but not before telling his father, 'Mind your own shagging business'. David's distress at these developments was understood by warm-hearted Norma causing her body to comfort him for three consecutive nights. David took up his appointment immediately, and was visited and congratulated by Mr. Cavendish. A genuine body of opinion in Cavendish's believed the position was fitting recompense for his sacking.

David was but a few days back in Cavendish's when one morning, beset by a nasty bout of righteousness, he went to Trish without consulting Norma, and confessed to their affair and the seriousness of it. Not once looking at him, Trish listened in silence to his bleating. He begged her continued friendship and hoped she could find it in her heart to wish them well. He left without extracting one word from Trish. Norma, later, not aware of David's debacle, breezed into the Mater to be met by a tirade of abuse. She listened unruffled for a few moments before snapping, "Grow up for Christ's sake!"

Norma left the room and the hospital, not returning the pleasantries expressed by a surprised nursing staff. Trish, having had time to reflect realised that both she and David had been played for suckers. Her usefulness was at an end but she reckoned David would have one more role to play, and that would be a supporting role in a business marriage.

Trish explained to Emma how she and David had been manipulated. Emma was shocked at Norma's ruthlessness and bemoaned her son's captivation. She entreated Trish not to shut David from her life.

The lid never stays put on these happenings. Where they are sourced cannot be pinned-down but the leak, inevitably contorted, spreads like wildfire. Larry Doherty's chuckle and knowing wink greeted David in the Cavendish foyer as he vigorously pumped David's reluctant hand. In glee, Larry remarked in his confidential tone, "O'Leary, fair play O'Leary, breeding is better than feeding, you put your dick to work when my Gloria would have nothing to do with that lowdown licking stuff, nothing! You're one cute West Cork hoor you are. Ha ha haa!"

His, 'breeding is better than feeding', gutted David. David had gutted the principles of clan O'Leary.

Larry was having a ball on the strength of his daily bulletins to Gloria. Harmony re-emerged between their gables. No longer a stalker, they linked to church on Sundays where on bended knees Larry thanked the Lord for the miracle of all miracles that had him swamped in Gloria's brownie points. Pre-prandial pints and the late drink re-instated and a new vase, as near to Ming as Larry could hawk from a friend of a friend, was installed.

CHAPTER 24

Condemned by his mother, ostracised by his father, grandmother, and Trish, made David's plush office a seat of bitterness. That the burglaries were continuing in Fitzwilliam did not cost him a thought. Norma, who had rarely visited the building, was now a frequent visitor. Her relationship with old man Cavendish was common knowledge, and David's emergence had tongues savouring a quite absurd ménage à trois'.

David became paranoid. He shut himself off from friends and associates correctly assuming they were spewing derision on his activities. He made his Saturday morning game of golf the only exception. Leslie was invariably drunk the seldom time he did turn-up for work.

Norma had more than enough to contend with in juggling time between Bartholomew, David, and her boutique, without mother Ann preaching ones goal in life should be the attaining of the next, not just for ones self but for the whole of mankind. Like a contagion, Norma and Constance had scuppered Ann's innocence.

Norma dismissed David's reluctance to visit her home for dinner as nonsense. Grandmother would ensure he was made welcome. But, when the day arrived, mother Ann's silence and exaggerated attention to kitchen matters made her disapproval of his rejection of Trish and affair with Norma abundantly clear.

In stark contrast, David listened to Norma and Constance heralding the wonderful times that lay ahead for the Newman's, with never a mention made of his family. This insult had David feeling like a Judas to the house of O'Leary. Innate decency had David's blood boiling. Knowing that topics Norma and grandmother Constance would prefer not to be mentioned and he himself would be embarrassed about but needed airing, one evening he chopped their gibberish when he asked, "How is Trish, Mrs. Newman?"

Ann, caught off-guard by the unexpected question, answered, "Miserable, terribly upset, at your conduct, all of your conduct!"

Norma, wanting to deflect from the word 'conduct' defensively replied, "We are all miserable and terribly upset, mummy. I too have lost a father."

David had enough, he was having none of Norma's deflecting, "I had to tell Trish the truth, Mrs. Newman. I mean about Norma and myself. I could not live a lie."

"If you couldn't you should have had the decency to wait until she was better, stronger at least. Both of you should have."

Ann was as much taken aback at her own frankness as were the two women. She would hold her ground and not dilute her disgust as previously she would have.

Grandmother Constance looked askance at daughter-in-law Ann whom she had never rated as other than a good wife and mother. Now, being a widow, Ann was turning out to be a different kettle of fish. Confident.

Constance questioned, "Was Trish not better off hearing it from one of themselves rather than a third party, as most assuredly she would have?"

Norma had to support grandmother's logic.

"David and I are both single. We have nothing to hide, and as grandmother properly points out, coming from a third party would make our relationship sound somewhat unsavoury."

"Would this have happened if Trish had not been injured?"

"Could what have happened if Trish had not been injured?" asked Norma in the certainty her mother would not go there. Her certainty was misplaced.

"I never got the impression you had feelings for David, not to mind loving him. Then you didn't mention the word love, did you?

Cavendish is another matter!"

On hearing himself being mentioned in the same context as Cavendish disgusted David.

When Ann had given her scathing opinion on David's relationship with Norma to Trish in her hospital bed, Trish did not comment other than remarking, "David's mother, Emma, is of the same opinion."

This was Ann's first blooding in battle; she was on her own and fighting on behalf of her Trish.

"Your remarks are most insulting, Mother. David, please do not take offence. Mother has to be suffering from post traumatic stress."

"Stop using language you are in no way qualified to identify with, and never will be if money, in one form or another, isn't involved."

Though David again cringed, Norma's body came in the way of his confronting the facts. No more than Constance or Norma suspected this reborn-in-widowhood Ann, was one and the same person, equally surprised was David.

Grandmother thought it time she went to bat on Norma's behalf.

"Ann, you are expecting too much from widowhood if you think Norma and David are going to listen to your outrageous suggestions."

Ann wasn't listening.

"Ann is not alone in her thinking and Ann hasn't time to grieve or suffer from post traumatic stress with this disgusting carry-on."

Embarrassed, David, anxious and as powerless as a patient on an operating table, listened, his head swivelling from one protagonist to another.

Grandmother, calling on the jib of her jaw and arching eyebrows to give full expression to her disdain, lectured, "Disgraceful, disgraceful! Those meddlers, whomsoever they are, they should be told to mind their own business. Norma and David are adults. Adults and not light-headed youngsters. Who are these meddlers?"

"I am one of those meddlers and another meddler is David's mother Emma, and as parents we have every right to say what we feel about our children's activities no matter what age they are or how adult they think they are. Poor James pushed and bullied by you two until the poor man was saturated by your ambition. You made my James other than what he was. And for what? A few shillings more and people of no importance stumbling over each other to tip their cap to him." declared Ann, her fury keeping grief's tears at bay.

Silence followed before David calmly said, "I agree parents have a right to a say in their children's lives, but as adults we cannot be denied our freedom to choose, Mrs. Newman."

"James has no future or freedom to choose," said Ann.

"You keep reminding Leslie of that accident and I could lose a brother and you a son. Cavendish's had nothing got to do with the accident. You are being hard on us and hard on yourself." said Norma, in a tone most placatory.

"Would you have freedom of choice denied to David and Norma?" asked grandmother, repeating David's statement.

"It wasn't freedom that made David change his mind!" snapped Ann.

David and Norma apologised to each other as they both spoke simultaneously. David conceded to Norma, who challenged, "And what do you think made David change his mind?"

Ann, using her hands indicated the magnitude of her answer. "Your appetite for advancement leaves me bewildered. Bewildered! What has Mr. Cavendish got to say about … about all this?"

When Constance asked Ann, "What exactly is it you want to know?"

David, fearful of Ann's answer, got smartly to his feet saying, "More than enough has been said. My future is with Norma. Thank you for the very nice meal, Mrs. Newman, and I ask that we be excused, now."

Constance caustically remarked, "Hopefully a degree of normality will have been restored before next you visit, David."

Ann, registering disapproval of the invitation, left the room.

Constance accepted the slim chance of her friendship being

rekindled with Heather Dempsey had been quenched by David's involvement with Norma for whom Heather had never concealed her disdain. Constance was well on her way to convincing herself she did not need the friendship she could not have.

As Norma drove her Porsche 911 towards David's apartment she tried some light banter to diffuse the import of her Mother's declarations. David's sullenness registered her lack of success. Grasping the nettle, Norma asked, "You did not like what mummy said about Mr Cavendish, or was it the answer you were fearful of?"

"Your mother is a very honourable woman. It took courage to say what she said."

"It doesn't take courage to repeat malicious gossip. Gossip begotten in jealousy. David, you are going to be unhappy, we are both going to be unhappy if you doubt what I am telling you. There is absolutely nothing physical in the relationship between myself and Mr. Cavendish. Now, David, if you do not believe me there is no future, absolutely no future for us. We had better end our relationship immediately; O'Leary, I love you."

While Norma never doubted that the potent force of her aggressive delivery combined with her body language would crumble David's doubting, it was her clever use of 'O'Leary' that clinched the deal.

"O'Leary should have been christened Thomas. Norma, forgive me. I have this terrible morbid jealousy that heightens my anxiety. I know my jealousy is unreasonable. Discussing, or confessing it has helped."

"I suppose I should be flattered, but seeing as the cause of your anxiety is a septuagenarian your Norma doesn't know how to handle it. It's… it's just ridiculous, David, ridiculous!"

Five months had passed since David had rejoined Cavendish's. Infatuated by Norma, the loss of communication from those once near and dear to him was nothing more than a light burden. He was, however, disgruntled by the short periods of time Norma and himself were spending together. Norma was forever travelling to fashion shows and trade fairs that invariably kept her overnight, but not contactable, in different cities, mostly in England. He trusted her implicitly and would have been quite content if she had allowed him move in with her, but she had firmly refused. "Not yet!" she insisted. "Dearest David, I would thank you to allow me a decent period of time to grieve. Grieving time is important for your Norma.'

No contest. David accepted Norma's grieving time came before his bedding time.

One Friday they had been out for a meal when Norma, invoking a migraine, had gone home on her own to Rathgar. A good night's sleep was required as Saturday was her day in the boutique; she would work from eight till eight. Business, always business with Norma. David was chuffed in admiration of his Norma's dedication to work.

Coming as she did from a golfing background, Norma knew how sacrosanct that fraternity's appointments were. David would fulfil his Saturday morning engagement, lunch in the club, have a few drinks, and meet her at eight in Dawson Street.

A seven thirty a.m. phone call informed David of the necessary golfing cancellation due to death of a close relative of one of his fourball. It was raining; he would lie in, make contact with Norma, and have lunch with her. He rang the boutique and was told by a new employee that she had not been in. He rang Rathgar but the phone was engaged. Uneasy about Norma's migraine, he drove to Rathgar. When he saw the blinds drawn he worried. On opening the hall door Norma's hysterical screams assailed his ears, "Yes, yes, coronary ambulance".

Bounding up the stairs David dashed into the bedroom. Stunned, David gawked at a prostrate Cavendish who bore a stark resemblance to Miss Piggy's great-grand-pappy, in his frilly bonnet and cute matching pinafore, nothing else; scrotum sack in proportion to his huge hind-quarters had its wrinkled appendage lying in repose, nothing cute about either. Dead eyes stared with the same dead interest all eyes stare from butchers' blocks. A coiled leather whip lay next his folds of belly-blubber, waiting to be cracked into action. Dominatrix Norma stood with a gloved hand either side of scarlet lips on an ashen face, her open PVC jacket exposing all that David had fallen in love with.

David's first impulse was to fall on his knees and administer mouth-to-mouth resuscitation- first opportunity he ever had of so doing and by God he was going to puff and puff until he got this hulk winging back down out of the clouds into the land of the living. Enthusiasm had him puffing and puffing and puffing before his head jerked violently away from its puffing; spitting and spitting and spitting, he shouted, "Piss fucking piss fucking piss fucking piss!" and continued his spitting.

Hysterical Norma screamed, "Not me, not me, not me, don't look at me!"

To which David replied as he wheeled towards the door, "Never again will I. Piss-piss-fucking piss!"

The silver Derringer lying on the dressing table caught his eye; grabbing it he rammed it against Norma's temple. Anything could have happened right then as his mind seized in its confusion. Slowly, down fell his arm until the Derringer pointed at the floor. Traumatised, Norma did not move; she seemed more a theatre prop than a person in imminent danger of having their head blown to pieces. David's swift exit from the bedroom was prevented when the fear of abandonment snapped Norma back to reality. With both hands she clung to the sleeve of his gabardine and yanked him back into the bedroom, shrieking, "You can't leave me, you can't leave me, ambulance is coming, ambulance is coming!"

Righting himself, David violently hurled Dominatrix backwards sending her sprawling on top of dead Bartholomew causing her hysterical screams to reach many octaves beyond hysterical.

Not like security-conscious David to leave the front door of a house open but that he did. Sticking the Derringer into the pocket of his gabardine, he got into his car.

CHAPTER 25

The pipe-smoking man who had spoken at David in the GPO, having posted his letter, dawdled clockwise round Cu Chulainn scanning notices, pamphlets, and anything else that was there to be scanned including other customers. Arriving back near David, who still had his pen poised over the blank letter-card on the octagonal writing desk, sidled up close to him, and, while seemingly giving the refilling of his pipe his full attention, the philosopher in him again spoke at David.

"Best you deliver that bulletin in person, son. Better still, sleep on bulletin. Everyone's wiser the day after, but 'wiser' never stopped this genius from making the same mistakes over and over again. Talk about intelligence! Then again without mistakes they'd be no wars - not that wars need mistakes to get them off the ground; that's the way 'tis in my house anyway. Myself now, as regards problems, not that I have any - important you know that - but if I did have any, I'd have me a few quiet pints in a strange boozer, cogitate, chat to a stranger - the further away the stranger the better. Now, if said stranger wasn't there at that particular point in time, to myself I'd hum-sing sing-hum, 'Red Sails In The Sunset'- my all time favourite. You know 'Red Sails'? Never heard of 'Red Sails'? Ok. Pity! You don't know what you're missing! Spent all my natural in the bar trade, never stopped no one from humming. Humming's okay with barmen once humming's not brought to their attention if you get my drift. All kinds out there, you know yourself. Ever on a cruise? No! Neither was I. But my dreams are chocker-block with horizons and sails, everywhere sails and horizons, Red Sails, Red Sails! Herself can't take rocking; get sick stepping on a weighing scales, but she'd drink Lough Erne dry. Isn't that a puzzler to beat all puzzles? That's women for you. Women and their agendas-agendas. Us men haven't a clue, not … a … clue! You know what the Queen told me the other night? Pissed of course! This'll tickle you no end; 'married her mother's agenda'! Her words not mine, married the mother's agenda! The way I figure it, to her mother I was a commodity of sorts before I married the daughter. Whatever that makes me now, I can do without knowing, but herself, yap, yap, yap, glug, glug, glug. You know the story. Meself and me Meerschaum. If you're ever thinking of investing in a pipe, think Meerschaum! Meerschaum is your only man. Anyway, scout, Meerschaum, and me gotta go puff-puffing into the sunset. Meeting the Queen. You guessed it, our Local. No strangers in our local, none, except the odd time. Sing-along Saturday nights. Big drawback with humming: no can sing-along, no sing-along with humming! Under duress, mind, under duress, I gives an airing to me old fav. 'Red Sails, Red Sails' … Pipe smoking men aren't much given to talking, but 'tis well known we're worth listening to when we do. Because we're contented, that's why, son, we're contented. I'd be thinking even tomorrow will be a day too soon to post that card. Go find yourself a far away stranger, a far far away stranger, have yourself an oul chin wag. Unload!"

Filling having been completed, Meerschaum was reddened. Scented puffs of smoke chased each other before drifting and dissipating round the raven and shoulders of Cu Chulainn's. Only then was Meerschaum's bowl ceremoniously capped. Contented he stepped away from David humming his all-time-great before seamlessly switching to lyrics, 'Oh carry my loved one, home safely to me!'

No more than David had noticed affable man's presence did David smell the scented air, did David notice his leaving, did David hear 'Red Sails In The Sunset'.

David's balling and tossing of his letter-card into a waste-basket had nothing got to do with the advice seriously given by the retired barman but not heard.

With firm purpose, David left the GPO and went in the direction of

Camden Street. Children begging on O'Connell Bridge homed in on David's stride and would have been trampled but for previous engagements with cold charity.

From the rubbish pile in Camden Street a newspaper escaped; scurrying, it lashed round David's legs and did not release until becalmed in the sheltered Camden Place. Camden Place, half open to sky, half archway, a lane connecting Camden Street with Harcourt Street was as lifeless as a vacant morgue. Diffused amber lighting and large circular mirror at arch's entrance gives vision of traffic coming from cul-de-sacs to left and right. Rarely is this connecting lane used at night and the dark cul-de-sacs that service the rear of business premises – never.

David turned into the left, stood, and waited for his eyes to adjust. It had been clean and dry when he had visited earlier that day and he had no reason to believe this - sheltered from the elements location - was otherwise now. In the semi-darkness, he saw objects placed against a door. Gingerly, he examined and discovered the objects were large flattened cardboard boxes. Makings of a wry smile stirred his lips as he considered fortune favouring him at last. Rats he detested; he listened for their presence, listened hard. For a long time, he listened and heard nothing but city noises.

Close against a doorway David carefully laid the flattened boxes. Standing at either end, he envisaged the view when lying on his back.

He settled for facing Camden Place whose diffused lighting changed colour's primary and all other colours to a bland amber. Taking off his shoes but leaving his socks on, he precisely placed them near where his head would rest. Opening the belt in his gabardine, he lay down. Not satisfied with his position, he turned and faced the Plough in the high heavens to the darker north and resolved this to be his final resting place. His shoes he relocated before lying down. The two holy pictures and Derringer he placed on his chest. As he fervently prayed, all ten fingers fondled the rosary beads, his mind and closed eyes oblivious to the world and the four shuffling down-and-outs who entered his darkness - their nocturnal domain.

Of these four, Limerick McCoy was first to react by sinking his boot into the horizontal intruder, "I'll ruck the bollox from your bag if you don't fuck off out of here."

Reacting to the unexpected kick David's body jerked violently sending the Derringer clattering across the concrete into darkness.

When the overcoated shortest of the four anxiously enquired in a midlands accent, "What was that, what was that?" he was assured by his tall thin Dublin companion, who was already on his way to finding out.

"Leave it to Limbo, Doc, leave it to Limbo!"

Terrified, David heard Midland's Doc declare his ranking. "Permission to search granted, Limbo."

The fourth, picking up David's shoes appeared to smell them before reporting in his lyrical Cork accent, "Clean, polished, going nowhere. A langer, Doc, a langer!"

David had heard the appendage langer used in Cork city and it wasn't at all meant to be complimentary.

"For your observation, I thank you, Langer!"

When goaded by the toe of McCoy's not too delicate boot, David sprang to his feet.

"Get up! Get up! Get up!"

Langer, wondering was there an ulterior motive to this intruder's visit, demanded, "What's the likes of you doing in the likes of here, Langer?"

Ex-rugby player McCoy of the cauliflower ears who had had his head squeezed once too often by mountainous rumps, repeated, "Yeah, what's the likes of you doing in the likes of here, shit-head?"

"No call for bad language, McCoy. Langer, calm yourself! Good Sir, as you will have noticed, you have distressed my territorial friends by invading their space. A prior reservation would have been appreciated, but now that you are here perhaps a word or two by way of explanation?"

"That's telling him, Doc, that's telling him," said Langer, who was not pleased when mimicked by McCoy.

"That's telling him, Doc, that's telling him."

One pair of ears was an audience for Langer who was himself gifted with the power of aggravation and wallowed in its dispensing. McCoy shouldn't have ridiculed him in front of this stranger; he would give better than he got.

"Keep your brains warm McCoy; shove the smallest toe you have up your arse."

The slightest raising of Doc's hand accompanied by the instruction, "Enough, enough!" quenched the budding of an argument between the two.

Doc would not abide violence in any of his group no more than he would tolerate the company of anyone who had perfected the art of misery.

David would have expected the leader of such a group to be the physically strongest, but here was Doc, a wee tub of a man, in command.

All turned and looked at Limbo emerging from the darker shadows brandishing a small object and calling out, "Boom-boom, boom- boom, we got ourselves a situation here, Doc."

"What boom-boom, whose boom-boom, I sees no boom-boom?"

"It's a gun, Langer, a gun. Our friend was on his way to hara-kiri; that's the situation we got ourselves, a boom-boom hara-kiri Derringer situation."

McCoy, from previous experience, pointed out the catastrophic consequences such a happening would have on their envied winter habitat.

"Cops crawling all over shagging Camden, statements, courts, cordoned off for days … and nights. Nights! Think about the freezing nights my friends. This guy is trouble. Doc, tell him to get the fuck out of here; or if he don't, we'll kill him. I'd kill for my bed, I would, I would."

"No hiding from those brassy stars," shivered Limbo.

Langer gave David some free advice.

"Come in the summer next time, you langer!"

Everything that is of fear was to be heard in David's tremulous voice when he asked, "If I could have my shoes and gun, I will leave immediately."

To which Doc calmly replied, "My good man, commonsense ordains the returning of a firearm to you at this time is not an option open to us. While us sane have possession of Derringer, your destiny is in our responsible hands. Agreed?"

"My reason for being here does not now have the same importance."

"Of course it doesn't. Now you fear for your safety. Friend, a contradiction exists, does it not?"

"As you say, my destiny is in your hands."

"Shall we say it's out of yours. A shot in the dark - pun not intended - would I be right in thinking pride had you come to this back lane, and now embarrassment wants you away post haste?"

"Right."

"Under the circumstances you would agree with anything I would say, wouldn't you?"

"Yes."

"Limbo is waiting on a liver transplant this past five years; his destiny isn't in his hands or ours, but could very well have been in yours. You do carry an organ donor card?"

"No, I don't!"

"Happens to be a prerequisite of joining our little group. Not that I'm expecting you to apply for membership in the immediate future, but please get a card tomorrow, and do keep it on your person, particularly when taking Derringer for walkies."

"I promise."

Taking three ten pound notes notes from his wallet, David offered them to Doc, saying, "I don't expect to get my gun and shoes back for nothing, please take it … as a token of my appreciation."

"Giving to receive cannot be construed as appreciation no more than it can be construed as charity."

His father's tongue had David inadvertently begin, "Beggars can't …"

To which Doc calmly replied, "The exception proves the rule, does it not?"

David put his father's wisdom to better use: when in a hole stop digging - his tongue stayed silent.

Langer couldn't believe what he was witnessing. "Doc, take it, take it. Limbo, tell Doc take it, he'll listen to you, Limbo."

"Langer has a point, Doc. The ins and outs of three ten pound notes shouldn't be lost through a hole in your philosophy hat."

McCoy brought his logic to bear on the situation.

"Take the wallet, Doc, the whole fucking lot! Hari-Cari can't very well go to the cop-shop. We've got his bollox over a barrel."

"Eejit, there isn't the making of a nose not to mind a barrel in a Derringer," snapped Langer. "There isn't the makings of a fucken bowran in the whole of your pelt you, you miserable langer!" snapped McCoy.

"Enough out of both of you. McCoy, you are on your last warning. House rules: under no circumstance do we rob from the weak."

David, wanting to protest at being so described, stuttered, "But… but …"

His 'But…but' was cut short by Doc.

"Yes, you are! Your name, what is it?"

"O'Leary, David O'Leary!"

"Verification, please?"

David, not wanting to divulge other than his name nodded in the negative while placing his hands against his pockets hoping to imply he did not have verification on him. McCoy barked, "Your wallet donkey, your wallet. Neddy. Snappy, snappy, snappy. Our leader has spoken!"

Doc, holding out his hand in expectation of receiving the wallet, corrected McCoy, "Always use the magic word 'please', McCoy, otherwise our curiosity could be construed as intimidation and we wouldn't want that to happen now, would we?"

When David handed over his wallet, Doc walked into the amber light of Camden Place. Taking a business card from the wallet Doc positioned it for maximum visibility and read with a court clerk's measured tone, "David O'Leary, M.C.A, Accountant!"

Prudence had Doc stop at that. To have continued reading the address could adversely affect their guest's future privacy. Langer and Limbo would not take advantage, but McCoy was not be trusted, hence, Doc's ending of his information-giving with the universally understood, "blah-blah-blah". David appreciated what Doc had obviously, on purpose, left out.

A serious Doc, looking up from the card, in judge-fashion, addressed his respectful audience some nine paces away, knowing the three tenners would have already been calculated by his comrades in flagons and bottles.

"Gentlemen of the jury, this court has been told the truth by this witness and this most unique of experiences justifies a celebration to equal that truth. Let the word go forth from Camden Place that the Right Honourable David O'Leary MCA insists on sponsoring our purchase of ten flagons of vintage Scrumpy Jack, all who disagree remain silent!... Verdict unanimous! Carried! American papers, please copy!"

David's concept of 'wino" was in total disarray when Doc returned the well stuffed wallet to him leaving the taking and giving of the three tenners to David. On handing over the money, David was again shocked by Doc's refusal when David enquired, "Enough?"

"Viaticum sufficient, thanking you, Sir David! Langer, you're in charge of shopping; McCoy, ride shotgun!"

When the pair had departed, Doc ordered, "Limbo, firing! Quickly, quickly, our benefactor must be kept in the warmth to which, no doubt, he is accustomed."

When Limbo had scurried round the corner, David, believing the wind was favourable for him to attempt his exit, again asked, "Please Doc, may I leave, now?"

"Neither prisoner nor in protective custody are you; you can leave whenever you like with your shoes David, though Langer might claim they were abandoned when he found them, but you are not leaving with the gun. You do understand?"

David understood Doc's position, but he could not leave without the gun. If it should be recovered at a the scene of a crime, there would inevitably be an investigation into its origins; worse still, it could be used to take someone's life. The irony of his thinking had him smile, a smile he welcomed.

Limbo hauled several deliveries of crates from the mounds left by the stall traders; some would be used as seating, the remainder would go into the fire. In gig-time, Limbo had the fire crackling to the tune of a zillion frying rashers.

Looking south over the high roofs, Limbo remarked, "Right now our moon should be down over Wicklow sitting on Sugar Loaf Mountain, or if it isn't, us and the heavens are in deep, deep trouble. Never been to Wicklow, never seen a real country field, never seen a farmer plough; in pictures, calendars, and the likes, I've seen ploughing. Horses, crows, seagulls, collie dogs: I've seen them all I have, and that they're there, of that I'm certain. But of God's Plough, Limbo's even more certain. Every night, Big Dipper is up there with its seven polished diamonds, that's my plough. Life is great! Great! Right now Limbo wouldn't call the Queen his aunt. Limbo don't keep Queen awake, Queen don't keep Limbo awake. We've come to that agreement a long, long time ago. The Queen and Limbo!"

David's concept of winos was now in absolute disarray. He had walked round them, stepped over them, never a kind word for them, and definitely no coins placed into those outstretched hands.

"Like me, the Queen doesn't carry a donor card."

214

When David had offered his own two-pence-halfpenny worth of what he reasonably considered to be humorous, it provided Doc with a soap-box, a soap-box on later reflection David was privileged to have provoked.

"But you don't know, do you?" enquired Doc.

"A reasonable assumption I would have thought?"

"An accountant an advocate of reasonable assumption? Whatever is your profession descending to, David O'Leary?"

Pedantic, thought David. Doc had his own story to tell. David would give him his full attention. He had to; his manners rather than his absent Derringer saw to that. David agreed with Doc.

"In relation to people we meet, where we meet, the positions they hold or don't hold, assumptions can indeed be erroneous."

With his fellow winos in mind, Doc qualified, "Be those persons horizontal or vertical!"

"Indeed, Doc."

David was quite pleased with himself. He was having a say in the direction the conversation was taking, which he could not say about his own. Doc proved David's read of the situation correct when he continued,

"Limbo, Langer, McCoy, Doc, aliases all. Collectively, David, you are in the company of future John Does whose bones will people paupers' graves; but until those mass graves open, we are about drinking the memory of our previous lives into oblivion. I, Daniel Lawlor, BA, H Dip, was a contented teacher until I became the beneficiary of two legacies: two substantial farms, one of which was swallowed by a hole dug in water off our southern coast in search of black gold; the other, in my grieving, I swallowed aided and abetted by a swarm of bar-flies who have long abandoned my exhausted gold mine. Mortarboards do not sit long on whiskey wobbling heads, and the rest, as they say, is history. Teacher can tell there is something radically wrong with the accounting that had you attempt what you did in your sober state, emphasis on sober, please. Teacher now insists on extending to you our hospitality at your expense, and I caution a refusal will most definitely offend. What refreshment would you care to indulge in, Mr. O'Leary?"

David's preferred option would be a pint of loose porter, so described by his father Tim Pat, but that wasn't an option no more than was the unhygienic swigging from a bottle whose neck had been circled by a vagrant's lips. Though it gave him wind, he opted for bottled Guinness. He could not recall ever having stepped over, walked around, vagrants gripping bottled Guinness, which he hoped would guarantee his not having to share.

"Guinness, bottled, please."

"Limbo, you heard the man. Comrades Langer and McCoy will still be at the Off-Licence. Scurry-hurry, hurry scurry, Limbo: two large bottles, please."

Limbo exited as Doc explained, "I'm not being stingy, David, but there are those who are blessed like our good selves who can handle Bacchus, and there are those not so blessed. Doc is erring on the side of caution. David, put your shoes on."

"Freezing," remarked David as he did so.

"Be grateful, you've earned your freezing; and be assured my brothers are just as alive to freezing as you are. Fiddling the accounts?"

"Definitely not!"

"Caught offside?"

"Not married!"

"One doesn't have to be married to have a partner."

"Speaking from experience?"

"I liked a girl and a girl liked me, but my absolute dedication to booze and bar-flies drove her into the arms of a happy marriage. Your turn, David?"

"Thanks for not reading out my business address."

"Who you work for, or with, is no one's business. Certainly isn't ours. For a consideration, I could however convince the boys to switch their accounts to Cavendish's. Cavendish's? Architecturally very impressive. Before the cargo arrives, David, talk to Doc!"

"As they say in Cork, I've made a pig's arse of my life. One sister: wholesome, intelligent. The one I now know I love, and not being big-headed, but I do know she loves me. The other, a conniving whore of a painted bitch."

"And the pig's arse did what pigs' arses do: you went for the muck and your arse happily rolled in the muck until your brain told you other piggies were sticking their snouts into your trough. Doc is not right? No, Doc is wrong! Brain doesn't function in love or liquor. Someone, not necessarily a friend, told you she was playing around. You wouldn't believe them; in no uncertain terms you told them so. Too late you found out they were telling you the truth. You've made enemies. O'Leary, how is Midland's teacher doing so far?" To which David replied, "Me thinks Midland's teacher writes for Mills and Boon. This pig can thank a migraine for finding her with another; facts too sordid to relate. But you are right, I've made enemies of my own family; her family have used me, made a fool of me. I was naïve, stupid. But for you, this clown would now be one dead clown."

"There's a nasty tang off the word 'sordid' that 'embarrassing' does not have. Me thinks O'Leary missed out on some of life's semesters." Said midland's master.

"Teacher man, you got that right. I've got this father, wiley fox of a West Cork man, who would agree with you. Not sure whether it is pride or shame, or perhaps a strong mixture of both that has me in this laneway."

"By violence pride kills. Make no mistake about that. Shame on the other hand can be internalised. Difficult? Yes, but can be lived with, even in the community one lives in when one is tough. Some of us don't have that toughness, much easier for us to hide in these back lanes where drink will waste away our miserable lives and livers. Anonymity we welcome and embrace. These hands, hands father and mother once held so lovingly have been shaped into begging bowls. Close your eyes David, smell me. Hear the lice marching on teacher Lawlor's skin, feel

217

the texture of Simon clothing, and all those other wonderful agencies who clothe and feed us and without whose help we would be dead long before our livers are given the opportunity to rot. But you had the gun, David. Lead makes a difference. Simon are good, but not even Simon can sit on a bullet and throw it into reverse. Limbo has you intrigued, hasn't he?"

Limbo did not occupy David's thinking to the extent of being intrigued, but casually curious he certainly was. It was Doc's way of saying David's crisis had been moved, in his thinking, from Intensive Care to Out Patients.

When David replied, "Interesting man, Limbo!" Teacher encapsulated Limbo's life in the following few short sentences, "Limbo had a menial job, a job he loved, gave him reason for living, gave him worth, dignity. One day a suit, pinstripe, arrived and decided Limbo was surplus to requirements. Sacked! Just like that. Limbo sacked by pinstripe! A beautiful human being who can tell where the moon will be at any given time on any given night of the year. Sacked! Cracked, cracked badly. His lady went off with another. Easy for us outsiders to be judgemental, but Limbo may have been impossible to live with. Who knows? These are mostly the people you find in these back-lanes. People with brittle minds, some of whom find solace in the likes of a teacher being here. But if it does, it gives teacher some status; bogus clap-trap you may say but everything is relative, is it not? Because of this status, I refuse to describe it as flimsy, means too much to me. I have managed to convince myself that I have successfully straddled the gulf between 'Hobo Lawlor' and 'Teacher Lawlor' - some trick, O'Leary, some trick you must admit."

"You find it in your soul to call spades beautiful spades, Teacher Man."

"Easier is the shot when Teacher doesn't have a bell to ring."

"Accepted. But your mind has all but made Elysian Fields of these lane-ways."

"Elysian Fields! With marching lice and rats? O'Leary, go to the

West Cork man, talk to him! He will tell you never look down for advice. Have you thought of the terrible violence you would have inflicted on your family, your loved ones, friends, and the wider community if you had succeeded in making a dead fool out of a thick mule over a painted whore, so described by your good self. David, education is lost on those who are not stronger in their beliefs having had the benefit of education. Where does that leave me? What was the purpose in my saying that? The fool, the mule, the whore, must have something to do with one of those, maybe all three. Must think about that."

"Education or no, we are but human: appetites, frailties, loves, hurts, pride, egos, envies; they are all there and we all have them. I am searching for a rational explanation for my overreaction. Stupidity, yes, stupidity. Whenever was stupidity rational or asked to be rational? You tell me? The likelihood of our paths ever crossing again is non-existent though your shoes stepping over Daniel Lawlor on some footpath cannot be ruled out."

"Next time there will be no stepping over. I will see the hand, and the person whose hand it is. Limbo knows the Moon!"

Simultaneous with his messenger's arrival round the corner, Doc was expressing his concern.

"Have those reprobates honoured their reputation by absconding with loot and booze?"

Langer, crouching, shook a box in front of Doc, saying, "Shaking booze here, Doc, shaking booze here, Doc."

Doc, at a time, considered himself to be a connoisseur of good porter, and Langer's shaking of the porter he considered to be nothing short of sacrilegious, which in turn had him lecture, " I've told you before, Langer, yeast is a living organism. You do not agitate Guinness; Guinness has to be treated ever so lovingly like …"

"A lady! All women aren't ladies no more than all men are gentlemen," interjected David.

"Bad porter has to be lived with too. You are a veritable mine of information, David, a mine!" said Doc. Lots of jockeying and box-manoeuvring ensued before all had red flames licking their faces. David was flanked on either side by Doc and Langer. On life's compost heap in that laneway David was more than conscious of his worldly importance dissolving to nothingness; his presence all but forgotten as booze and banter flowed there among fellow human beings, all heirs to the Kingdom of God if one happened to believe in the hereafter.

When a disappointed Langer pointed at David's shoes and remarked, "I wouldn't be caught dead in them, anyhow." David replied, "Neither would I; that's why I took them off." Langer enquired, "Going somewhere now are they?"

"Not my shoes' decision, Langer. Doc, I give you my word my crisis is well passed, trust me."

With a headmaster's calculating eye, Doc scrutinized David. When he asked David, "Is that cannon loaded?" Langer answered, "Course 'tis loaded, he's not a total jackass!"

Langer and Doc were taken aback by David's reply, "I expect it is."

"A langer, Doc. A total fuckin' langer!"

"You mean you don't know?" asked an astonished Doc.

"But for you happening along we would all know, wouldn't we?" replied David.

"Fucking stupid langer!" repeated Langer.

"Doc, proposition?"

"Education also teaches one to be a listener; let your proposition proceed."

Langer would not transgress Doc's house rules as McCoy had done, but sniffing another possible windfall, offered his clueless opinion, "That gun is worth a load of shekels, Doc, shekels, a load. Langer might know nothing but Langer knows guns!"

Doc, contemptuous of Langer's greedy thinking, continued, "David, Doc is listening!"

"I am setting up my own company. From day one phones will need answering, correspondence filed, clients chatted-up, while waiting on appointments, that sort of necessary business. Doc, you've got the lot, full package; you're coming with me. O' Leary just might need rescuing again!"

Doc couched his response in a language his followers had come to expect from their leader while at the same time signalling his interest to David.

"You've had your brush with that nonsense. Losing your life for loss of face is in the past. Forget it ever happened. Doc is doubly blessed with two wood-pecking fingers that have been favourably compared with the breathless motion of a sewing machine in full flight."

Langer, lifting himself off his crate, pointed at Doc, begged attention.

"Doc, listen, … will you listen Doc!"

Doc was listening, but it was Langer's way of getting the others' attention by first addressing their leader.

"Doc is listening, Langer. Langer, be assured all ears are listening."

"What you said there, now, like, I heard a man with a limp down in Skib calling that impromptu- would that be impromptu, like? Down our way in Skib, 'twould be impromptu, like."

McCoy again antagonised Langer.

"An impromptu called limp in Langer country, ha-hah-haah." No one else laughed.

Doc assured Langer, "Langer, it is very important it would not be called other than impromptu down your country."

A frustrated McCoy again mimicked,

"Would Langer be an impromptu version of a man, that would be down your way like, Langer like?"

Langer spat back, 'If you had cleaned your arse, they'd have left you play in the scrum, but you couldn't get that much right- you still don't clean your arse, you langer-langeruuh."

Doc, raising his hand, ordered, "Enough, enough, molecules settle, molecules settle."

"Doc's right, you're one poisonous rat of a molecule, Langer."

Doc pleaded, "Please, please, please, gentlemen, please! David, you have progressed from being an advocate of reasonable assumption to an advocate of ridiculous decisions; am I not what I am? Am I not what you see?"

"O'Leary knows what he is doing and I assure you O'Leary is not a gambler. The 'you' my eyes are looking at is not the person I see. Daniel Lawlor has punished himself enough, time Daniel came into the light. Time we both walked back into the light, together".

McCoy, Limbo and Langer had suspended their swigging knowing Doc's decision would impact greatly on their lives. Each in his own way wished Doc well, believing he would not abandon them no matter his decision. Doc continued, "Without a bottle or a gun, these lanes don't bring forgetfulness. The drunk leading the blind into the light; no full-faced moon on high to blame. Let your appointments be reasoned or your company is doomed to failure; no one knows that better than accountants, and you haven't considered the power of knowledge, have you? Do I not know too much about you? And there is the small matter of my large capacity for alcohol."

"Where there is a will there's a way- capacity is curable. You tell me how forgiveness can be induced from a family who have been grievously wronged?"

"Maximum attention to the most seriously injured and you will find the rest can be dealt with from the first-aid box."

David was giving Doc's suggested remedy a lot of thought when McCoy said, "Tears on their shoulder and balls in their hands - winner alright!"

Doc, David and Limbo had a fair idea what McCoy had in mind, but Langer's thinking had taken him elsewhere.

"The more Langer hears about the goings-on in them rugby scrums the more confused Langer gets."

Limbo, recalling the undignified haste with which his partner abandoned him after his sacking, remarked, "Petals with claws!"

Prompting David to again divulge, "Sisters, one who was honest and true the other – well, you know the story, Doc."

"Tits and bum may win the battle but constant wins the war".

"Doc, did you say Constance?" asked David.

"I said constant, as the Northern star constant".

Limbo mused, "Big Dipper, Little Dipper, all stars constant!"

Langer accused, "Wasn't the world tight on you, sisters! Worse than eating your cake and wanting it. Not even shitty-arsed-scrum-down McCoy would be lunatic enough to try that."

"Wouldn't he? Mother to boot! McCoy did!" boasted McCoy.

"Suffering cow, mother to boot? The father, how did pops escape?"

"Pops was bent and McCoy wasn't, that's why, Langer!"

"In fairness, McCoy, you're not one to hide your madness. Two sisters, a mother, and one mad McCoy, some treble-barrel shotgun wedding that would make. Doc, cut your stick, fly from this place pronto, fly!"

Limbo, Langer and McCoy chanted. "Give it a lash, Doc, give it a lash."

More than the others, sick Limbo regretted Doc's leaving, "We will miss our leader but our leader need have no worries, we will stagger to the paupers' grave on our own. Headstone for Doc, headstone for Doc!"

"Give us a voice, Doc, give us a voice. You're the man, you're the man, you're the man," pleaded Langer, who was never satisfied with what he received from any quarter and believed Doc, if given the opportunity, would favour them with preferential treatment.

Into the palms of his stained hands Doc hid his silver tears. David tried assuaging Doc's dilemma.

"Langer is correct, you can be their voice, you must be their voice. With your experience, you will be in position to help not alone your friends, but the hundreds of others if you involve yourself in the many different agencies."

Wanting to end the discussion focusing on him, Doc demanded,

"Limbo, the gun, give it to me. Be extremely careful!"

With the reverence associated with the receiving of a sacrament, Limbo placed the Derringer in Doc's hands.

"Langer, your coat!" demanded Doc.

"My coat, for why, for why my coat, Doc?"

"Your coat!" Doc imperiously demanded.

"McCoy's would fit you better, Doc!"

Doc would not ask McCoy for his coat: McCoy was a tricky customer, needed delicate handling. Limbo needed his warmth and David's gabardine was out of the question as was his own coat.

"Give me your coat, Langer. Doc is not asking you again!"

"All right so, Doc, but 'twon't fit, I'm telling you 'twon't fit."

Turning away from the fire, Doc wrapped the coat round his gun hand and pulled the trigger. The muffled bark confirmed the gun had been loaded. Having no idea how many bullets the Derringer could hold Doc pulled the trigger several times before handing it to David.

Langer, eyes out on stalks but not dropping his flagon of Scrumpy Jack, exclaimed, "He shot, he shot my coat, my good coat he shot. No call for that, Doc, no call for that!"

McCoy, who was not above passing on an opportunity to snipe at Langer, asked, "Tell me now, what would ye be calling the killing of an empty coat down your way like? I mean down below like? You know like? Down your way like?"

"Fucking good coat it was!"

"Pity 'twasn't up on Langer's scrawny back when 'twas shot dead, like!"

Midst all the commotion a white Renault Four Van sped up and reversed into the cul-de-sac opposite. Its dimmed headlights lit up the gathering before David had time to hide. Two men got out and went to the rear of the van. Doc placed his hand on David's shoulder indicating for him to stay still. In severe school-master fashion, he informed David and commanded the others,

"Simon! Any questions about David, I answer them, and no one disagrees with my answers. Does Doc make himself clear?"

All mumbled obedience; Doc sat down.

The two Simon men re-emerged into the light carrying gallons and parcels. The exaggerated shoulder swagger of the smaller man registered with David as McCoy said, "Din ah Din Dinner Dinny, Clonakilty's own leprechaun! Tall Simon, new Simon!"

Recognition dawned on David. In fear of discovery, he whispered to Doc, "I know small Simon, postman!"

Doc, rising, positioned himself between David and the two Simon arrivals. Tall Simon stayed in the background leaving the dispensing of the soup, tea, sandwiches to small Simon who had responsibility for this Camden beat.

Piously, Doc greeted, "Ah welcome to you Tall Simon and to you Brother Theresa of the Rolling Kitchen. Once again, Brother Theresa raises the siege on the ravaged ramparts of our tucker bags. Together, together brethren, a great big Heavenly Amen for our dearly beloved Brother Theresa and his acolyte Tall Simon!"

Doc raised his open hands to the heavens, all eyes fixed on their own stars; at the dropping of Doc's hands, they chanted, "Fuck you brother Theresa, fuck you brother Theresa, fuck you our Dear brother Theresa from Clon!"

Dinny enjoyed this unique group. This was their welcoming bash at him each night. No other of his Simon volunteer- colleagues were accorded this importance.

"And fucks a plenty be to you lot, too. Dinner Dinny's most grateful fucking brethren".

Proud Dinny's Cork accent irreverently pierced Dublin's night. Langer envied Dinny, he could not reach that high pitch that just about stopped short of a screech without losing its lilt. That he was from Cork was enough for Limerick McCoy to hate him, but it was Dinny's blatant arrogance that drove McCoy wild.

"Pray, what nibbles are you scattering to your hated swine tonight, Din ah Din Dinner Dinny?" enquired McCoy, caustically.

"Meat sandwiches, my beloved Limerick Muck. And, Muck, if you take out the meat, you are left with a ready-made bread sandwich, and how is it all you smart fucking mucks are here in the shite and Dinner Dinny ..."

The gathering, chorused, "Is driving a Renault Four he got on the drip-ah-drip-drip, yeah, yeah and ah yeah, yeah".

"Exactly, my beloved hobos and nobose!" lilted Dinny.

"Don't you mind those bold nobose, Din ah Din Dinner Dinny. As long as you scatter unto these Mucks, you scatter unto McCoy," growled McCoy as he wolfed the solids.

Dinny, smiling, not much taller standing than those sitting, said, "Why I put up with you shower of nobose I will never ever know".

Dinny and Langer, both Cork men, both small in stature, never had a moderate word for each other. Langer squeaked his explanation.

"It's for the indulgences you puts up with nobose, Din ah Din Dinner Dinny. Indulgences short'ee - you collects them in your postman's bag, fucks the lot into the back of your little white vaneen, and hands them over to the angels and saints for counting, you miserable little git of a Clonakilty langer."

Dinny's head swivelled in all directions pretending to be looking for the speaker. Catching the fork in his trousers, he bends and peering beneath, cried, "Ah, there you are Langer! Hanging out with the big knobs, partying with your betters!"

The guffaws of his comrades told Langer he had again come second-best in his verbal skirmish with his fellow Cork man. Dinny, encouraged by their reaction, continued his slagging of Langer as he pointed at each in turn and demanded, "Which one of you mucks didn't keep your cuts of bread together? – Come on, own up! This little prick is after jumping out of someone's sandwich. Owner can reclaim same in Dinner Dinny's inglenook; nit rack will be required".

The severity of the slagging shocked David as it did Tall Simon who, in the interest of self-preservation took a further step to the rear.

Not wanting to be identified restricted David's enjoyment, but sharp Dinny had spotted David, "Who is this we have here?"

"Giving us a dig out with our tax returns," barked McCoy. "McCoy!" snapped Doc, not pleased his instruction for silence had been disobeyed.

"Friend of a friend, he is trying to rescue me back into a society where I would be guaranteed the privilege of meeting your likes, Dinny, praise the Lord. David O'Leary, I want you to meet Mother Din ah Din Dinner Dinny O'Donovan from Clonakilty.

"I knows you, O'Leary! Remember Bald Tyres Donovan? Postman Dinny? You must remember? Fitzwilliam? Brass plate? Ould one? Brass balls? Swanky accent? MD. GAA. and whatever you're having yourself. My ould fella was a true blue badger of the peace, Bald Tyres Donovan. Garda! Remember?"

"Course I remember, you knew about my grandfather, Dave!"

"Whips shit meeting you here. What are you at?"

"As Doc said, we have this mutual friend."

Cute Dinny wasn't buying that yarn. The fact that Doc was telling him to back-off the questioning Dinny was certain O'Leary had something to hide. To pry would be wrong. Dinny would ask an innocent question about David's grandmother. "Is vinegar still to the good?"

David couldn't help but laugh at Dinny referring to his grandmother as vinegar.

David answered, "Vinegar still to the good but himself has passed on."

Dinny, "A miracle he lasted that long with her." Looking at Doc, Dinny remarked, "Doc's full of brains just like the O'Learys. If only he'd stop flushing them down the drain with lunatic soap. Can be rescued, O'Leary, you know what I'm getting at?"

Langer, smarting from Dinny's assaults hurled back, "No, we don't know what you're getting at! How could we know what you're getting at when you don't know what you're getting at yourself? And you wouldn't know a swanky accent from that of a hoarse corncrake, you,

you, you Clonakilty gander! And like all your seed and breed, this soup of yours is perished".

McCoy couldn't resist a dig at Langer. "Will you lie down Langer! Lie down! Your ankles Mother Dinny of Clon, tuck ankles into boots, inclined to snap you know; inbreeding! Clonakilty leprechauns are hoors altogether for the incest, hoors!"

Doc, conscious of the presence of Tall Simon, and wanting to make him feel at home and safe in their muddy midst, asked "Please introduce us to Simon's new apostle, Dinner Dinny."

"Jack here is a taxidermist – that's a fellow who stuffs weasels, Langer. But Langer you can tell your cheeks to relax; you'll not be seeing him again, forced into service tonight, short-handed as usual."

While the group gave him an energetic welcome, "Hi-Hi-Hi-Hi-Hi taxidermist Jack", taxidermist-Jack acknowledged their salutation with the slightest movement of his seemingly exhausted stuffing right hand.

Doc and David exchanged knowing glances when Dinny, not one to miss out on an opportunity to recruit, continued, "The right man in the right place! Dave, your big chance to break with O'Leary tradition, give working for nothing a chance. Simon are forever short of helpers, especially helpers with wheels. How're you fixed?"

"No problem, if at all possible. Here's my card. Ring my apartment, not my office number."

"And I'll give you my number. Any of your friends with cars who want their tanks filled with indulgences, Dinner Dinny is your man. Anyone a biro?"

David handed his biro to Doc who passed it on to Dinny. Flames from the fire set the biro alight. Dinny admired.

"Gold, fucking gold!"

As Dinny handed the biro back to Doc he winked and said, "One thing about Bald Tyres, he'd send you a summons alright, but he never said nothing about no one. Bald Tyres no talk. I'd be the same myself. Get my drift, Doc?"

"Gotcha!"

"Until tomorrow night, my beloved nobose and hobos, Dinner Dinny bids you fucks adieu. Dinny's drip-drip van has lanes to visit and bellies to fill. David O'Leary, don't disappear without Doc. By the way, bush telegraph told me your brother, teacher Tom, has townie children out on his mountain-field picking stones. Work experience! The naïve say he's ahead of his time but the all knowing majority say another cute hoor of an O'Leary!"

"Beware an O'Leary bearing gifts. Thanks for the warning, Dinner Dinny."

As the van sped away, Doc went to hand back the biro to David who suggested,

"You'll be needing that, Doc, hold onto it!"

Though life in the rough had long since hacked emotion from Doc, a lump, long gone, near choked him. Humbled, he asked, "Where does gratitude begin?"

"Follow me!" said David. Handing Doc one of his business cards he repeated, "My apartment."

As David walked away from them and the fire, Limbo said, "Headstone for Doc! Dogs bark and caravans roll on! Headstone for Doc!"

CHAPTER 26

The phone ringing woke David next morning. "Did that one ring you?" barked the voice of Tim Pat.

There had been no communication since the day he told his father to shag-off and his mother to mind her own business.

David knew it had to be Norma who supplied them with his number. Feigning ignorance he enquired, "Which one are you talking about?"

An angry Tim Pat belched, "Cut the horse-shit, Tim Pat you're talking to. That Newman bitch, who else?"

David did not consider testing his father's tolerance further by asking which Newman bitch, Constance or Norma. Conversing with his father was going to be rough. The only phone call that would have pleased David more than a phone call from his mother Emma would have been a phone call from Trish, but that, he knew, was a hope beyond dreamland. David knew Emma; if she had been at home, she would not have allowed combustible Tim Pat to ring her darling David; she would have rung herself. Tim Pat was a jugular man, diplomacy wasn't in his vocabulary. Knowing the answer would be in the negative, David asked, "Is mother there? I've been away from my apartment?"

"Mother is not here! That bitch had gall ringing here! She gave us your number. We didn't have it, remember?"

"What did she want?"

"She wanted to speak to you, urgently. Cavendish is dead!"

Tim Pat listened for David's surprise and when none was forthcoming he said, "You know, don't you?"

"Yes."

"Well, we didn't have to wait for you or her to tell us, Whiskey Larry saw to that. He had been on earlier looking for your number, which, as I said, this house did not have!"

Tim Pat registered David's estrangement with emphasis on his last few words. David knew Doherty's source of information was the ubiquitous 'someone from home' he seemed to have on tap in all services - be it telephone exchange, police, press, fire brigade, ambulance, as assuredly it must have been the ambulance service in Cavendish's case.

All salient 'Piggy Whip and Leather' details were in Larry's possession, and he gloried in relating those detals to his Gloria in the first place; then, at Gloria's insistence, to the O'Leary household next; and after that, his workplace. So convinced was Gloria of the story's currency, she took to going to the pub with him where the retelling guaranteed not alone late drinks, but free drinks. Larry bent the ears of all with his tale, from men in carts going the road, men of art, to priests in robes. Ensuring his tale would not go stale at each retelling he tagged embellishments, like the added strips of wishing rags that coloured and fluttered on bushes at the site of holy wells. These additions were mostly of his-own making but a triumphant Gloria was ever eager to pitch-in.

Wanting to find out just how much Larry had told his father, David asked, "Doherty said Cavendish was dead?"

Not feeling any sympathy for his fool of a son, Tim Pat related the story as it was told to him by Larry. "To the last squirt Doherty milked the disgusting tale into your father's eardrum. The embarrassment, said Doherty, of having the boss collapse down dead on the floor of your son's girl friend's bedroom without a stitch: starkers, a bonnet and… and a bit of a bib! Fancy that! Bonnet and bib! No way will Miss Piggy get into Heaven in that rig-out. 'No way,' said he. 'Don't fret, don't fret,' said he. The information was dead with him, his lips were sealed, on his mother's grave his lips were sealed. Did I want to know about my daughter-in-law's whip and leathers, he asked? I told that sniggering bastard to go fuck himself all the way to Timbuktu."

Though Tim Pat was relieved to hear David laughing, his son's stupidity was an insult to Clan O'Leary. As best he could, Tim Pat would hold his fire.

"You don't seem too upset?"

David was immensely relived at his father's attitude.

"Not anymore I'm not. Hold on, Dad, someone at the door." David immediately returned saying, "I'll ring back in a minute".

"It's the bitch, isn't it?"

"Yes."

"You're a certified fucking idiot if you listen to that bitch. Kick the bitch's leather arse out the door; that's if you're fool enough to let her in?"

"I'll ring back."

David expected a contrite Norma, but was perplexed by her exquisite smile.

"When you weren't answering your phone, I worried".

"Yes, my death by his Derringer would have caused you problems. Enquires by the police and the attendant publicity, not what an ambitious businesswoman would want."

"David, you're behind the times. Norma is now a most successful businesswoman. Norma Newman is the major shareholder in Cavendish's!"

David's derisory laugh greeted this news. He asked, "Can we expect to see your thighs foreclosing on the sexual depravities of other proprietors?"

"Proclivities is the word you're looking for, and spare me your moralising. Grow up for Christ's sake. What has transpired is unfortunate. We could have made a good team, you and I."

"Never! Your 'have leathers and lash will travel' style is anathema to me. However, I caution one of your employees is in possession of all the salacious details surrounding your whipping of grunter Cavendish, not across a stile but the Styx. I suggest another expeditious dropping of your business trousers will have Doherty's dick and tongue copper fastened to the roof of his filthy mouth."

Not a flicker of reaction from the still-smiling Norma

"You still have the gun?"

"Fearing you might do someone an injury I took the gun, though Cavendish was safe, he had death to protect him and a pig dead is just that, a dead pig. The gun is in the Liffey."

Again not a flicker of reaction from Norma. Calmly she asked, "Are you interested in the funeral arrangements?"

"Definitely not. The sight of you grieving would be altogether too much for my innocence."

"It was Doherty who told your father?"

"He is calling shortly – my father that is."

David lied knowing Norma would make a quick exit.

"I had best be going then. That man was so rude when I rang looking for you".

"He does have a tendency to call a spade a spade".

"Do you mind me asking where you've been since the incident?"

"Interviewing prospective employees."

"You anticipated being sacked?"

"Not being a rocket scientist, I'd never have figured that out. It's best you leave now and prepare leathers and lash for Lars Doherty".

"Your insulting remedy won't be necessary. Leslie will be taking care of Mr. Doherty in due course. O'Leary, you are nothing more than a figures' manipulator: figures dumped on your lap by those who generate wealth, people like me. Bartholomew, for all his years, knew how to please a woman. I got more pleasure being in his company for one hour, in bed or out of bed, than all those dreary drooling hours spent with you, you slob. I've finished with you, run back to Trish, you two deserve each other."

David, smarting from Norma's indictment of him as a lover, held the door open as she, still smiling contemptuously, swaggered her arse ensuring it brushed off him for the last time as she passed. It took minutes for David to gain composure, and when he did, he rang Dinny Donovan in the hope he had been pressed into service by Simon before returning his father's call. His soul needed a night working with Simon.

When David did ring home, a delighted Emma answered, not enquiring who the caller might be, she blurted out, "Marvellous, marvellous! I'm not interested in details, explanations, reasons, nothing. Thank God you rang. Dad is gone to a friend to advise on plant potting."

"Maybe this isn't David!"

"For too long we've been waiting for you to ring. When father told me you would be ringing, I was waiting to pounce at first tinkle."

"Out doing house calls?"

"For my own peace of mind I pop in to check on a few patients, and visit one very special patient in the Mater. But it wasn't the visiting that delayed me. A wonder your father didn't tell you".

The debacle with Norma prevented David from asking after Trish's welfare, though he very much wanted to. Instead he enquired, "If it wasn't the visiting, then what delayed you?"

"My car stopped dead in the middle of traffic. Inconsiderate male drivers honked and honked; what was I to do? I sat there in the traffic, what else could I do? Unceremoniously my little car was shoved, pushed, bumped up onto the footpath by a pack of raging drivers, all heart attack candidates with their bulging red necks and redder heads. Their sexist language was on a par with Tim Pat's worst - or best, as he would see it. Those drivers are a danger to themselves and all other road users."

David, familiar with his mother's rigmarole of storytelling, attempted to hasten her to a finale. "You are on the footpath in your car, what happened next, Mother?"

"David, Mother was coming to that. You are getting more like your father every day!"

"Not before time!"

Emma, personalising David's interjection, asked, "What are you saying, David?"

"Mother, I didn't mean it in that sense. Please carry on!"

"Very well. I rang Tim Pat. He asked if I had checked the petrol guage. When I saw him coming on his bike with a gallon hanging by his side I could not help thinking of poor Blessed Oliver Plunkett with all those gallons hanging out of him ..."

"I believe it was chains he had hanging out of him, Mother, chains. Even for an aspiring saint, gallons would have been much too expensive back then."

"Accountants are a bore, I don't mean you, David- in general."

"Of course not, Mother. You are truly objective."

" Money buys pleasure, David, not happiness. Now, please allow your mother get on with her story: what your father didn't say about women drivers wasn't worth saying; he was raging, raging, and he had to cycle home! David, there isn't a bone of a suffragette in your mother's body, not one bone. I was sure my ordeal - or as he would see it, his ordeal - would have been the first item of news he would have told you, he must be mellowing. "

His mother's subtlety wasn't lost on David. His father's absence of the same subtlety had David many times witness his mother indulging in convoluted explanations of the indefensible. Now he was witnessing his adoring mother relegating his own involvement with Norma to a division well below an empty petrol tank.

"Your ringing has knocked at least twenty years off your dad. His head is on its way back to Tim Pat's own standard of normality. And you've given your mother back her reason for living. David, I insist you come to dinner tonight, nothing fancy, please come!"

"Honestly mother, I've an appointment at eight fifteen, I just have to be there."

"You be here at six, and I promise you will be out of here at the latest seven fifteen."

"I'll be there. Mother, what had Dad to say about my involvement with you-know-who?"

"I believe he said, you-know-who had you beguiled."

"Tim Pat wouldn't know beguile if he had it impaled and screeching on both prongs of a hay-fork. The truth, Mother, I'll settle for one of Dad's milder comments."

"One of Dad's milder? Try this one, 'The bitch has the balls of the bollox captivated!'"

"Father's subtlety got it in one. It is Trish my heart loves!"

"Begging is best done on one's own. A lot can be learned from those on the street."

"I have this friend who told me never look down for advice!"

"Observe, David, observe."

Though David had the key in his pocket, he considered it proper to ring the doorbell.

"Sorry Mother, forgot my key!"

Emma appraised David at arms length asking in bewilderment. "Where in God's name are you going in polo-neck, jeans, runners?"

David, attempting to give the impression he had never left home, flopped into his father's favourite armchair. He did not satisfy his mother's reasonable curiosity but instead asked. "Father not here?"

"Good has come from all that has happened!"

"Good from my madness or badness?"

"You can judge for yourself shortly"

"The plot thickens!"

"Trish keeps asking for you. Silly girl!"

"I'm ashamed, guilty, my selfishness is unforgivable."

"Any woman with sense would be loath to extend forgiveness but Trish is Trish. I'm not saying Trish is pining, Trish is furious, not at you, Norma gets all the blame!"

"By her blaming Norma says very little for me. I do have my own mind, I knew what I was doing, David is a big boy!"

"As a GP it never surprises me the number of men who are boys, G.P.'s included. 'You were beguiled and you did eat.' Genesis 3.13. I've purposely omitted 'serpent'; let those without sin, etc., etc!"

"God nor prophet never stopped Tim Pat from pebble-dashing someone's character."

"Tim Pat is Tim Pat, and I thank God or prophet for Tim Pat!"

The front door opened; familiar voices came from the hall.

"The miracle of flower potting, Gran has contracted Tim Pat's green fingers!"

"Regeneration, David. A time comes to forgive, forget and grow anew." Grandmother Heather preceded Tim Pat into the kitchen.

"Ah David' – thank you for dressing for dinner!" saluted Heather as David kissed her on both cheeks.

Tim Pat pucked David in the shoulder before grasping him in a firm handshake, "You have to feel the flesh, son, you have to feel the flesh!"

David acknowledged his mess.

"Cause of my downfall, Sir!"

"Some have all the luck," quipped Tim Pat.

Emma was about to ridicule her husband, but Heather informed in a language most un-Heather-like, "Veterinarians ascribe the term 'bullocks notions' to your father's condition."

While Heather experienced discomfort in articulating Tim Pat's condition so rudely, it was as much a sop to Tim Pat as a palliative to what could possibly turn out to be a fraught evening.

No more was her mother's sacrifice lost on Emma, than it was lost on Tim Pat or David, causing Emma to wonder whether Tim Pat's influence on her mother to be a good thing or a bad thing. All laughed as all would laugh at every opportunity during the meal. The discussion format had been prearranged – it was to be one of levity; if David decided to take it elsewhere, he was to be listened to but in no way chastised.

Grandmother would be expecting one of the party to make comment on her out-of-character contribution. David did the necessary knowing the comment could not come from Tim Pat and believing it would not be easy for mother Emma to do so.

"Grandmother, one's vocabulary becomes blemished rather than embellished from listening to my father."

"David, what has proven excellent medicine for my dear daughter Emma cannot be at all bad for grandmother. Everyone makes stupid mistakes, for whatever reason, going through life. Thanks in no small part to your forgiving parents, I have lived to see one of my major mistakes laid to rest,

Patronising Tim Pat was like waving a red rag at a bull. Neither was he a respecter of pre-arranged formats, discussion or otherwise. Wise Emma ordered "To the dining room, please! David has an eight fifteen appointment".

This disclosure brushed aside Tim Pat's and Heather's relaxed façade as both, by their peering, made it obvious they would welcome further information. When seated for dinner David casually informed, to their relief, "I am doing work for the Simon Community – it's really my car they want. That's my mission".

While Tim Pat laughed, Heather exclaimed, "Oh my God!" while Emma complimented "Marvellous David, that organisation does wonderful work."

Tim Pat viewed recipients of charity with at least one jaundiced eye.

"How did you manage to get roped into that outfit?"

"Pure luck – nothing but luck, Dad," smiled David.

Tim Pat wasn't finished; saying without kindness,

"I thought 'twas student crusaders staved off death from that shower armed with flask and sliced pan after whipping the meat from the sandwiches to feed themselves."

"Those helpers are much appreciated by those casualties, I assure you."

Tim Pat's response was everything David expected it would be,

"Casualties my arse; bone-idle lazy shower of hoors!"

David's instinct was to defend the Limbos, Langers, McCoys, and Docs of the world, but in the interest of harmony he decided another day, another time.

Emma rebuked, "But for the Grace of God ... Please have a modicum of charity, Tim Pat".

"You'll not find an O'Leary huddled in the muck guzzling plonk with that shower of wasters! Right David? Not likely my son, not likely!"

While noting his father's toning down of adjectives, David nearly choked on a slice of beef with the laughter. In no condition to excuse himself, hurriedly he left the table. On returning, he apologised for his rudeness. This episode gnawed at Tim Pat's curiosity; he too decided another day, another time. Lest the subject of Simon be resumed grandmother requested, "Please, let there be an end to this discussion; Simon is not a subject for the dinner table".

Lifting the decanter, David would have loved to share this dramatic irony while enquiring, "More wine anyone?"

Grandmother's wish was obeyed; silence reigned as justice was done to Emma's cooking. David's sketching of his future plans was welcomed when he informed, "As you will have guessed I am forming my own company".

"Good on you, son, good on you!" approved Tim Pat sticking out his hand to feel the flesh as David expected he would.

"I know someone who will be very happy when they hear this news," said Emma.

Fearing capture in David's trawl for staff not requiring remuneration or stamp, Grandmother placed her non-availability firmly in place.

"Serving as secretary would leave me cold. Count grandmother out, David"

"Position already filled, Gran.'

"Anyone we know?" asked Emma.

"If it's Tim Pat you have in mind, Tim Pat has no intention of retiring."

Emma could not have been more serious when she said, "Tim Pat is definitely not retiring; idle Tim Pat would drive Emma and the world crazy!"

"The bad news for all you volunteers is, that position is filled. Secretary's name is Daniel Moore, a very private, efficient man. Minds his own business and welcomes reciprocation".

" That's telling us to mind our own business, Heather!" said Tim Pat.

"His privacy will be respected, David," Emma assured.

"Where do you intend setting out your stall?" enquired Tim Pat.

"Nothing pretentious to start with, on the look out at the moment".

"That rules out Fitzwilliam Square," said Heather mischievously.

"Are you offering David space as well in Fitzwilliam, Mummy?"

"Why not? He won't be interfering with your surgery."

"No, no, I couldn't have that, couldn't!" exclaimed David, believing it proper he should refuse at least once in the certainty grandmother would repeat her offer.

Tim Pat would have snatched the offer with both hands. "Stupid, stupid, stupid," he thought. Then David was an O'Leary, he was guaranteed to have a recovery strategy in place. Tim Pat would withhold marking David's strategy out of ten until the game was played.

When stern faced grandmother answered, "Suit yourself young man!" David did not respond, stayed silent. Tim Pat was gutted; what had he reared? Not a whisper of a recovery plan from an O'Leary. His own ould-fellah would have kicked the arse off him from the haggard to the high field if he ever let a shilling or shilling's worth escape.

Knowing exactly what was going through her husband's mind Emma, in her wisdom, got the ball rolling again when she pointed out, "No shortage of space, David; Grandmother is being generous in the extreme."

Tim Pat had choice adjectives, in no particular order, clustered on the tip of his tongue to hurl at son David if he again refused. David clearly understood his father's inherent threat when Tim Pat demanded an answer in the positive, "O'Leary?"

"Well?" demanded Heather, staring from under arched eyebrows at David.

"Grandmother, I am delighted to accept your most generous offer, I truly am."

Grandmother, on purpose, pleased Tim Pat when she complimented David.

"O'Leary, you have come of age; common sense!"

"Common sense job, David, common sense. Thanks, Heather," said Tim Pat, awarding David zilch for his unguarded ploy and Emma ten out of ten for coming to his rescue.

Heather's right index, at half mast, signalled a codicil in the offing.

"Under one condition David: you move back to Fitzwilliam; I am not living there on my own."

While David had become very attached to his own apartment, he could feel the fury of his father's eyes boring into his skull demanding he do the right thing this time; to refuse would be his certain death by other than misadventure.

"Grandmother, I am truly blessed, thank you!"

Postman Dinny would have a new brass plate to contend with. Emma instructed Tim Pat to stay where he was when David got up to leave. She would see him to his car intending to afford him an opportunity to make mention of the sorry chapter of events that had him sunder his relationship with Trish. David knew that was the purpose of his mother escorting him. She would talk and talk and that would suit him. He initiated the conversation by giving expression to his disbelief at the togetherness of his father and grandmother. "In my wildest dreams, I could never see father and grandmother being civil to each other not to mind being so overtly friendly."

"David you have just witnessed the influence a common enemy can have on former enemies. Leaving those past negatives behind, your grandmother's new found passion for plants, shrubs, flowers, even compost, and her array of garden implements has to be seen to be believed. Father and herself have transformed the wilderness that was Fitzwilliam into a garden fit for the Chelsea Flower Show; a show, believe it or believe it not, that is being visited next season by the pair. Isn't that something? Nothing short of a miracle."

" Mother, right now I could well do with some of that same miracle."

David had opened the door for his mother to discuss the all important issue of his relationship with Trish. Emma wasn't found wanting; she pushed that door wide open.

"I am sorry for the man that is gone and the undignified if hilarious manner in which Miss Piggy went but his death aside, I am more than pleased at the way things are turning out. Though I caution Trish is not one bit pleased at the fool you have made of yourself and her, she blames Norma, so too does her mother Ann. We meet most evenings at the hospital."

"Mother, my dignity demands I assume ownership of my actions. Stupid and selfish they certainly were, but, nevertheless, those decisions were mine. Quite obviously my control wasn't what it should have been; Norma did not have to put a ring on my nose; I followed."

"Women never have to, David."

"But I was the man, Mother, I was the man."

"Men are so pathetic; the hand that rocks the cradle rules the world!"

"Cliché, Mother!"

"Proverb, David, as old as time itself. And mathematics, no matter how creative, won't change that. You mentioned control; of its nature, control does not allow for dialogue; a consequence of no dialogue is there can be no compromise, which in turn results in discontent, and discontent is followed by fracture, and the relationship founders. Control can be a blind for insecurity, meanness, a blind for many, many things".

David smiled at his mother's lecture.

"I doubt Tim Pat would approve of Doctor Emma writing an agony column."

"David, another not-so-mild quote from your father, 'Our Dublin son was easy meat for that harlot!' Tim Pat is firm in his belief that country people are away shrewder than their city counterparts. Your father is beyond redemption when it comes to bad language, but in the presence of grandmother he can be seen to make painful efforts to tone his language down."

"I've noticed."

"Go to your Simon and do not delay in visiting Trish."

"I will have to crawl."

"I should think so, and crawl on your own!"

David wanted solid progress to report when he visited Trish in the hope that it would somehow deflect from what would be his pathetic explanation of his tangle with Norma.

Doc Lawlor, with resolve dredged from times long past, abstained from alcohol that Sunday. Sprucing himself, he booked into the Salvation Army Hostel in York Street. His red eyes had smiled back at him as he shaved before stepping into Monday feeling lousy. He satisfied the police that his intentions were not criminally oriented when they arrived at the junction of Camden Row with Camden Street in response to a 999 call advising that a man was lurking suspiciously in the area. He apologized to the lady whom he suspected of placing the call for any distress caused. Her demeanour confirmed his suspicion that it had been her. At seven on that cold Monday evening, having spent his day on the lookout for David O' Leary, he ended his vigil and sloped towards Aungier Street where he met Limbo and Langer. Limbo properly surmised, "No show, Doc, sorry!"

"You after a major hose-down, spanking clean, and he didn't show. A langer, a langer, I knew it, a langer!"

Sensitive Limbo, unaccustomed as he was to giving orders but conscious of the magnitude of Doc's disappointment, ordered, "Langer, put a sock in it!"

Doc mused as his hand held the gold biro in his pocket, "David did not nominate a day, or an hour. At the time, I thought the arrangement loose, but I felt, 'in his own time, in his own time'. I still believe he will honour his commitment, of that I'm pretty certain, sure!"

Limbo encouraged, "That's the spirit Doc, that's the spirit. It isn't how our diaries are chocker-block with appointments this time of year. Stay in the Sally again tonight, Doc; steer clear of booze."

Doc, shrugging his shoulders, turned out his empty pockets. "No can stay in Sally, Limbo. Doc's pockets are shekels shy!"

Fearing he would have to provide Doc with a sub even for a one night stay in the Salvation Army Hostel, Langer magnified the hopelessness of Doc's financial situation, "Shekels-shy today, shekels-shy tomorrow, shekels shy the day after, a bleedin' millionaire couldn't stop in the Sally that long".

As Limbo mined coins from the tattered lining of his pockets, he demanded "Stump up, stump up, Langer!"

To which a panicking Langer said, "My arse I'll stump up. The few odds Langer has, he earned hard this long day. Shag Sally! Nothing personal now, Doc, but shag Sally, shag Sally!"

Limbo threatened, "I'll get McCoy to boot your miserable bones all the way down to your MacGillycuddy Reeks if you don't stump up!"

"Them Reeks are way down in the County Kerry, you Dublin jackass. Savages they are down there, savages! Doc, Langer's for your good, Sally-living will make Doc soft, Doc'll wind-up with every known disease and plenty more that aren't. Sally nearly killed me, I was saved, I was. Wasn't I lucky, I was."

Limbo, doing a McCoy on him, mimicked, "You was, you was, saved you was, and when you is dead, the whole world will shout, it will. Langer the shit is dead, he is. Long live Sally!"

Langer screeched, "Mocking is catching, mocking is catching, mocking is catching, Limbo!"

As a stressed Langer reluctantly counted coins into Doc's cupped hands, Doc promised, "You'll get your coins back with compound interest".

Langer responded, "Make my compound liquid, Doc, make

Langer's compound liquid!"

Early next morning as the Camden merchants went busily about setting out their stalls, Doc quickened his step when he saw a traffic cop with notebook in hand speaking to David through the window of his car.

"Officer Muldowney! Please, this gentlemen is a colleague of mine. I will look after him," said Doc authoritatively as he opened the passenger door and sat into the car.

The officer, observing the unlikely alliance he was presented with, advised, 'Master Lawlor, please be more selective in your choice of company, not like you to leave your standards drop!"

"Master Lawlor thanks Officer Muldowney for his timely advice."

"Till the next time then, Master, till the next time," said the officer, while stuffing his notebook back into his jacket pocket and nonchalantly mounting his bike without knocking it off its stand.

David, smiling, replied, "No next time for Master Lawlor. Officer Muldowney, no next time. Back to work time for Master."

Dismounting and ceremoniously taking off his glove Officer Muldowney reached in the window saying, as he shook Doc's hand, "About time, Master, about time. Every good luck to you and your colleague here, well done. And Doc, if colleague should persist in getting into trouble with the law give Muldowney a shout. You know where to get Muldowney!"

"Will do, Muldowney, will do."

As the cop sped away, Doc explained, "Ex-pupil, respectful, good stock. I could have been his father!"

David's fluttering heart accelerated to ninety mile an hour palpations as he waited to be connected to Trish's ward. Trish had to repeat "Hallo" before David meekly chanced, "It's David, Trish, me, David".

Of equal proportions was the hurricane that unleashed itself through Trish's veins as she screamed, "Damn you, damn you David O'Leary! Where have you been? I know where you've been, I mean where have you been since you've been?"

With childlike innocence David pleaded, "Out with Simon, Trish, I help out with Simon on their rounds; cars they are in need of, cars, Trish."

"You get in here, you great big stupid oaf, and if you must bring Simon with you, you bring Simon!"

"Begging has to be done on my own- that's what Emma said. I'm begging your forgiveness."

"Every day, every minute, I was expecting you to call."

"Trish, I did call, yesterday. I called but a nurse produced two lists, one with 'visitors welcome' the other with 'visitors barred'. As my name didn't appear on either, nurse asked me to leave saying Trish Newman didn't have a Limbo List. I could not help but notice your grandmother's name was circled in red in your barred list."

"Apart from my mother, Ann, all females in that house are arrogant bitches, horrible people. Incoming phone calls from my 'welcome' list I only accept. How did you manage to get through now?"

"When I told the man on the switch-board I loved Trish Newman he said he too was blind. He put me through."

"He was telling the truth, he is blind. That man has such a rich sense of humour. Fabulous!"

"Trish, how do I begin…"

"Enough, enough! You were no match for that tramp, no man is. Get you in here, O'Leary, get you in!"

When David entered the flower shop in Dorset Street, he was as high as a kite. While surveying the shop's presentation and mindless of the female shop assistant who shadowed his movements round the laden shelves, in a confessional way he spoke his story at the flowers.

"There is this very special patient who has forgiven a boy for his stupidity, and this boy wants to say 'thanks' in that very special way flowers say thanks."

Not taking his eyes from the flowers, he requested the help of the assistant, "In the matter of flowers appropriate for a very special occasion I would really appreciate your expert help, lady".

As David watched the lady's fingers carefully select different species of flowers while ensuring no damage was done to any other, he could not be more impressed by her dedication to duty. Her selection having been made and wrapped, the bouquet was carefully laid on the counter. David's hand moved towards his inside pocket for the gold biro; remembering, he checked and asked the loan of a biro to sign the greeting card. Having written a simple "I love you, Kisses David", he handed the biro back to the lady along with four ten-pound notes saying, "Please keep the change."

"Sir, that is the price!"

Their eyes met. There was that flash of mutual recognition. Her hair colouring wasn't the bright shade it now was, she had not been wearing the blue shop coat; the small crucifix was still hanging round her neck. He had worn a gabardine with collar turned up. They both clearly remembered.

David took another ten pound note from his wallet; handing it to the assistant, he said, "Thank you...and tomorrow is a lovely day!"

End.